Sophie's Children

PENELOPE ABBOTT

TABLE OF CONTENTS

CHAPTER ONE
CELEBRATIONS

BEN ENTERED FORGE COTTAGE, OPENING the kitchen door and letting in a cold wind. Sophie shivered and moved to get up from her seat to put the kettle on the range for tea. Before she could do so, Ben placed a newspaper on the kitchen table in front of her.

"IT'S OVER! JOY AND THANKSGIVING MARK START OF THE ARMISTICE ON THE GREATEST DAY IN OUR HISTORY," the headline announced.

Sophie jumped up and flung her arms round Ben's neck. "Oh, thank God! Our boys are safe! They are safe, aren't they, Ben?"

Her husband held her tightly. "They're safe now," he said reassuringly.

She picked up the *Daily Mail*, which was dated Tuesday, the 12th of November, 1918, and studied the photographs on the front page. Cheering soldiers and civilians were waving flags and celebrating in the streets. As she turned each page, she eagerly read out parts to Ben that she thought would interest him. The headlines were joyful, but the descriptions of the aftermath were devastating.

Finally, she took off her reading glasses and let out a sigh. "All that dreadful waste of life," she said, shaking her head slowly. She and Ben knew of several families in their village of Clayden who had suffered losses—husbands, sons, brothers, gone forever. She looked up at Ben. "When do you think we'll see Charles and Florrie again?" she asked.

"I've no idea. I suppose Charles's work at the hospital will continue for some time as they continue to bring back the wounded. He'll be kept busy. I hope he and his sister can come home now. Florrie will probably want to give up her voluntary nursing to complete her teacher training."

"Perhaps Charles will be able to finish his studies now and finally become a qualified doctor. Did Millie have any news of their Tom when you were at the shop? Is he recovering from his wounds?"

"She said they were not life-threatening but he would need time recuperating. She and Harry plan to visit him as soon as possible. He's in a military hospital in Plymouth."

"He was so young when he joined up, barely eighteen."

"She also told me that Billy is still in France, overseeing the return of horses back to England. He was fortunate not to have been fighting at the front."

"I'm glad he managed to finish his veterinary training before the war." Sophie leant back in her chair and closed her eyes.

She had always been fond of Ben's nephew. Billy had loved animals as a child, and she remembered the time when Ben had arranged for him to have a ride on one of the shire horses outside the forge on his fourth birthday. That was before she'd had their own son, Charles, the quiet, studious boy who had begun his education with her at the same kitchen table she was sitting at now.

She opened her eyes and sat up, feeling a glow of excitement at the thought of seeing her children home again.

Rosa, their youngest daughter, was due back at the end of the week. She had continued to live at home, staying at the hospital, where she worked during the week, because of her night duties. After the war began, she had, like many other young women, volunteered to join the Voluntary Aid Detachment as a nurse and was helping with the recuperation of wounded servicemen in a hospital in Kingsbridge.

The cottage had been too quiet with two of Sophie's children gone, but now that the war had ended, she hoped to see more of them.

"We ought to celebrate," she said. "I think we still have some bunting somewhere. Do you remember when we put it up in 1900 to welcome in the new century? I wonder what celebrations there will be in the village. There'll probably be a service of thanksgiving at church."

"Put the flags up, by all means, but we'll leave our own celebrations until all the family are back together again," Ben said. "Let's hope we don't have to wait too long."

Charles and Florrie arrived four weeks later for Christmas. Sophie wept as she welcomed her son and daughter, thankful to have them back home at last. Florrie was also near to tears as she hugged her mother. She had come with two large suitcases, which her brother heaved into the kitchen.

Charles embraced his mother. "No need to worry anymore, Ma. It's all over now, and I want to forget work for a while."

Sophie nodded as she stepped back, studying her tall son while she held him at arms' length. His face was drawn, and he looked older than when she had last seen him. "You look worn out, darling. You need a good rest."

"No chance of that!" said Ben, laughing. "I've a few jobs lined up for him to help me with."

Florrie kissed both her parents and slumped down into a chair. "I'm pretty exhausted too," she said. "It's been nonstop, hasn't it, Charles?" She looked round the familiar kitchen, the blue-and-white plates on the dresser and the kettle puffing away on the range. "It's good to be back home," she said.

Rosa arrived five days later, on Christmas Eve, and that evening, the family gathered round the roaring fire in the parlour. Ben piled it with logs that crackled and blazed, spreading a welcome warmth into the room. Sophie had devised some games and quizzes, wanting them all to have fun together. The three siblings won most of them with a fair amount of friendly squabbling and banter.

"You lot haven't changed!" said their father as he retreated to his chair in the corner of the room.

Florrie tidied away the games back into their boxes while her mother brought in a plate of mince pies and some warm spiced wine in a jug. After handing it round, they raised their glasses and wished each other a Happy Christmas. Forge Cottage was full of joy that evening.

Sophie spent the following day with her daughters, preparing the Christmas dinner. She completed laying the table in the parlour, getting out her best dinner service and cutlery and placing a candelabra in the centre. There were eight places laid, and it would be a tight squeeze in the moderately sized room as Ben's sister Millie and her husband Harry had been invited, together with their daughter Agnes. They ran the village shop and post office and had been glad of a few days off for the Christmas festivities.

When the visitors arrived, Millie warmly embraced her nephew and nieces, asking them all about themselves, while Harry placed their presents under the tree in the corner of the parlour. He stood up, his head near to the low ceiling. He had always been tall but stooped slightly now he was getting older. He stood by the fire, rubbing his hands together. Charles asked him how Tom was.

"He's doing very well," he replied. "We've been so worried about him, but he's now improving, thank God, and we hope he'll be back home in a few weeks."

"I'd give anything to have our son here today," added Millie. "But we must be thankful he survived."

Sophie announced dinner was ready, and everyone sat down and began to pull the homemade crackers and read the jokes inside. Ben entered with the roast turkey on a platter, placing it on the table, and proceeded to carve. It took a while for plates to be filled with all the trimmings, and then the meal commenced.

"What are your plans, Charles?" asked his father as he poured gravy over his piled-up plate. "Are you returning to Portsmouth?"

"For the time being," he replied. "There's a lot to do. We're still receiving casualties. I'll probably commence my studies next year."

"What about you, Florrie?" asked Sophie.

"I'm leaving and going back to teacher training college. I wrote to my old college in Bristol and found out they were commencing the course but with a reduced teaching staff. I'll take my final exams this spring and then apply for a teaching job locally."

Rosa helped herself to more turkey. "I've decided to continue at the hospital," she announced. "We're also getting wounded soldiers."

Sophie looked proudly at her three children. They had all turned out well, and she was thankful they had all received a good education despite her and Ben's struggles with money over the years.

"I've heard from my old grammar school," Charles suddenly declared. "They've contacted all the old boys, and they want donations for a memorial for the fallen. I thought I would go over to Kingsbridge to see the headmaster while I'm here. He lives at the school."

"I don't think our school will be doing anything like that," remarked Florrie. "As Quakers, they are against war of any kind."

"I'm sure they'll be helping in some way to make a better future for us all," added Rosa.

"I think our decision to become nurses is thanks to the time we spent there," said Florrie, looking at her mother. "I'm glad Aunty Caroline helped to give us a good education. I shall be forever thankful to her and Dr. Bailey. They're good people."

Sophie smiled contentedly as she remembered her friend's kind offer to help pay for the girls to go away to the Quaker school where her own two daughters were being educated. She and Ben had scrimped and saved to help pay towards the fees, but they could not have done it without Caroline and Donald's help.

"I'll tell them when we see them again," she said. "I'm sure they'll be impressed with your service during the war, as your father and I are."

Ben asked Agnes if she was still enjoying her work at the post office. She had been there since leaving school.

"Yes, I love it, Uncle Ben. It's been difficult, at times, when I've had to deliver telegrams to folk in the village. I shall never forget the pain on their faces when they read the bad news. Now I just want my brother back home."

Ben reached out and patted her hand. "He'll be all right, and I'll do all I can to help him."

"Have you heard from Lionel?" asked Ben while he and Charles were together in the forge workshop a few days after Christmas.

Charles had been helping his father with a difficult repair job, and he put his spanner down onto the bench and replied, "Not for some time, Pa. I'm a bit concerned."

"I think we would have been notified if anything had happened to him," said Ben.

"Have you contacted his mother?"

"No, I've not seen Lucinda for a very long time. I've had to spare your mother's feelings, so I haven't written to her." Ben knew his affair with Lucinda would always be a source of pain to Sophie. She had valiantly allowed his and Lucinda's son to visit them in the school holidays, but when Lionel had begun to study law before the war, the visits had ceased. Charles had always known Lionel was his half-brother, but he had never been told all the details and had never asked.

"We've rather grown apart," said Charles. "Our lives have taken very different directions. I understand Lionel is a captain in the army."

"Yes, he's done well." Ben stopped tinkering with the bicycle wheel and looked at Charles. "I don't want to lose touch with my boy," he said, his eyes glistening slightly. "You'll let me know if you hear anything?"

"Yes, of course. Please don't worry, Pa."

CHAPTER TWO

TOM COMES HOME

CHARLES LEFT SHORTLY AFTER CHRISTMAS to resume duties at the hospital, and Florrie began preparing to recommence her college course. Ben and Sophie saw her off at the end of January.

Millie and Harry had gone to visit their son Tom at the hospital after Christmas and been told he was ready to be discharged. He had received treatment for injuries to his arm, side, and leg, caused by a hand grenade, and the doctor said he would need some time convalescing.

Millie thankfully emptied her son's bedside locker. It contained some old cigarette packets, a battered tin, and two worn-out books with their pages falling out. She bundled it all into his bag and helped Tom to his feet.

The doctor gave Tom's discharge papers to Harry and emphasised that he would need time to recover to be fully fit again. Then the doctor turned to Tom. "You've done your duty, young man, and you've done it well. Now is the time to get on with your life, and I wish you well." He shook his hand.

"Thanks for patching me up," said Tom.

His parents tried to engage him in conversation on the way to the railway station, but Tom answered only in monosyllables no matter how much they tried to engage him in conversation. He found it hard to walk, and his father had to support him. His mother exchanged an anxious glance with his father as they boarded the train back to Kingsbridge.

"The shop's doing very well," said Millie brightly, when they had settled into their seats. "We've had trouble getting supplies, of course, and it's been a problem managing the ration books. Folk always want extra. We've been short of sugar, butter, and cheese, although the local farms have helped with dairy produce, thankfully."

Tom stared out of the window blankly as his mother chattered on.

When they arrived back at the village store, he was surprised to see a small group of people outside, waving flags and cheering. He suddenly realised it was for him and tried to smile as he emerged from the taxicab. He knew Millie and Harry were popular as the village shopkeepers, and their grateful customers were expressing their joy that he had survived the war and finally returned home.

"Well done, lad!"

"Welcome home, love!"

Tom waved, acknowledging their well-meant messages as he limped into his home. Once inside, he sank into the nearest chair and said, "I didn't expect that, Ma!"

"The village is very proud of you," said his father.

Millie took some refreshments out to the welcoming-home party and stood chatting with them a short while. "Yes, thank you, thank you all. This was a lovely surprise. Yes, his injuries were bad, but the doctors say he should make a good recovery."

When she came back inside, she found her son fast asleep in the chair.

"The poor lad is exhausted," said Harry quietly. "It's going to take time to get him back to normal life. What can we do to help him, Millie?"

His wife looked tearful. "I'm just so thankful he's alive," she said. "All we can do is care for him and get him fit and well, then he can begin to think about his future."

Agnes had been looking after the shop while her parents were away, and she came in to see her brother. Millie put a finger to her lips so she would not disturb him.

"How is he?" whispered Agnes.

"He seems a bit down," replied Millie.

After a short sleep, Tom woke up.

His father brought him some tea. "Would you like to go and rest in bed when you've had this?" he asked as he placed the cup beside him.

"Yes, I still feel very tired."

"Do you think you can you manage the stairs?"

"I think so," he replied. "If I take it slowly."

"We could always make you a bed downstairs," offered Millie.

"I'll be all right, Ma. Don't fuss." As he drank his tea, Tom looked round.

Millie could see a bewildered look in his eyes. "It must feel strange being back home," she said.

"There were times when I thought I would never make it," he replied.

Millie tried to spend time with her son, but her duties running the shop prevented this. She could see he was bored.

After a few days, his father asked him if he had any plans.

"I have no idea. I'm sorry, Pa, but I don't want to work in the store. I did like working with Uncle Ben in his workshop before I went away."

"We could ask him if he wants to take you on, but I don't think he has much work now," replied Harry. "He tells me that the demand for bicycles has fallen off since the end of the war."

Tom sank deeper into the chair, the hint of a smile he'd worn a moment ago fading away. "Bloody war's ruined everything!" he muttered under his breath.

"I'll certainly have a word with him," added his father. "Don't worry, Tom. We'll sort something out. Better still, why don't you go over there when you feel up to it?"

Millie put her arm round Tom. "Pa and I will help you find something."

"What's the point?" he asked. "There's lots of able-bodied men looking for work. Who will employ me?"

In the days that followed, Millie tried to get him involved in the shop, asking him to slice the bacon or crush the cones of sugar, but he refused and spent most of his time sitting in the kitchen, reading the newspaper and smoking.

His cousin Rosa came to see him. "Florrie and Charles send their love," she told him. "Charles had to get back to his hospital, and Florrie has gone to rejoin her teacher training college."

"Lucky them," replied Tom wryly.

It was a frosty morning in February when Harry arrived breathless and distraught at Ben's workshop door, his breath like wisps of smoke in the cold air as he stood panting. "Tom's gone," he said, his face stricken in panic. He caught his breath before going on. "Millie found his bed had not been slept in last night. He's taken a few clothes, and she found some money missing from the till when she went to open the shop. She's beside herself with worry. We think he may have caught the early bus to Kingsbridge, as he still can't walk far."

Ben placed a strong arm round Harry's shoulders, his kind, round face showing concern. "Don't worry, he can't have gone far. I'll get the horse and trap out. Go and tell Millie we're going to look for him, and I'll pick you up back at the shop."

"He hasn't been right since he came home. I knew something was bothering him," said Harry as he turned to leave.

Ben hurried to the cottage to tell Sophie, and she said she would go and stay with Millie while they searched.

When he collected Harry, there was some more news. Agnes had told Harry that Tom spoke about going to sea, joining the merchant navy or something. Ben suggested the best place to start was Kingsbridge quay, so they set off to begin the search there. Millie and Agnes saw them off with worried looks, their arms firmly entwined as they held each other close. Ben shook the reins and urged the horse into a trot, and they rattled off down the hill.

Once they arrived in Kingsbridge, Ben tethered the horse, and he and Harry began looking round, walking up and down Fore Street and asking passers-by if they had seen a young lad with a limp. No one had anything to tell them.

Down at the quayside, the tide was out, so they decided that Tom would probably be waiting before he could board a ship.

"Where can he be?" asked Harry, looking distraught. They had now been looking round all morning for any sign of Tom. Both were feeling exhausted.

"If I had some time to kill, I'd be in there," Ben said, nodding towards the Harbour Inn. The black-and-white building was situated conveniently near the quayside and was a favourite haunt of sailors and crew. It was just after midday and the public house had just opened.

The two of them entered the noisy, smoky bar and looked round. They found Tom sitting at the back, tucked away in a dark corner, with a pint of ale in front of him. He looked up as his father and Ben approached.

"Hello, Tom," said Ben.

Tom scowled, clearly not pleased at seeing them.

Harry sat down beside his son.

"I'll get some drinks," said Ben, leaving Harry to reunite with his son.

Harry talked quietly to him. "You know, Tom, there never was a problem you could run away from and make it go away."

They sat in silence for a while until Ben returned with the drinks.

"I'm glad we've found you. Your mother's frantic," Ben said, placing the glasses of ale on the table. "Out with it, now, lad. Tell us exactly what you're feeling. We're here to listen and, I hope, help."

"I'm sick of this world with people killing each other," began Tom, thumping his fist on the table. "I've no idea what I want to do. There's no future out there. Billy has had all the luck, and I've had none. He's clever—I'm not. He has money—I haven't. He has a girl—I have nobody!"

"All that you say is true, Tom," said Ben. "Your brother has been very fortunate."

"Half-brother!" interjected Tom angrily.

"I know he's got through the war unscathed and has been left money by his grandmother," continued Ben. "It's not a fair world, and it's not a good world, either. Now, think on this. As you well know, there are many good men rotting under the mud in France, and you're here, drinking ale, with your father beside you. What do you think those poor men would be saying to you right now? That you're a lucky fellow, and you should be wanting to live your life to the fullest. You say Billy is clever, but you're as clever with your hands. You say he is rich, but you could make yourself a decent living, as I've been able to, if you've a mind to. You say he has a girl… Well, find one for yourself. There won't be much competition, with so many young men gone. I can offer you work at my workshop, and I can train you, and I would like to hand over my business to you eventually, when I retire. I was going to put all this to you before you did a runner. So now you must decide what you want to do, and I'm sure your father will respect your decision."

Tom slumped forwards and put his head down on his folded arms.

The two men each placed a hand on each of Tom's arms and waited patiently for him to think for a few moments.

Then Harry gently asked, "Are you coming home, son? Your mother's so worried."

Tom sat up slowly and, looking at Harry, nodded reluctantly, then the three of them finished their drinks and got up to go. Harry supported his son as he limped alongside on their way back to the horse and trap.

When they got home, Tom hugged his mother and blurted out, "Sorry, Ma."

Millie held him tightly, tears of relief streaming down her cheeks. "Oh, Tom, I'm so glad you're back! Please, please don't do that again. We all want what's best for you. Give it time, and we'll help you make something of your life when you're fully recovered."

Tom nodded silently, and the look on his face showed he would not be running away again.

He was late getting up the next morning and was sitting with his mother in the kitchen when the door opened, and Harry walked in, holding a lively young dog on a piece of string.

"Good Lord!" said Millie.

For the first time in a long while, Tom's face lit up with excitement and joy. The animal, with his tongue flopping and his tail wagging furiously, was straining to come towards him.

"Hello, boy!" he exclaimed, fondling the dog's head. "What's his name?"

"Digger," replied his father. "I got him from the farm. If you want him, he's yours."

Tom continued to make a fuss over the dog. "Thanks, Pa!" he answered.

Harry beamed.

"You'll have to walk him every day, Tom," said his mother. "And feed him. I won't have time."

The following day, Tom hobbled over to Forge Cottage with Digger for the first time since his return. As he entered the kitchen, he called out, "Look what I've got here, Aunt Sophie!"

Sophie came out of the scullery, drying her hands on a towel. "Tom, he's lovely! Is he yours?"

"Yes, Pa gave him to me. He's from the farm."

Sophie put her hands on her hips and took a good look. "He's very friendly. You should check him for fleas, though, if he's a farm dog."

"Yes, I will. I think we stock some powder in the shop." Digger dashed about, tugging excitedly on his string, making Tom hold on tightly as the dog jumped up at Sophie. Tom decided to take him outside. "Is Uncle Ben here?" he asked as the dog pulled him towards the door. "I'd like to see him about something."

"Yes, he's in his workshop."

Tom let Digger drag him outside, and they went off in the direction of the forge.

Ben came out of the workshop just as they approached. "Hello, Tom! Who's this?" He bent down to give Digger a stroke.

"Pa gave him to me. His name's Digger."

Ben stood up and gave his nephew a steady look. "How are you, Tom?" he asked.

"I'm not good. To be honest, I'm bored and fed up. Is there a chance I could help you, Uncle Ben? You don't have to pay me. I just want something to do."

"Of course! I said I would take you on, but there's not much work just now. Things usually pick up when the cycle clubs start up again at

Easter. Tell you what, I could show you how to build a bicycle. Then you can ride it to exercise that leg."

Tom looked pleased. "Thanks, Uncle Ben. I'll come tomorrow if that's all right." All this time, Digger had been straining to go for a walk, and Tom turned to leave.

Ben stood by the workshop door and waved them off, watching Tom limp up the lane, pulled by Digger. "And get that dog a decent lead!" he called after them.

The next morning, Tom turned up again at the workshop with his dog. "Is it okay if he comes too?" he asked.

"As long as he behaves."

Tom tied Digger up outside, and the animal flopped down to rest.

"You'll have to take him for a walk later."

"We'll go off after lunch," replied Tom.

Ben turned his attention to their work. He had put a few bicycle components out on the bench and began to show Tom how to put them together. Tom listened with interest, seeming to find all the different pieces that went into making up a bicycle fascinating.

The two men worked all morning, finally putting their tools down at midday. As they stepped outside into the fresh air, Digger looked up expectantly.

Tom untied him, cupping his hand round the dog's face to fondle him. Digger showed his delight by wagging his tail furiously. "Come on, boy!" he said, taking the young dog's lead and following his uncle towards the cottage for lunch.

On Saturday, Tom came back to Forge Cottage to see Rosa, bringing Digger. He introduced his new friend.

"He's lovely!" she said, patting him. "Has he done much digging?"

Tom laughed. "Only down a few rabbit holes on our walks. He's a bit lively, but I think he'll settle down. Ma makes him sleep outside. She reckons he has fleas, so I'm treating him."

Rosa backed off when she heard that, pulling a face.

They left the cottage and began walking slowly together down to the workshop.

"I want to ask you something, Tom," she began. "On my way home, I saw a poster advertising a Valentine's Day dance in Kingsbridge. I'd like to go. Would you come too?"

Tom suddenly felt all his despair returning. "It's no good, me going," he replied, looking swiftly away. "I won't be able to dance."

Rosa leant towards him, bending her head near his ear as if to divulge a secret. "There'll be lots of pretty girls there, Tom."

They won't be looking at some cripple like me, he thought. "You go, Rosa. You'll have no trouble finding someone to dance with. Your hair looks good like that."

"It's called a bob. All the girls are having their hair cut off. Long hair's such a nuisance. I'm sure you'd find a girl who would dance with you." She gave him a smile. "I wonder how many young men will be there? Not many, I should imagine. I wish you would come. Please think it over." Reaching the forge, she opened the workshop door and called out, "Pa! Tom's here!"

CHAPTER THREE
ROSA JOINS A CAUSE

"BEN, THE CYCLISTS WILL BE arriving at Easter, and I'm not sure we're ready for them," said Sophie as she prepared the vegetables for their evening meal. "Perhaps you and Tom could have a look at the tables and chairs in the outhouse. Some are getting a bit old now."

Ben and Sophie had been running a refreshment stop for cycle riders for some years. Groups of cyclists would stop at the cottage and congregate in the orchard. Ben and Sophie worked as representatives of the Cycle Touring Club, a countrywide organisation, and Ben had attached their emblem, depicting a bicycle wheel with three wings, on the wall of the old forge. Small groups had continued arriving even during the war years, but now the war had ended, and Sophie knew there would be more.

"I wonder who will turn up?" continued Sophie. "It will be lovely to see some old faces."

"I'll see to the furniture," replied Ben. "But it might be a bit chilly to sit outside."

"I won't have room for them all in my kitchen," said Sophie. "Especially if they arrive in groups."

Sophie had been advised by the CTC that some of the riders were forming themselves into small affiliated clubs, such as ladies only or those belonging to the same political persuasion.

On Easter Sunday, a group of lady riders arrived, and as the weather was dry, they sat outside. When Rosa went round with the tray of teas, one of them introduced herself.

"Hello there!" she called out heartily. "I'm Anthea. Jolly pleased to meet you!"

After she had finished serving the teas, Rosa spoke to her again, asking about the group she belonged to. Anthea explained about their organisation and what it stood for. Rosa was very interested and asked a few questions. She talked to some of the other young women and listened to their opinions.

Later at dinner, she told her parents about her new friend. "Her name's Anthea, and she's the leader of the local Women Workers Socialist Group," she began enthusiastically. "There's about six of them altogether."

"And what do they all believe in?" asked her father, leaning back in his chair and raising his eyebrows.

Sophie frowned at him, then asked Rosa to tell them more.

"Anthea believes we should all have equal rights, men and women, rich and poor," she explained. "We should all have the same opportunities, especially in education."

Sophie nodded in agreement and smiled at her daughter encouragingly, but Rosa could see her father was not convinced.

"That's all very well, Rosa," said Ben, looking sceptical. "But the world isn't like that. How can things be any different when it's the rich men who govern our country and they want to keep things unchanged?"

"Well, by giving women the vote, for a start," replied his daughter. "The suffragette movement was just getting somewhere before the war. The Act passed in Parliament last year has gone some way towards giving us the vote, but not all women are eligible. Women have been doing men's jobs while they were away fighting, and they should have a voice. I would like to see all women over twenty-one given the right to vote, the same as men, and then ordinary people can vote for a government that will reflect at least some of their demands for justice."

"It's a man's world and always will be as long as men work and women have babies," replied Ben. "Men and women have different roles in life, and that's how it should be."

Rosa could feel herself getting worked up. "Until there's a war, Pa. You must agree that many women can do men's jobs now."

"Yes! And take the jobs away from them if we're not careful. There's enough unemployment as it is." Ben banged his fist down on the arm of his chair.

"I think you two should agree to differ," Sophie said, trying to calm them both down.

"Sounds as if that Anthea doesn't know what she's talking about," said Ben gruffly, crossing his arms. "She should take a step back and view society as it really is."

"I think that's exactly what she is doing," replied Rosa quietly, getting up to help her mother with the dishes.

While they were washing up in the scullery, Rosa told her mother that she wanted to become more active in the socialist movement. Anthea had told her about a rally to take place in Exeter shortly. "Do you think Pa will let me go?" she asked anxiously.

"If he does, I think he should take you there," suggested her mother. "I don't think you should go on your own, among a lot of strangers."

"There won't be any men. It's really for women. Besides, Anthea will be there."

"We'll see what he says."

"I know—I'll ask Agnes to come with me," said Rosa. "I expect her parents will give her permission to go."

They went back into the kitchen. Ben looked up from his chair as Sophie mentioned the rally to him.

When his expression turned sour again, she implored, "We should be encouraging Rosa to care about what happens in the world. The war has changed everything."

Ben looked contrite. "I realise that. If Rosa and Anthea can make the world a better place, good for them." He turned to his daughter. "Yes, you can go to the rally, but don't get into any trouble like those suffragette women. I'll take you and Agnes there and collect you afterwards."

Rosa flung her arms round his neck. "Oh, Pa, thank you!"

The rally was the following Saturday morning, the first week in May, and Ben accompanied the girls on the train to Exeter. He left them by the cathedral after seeing that the rally appeared well organised.

Groups of young women, some with banners, were standing about on the green, and Rosa soon spotted Anthea. She reassured her father they would be safe and kissed him goodbye.

"Thank you for bringing us," added Agnes, giving her uncle a charming smile.

"I'll see you both later. I feel out of my depth among all these determined young women," he muttered as he left them.

He strolled along the busy High Street, looking for a pub where he could get a few beers, dodging honking motor cars that rumbled up and down the street.

Suddenly, he stopped in his tracks at the sight of Lucinda and her daughter, Sapphire, strolling towards him, arm in arm. Lucinda was in a smart-looking long coat fastened with two large buttons at the side. It had a large fur collar framing her pale, made-up face. She was wearing a close-fitting hat with a band round the crown. Sapphire was in a shorter red coat with matching cloche hat.

Before he had time to decide what to do, they spotted him and hurried over.

Ben removed his cloth cap, clutching it in both hands in front of him.

"Ben! How *lovely* to see you!" enthused Lucinda.

It had been some time since they had last met, but he could see she still had the same attractive looks. "Hello, Lucinda," he replied. "It's good to see you again."

"This is my daughter, Sapphire." Turning towards her, Lucinda said, "Ben is Lionel's father, darling."

Ben smiled at her. "Hello, Sapphire. It's nice to meet you at last."

Sapphire gave him a half-hearted smile.

"What brings you to Exeter?" asked Lucinda.

"My youngest daughter, Rosa, wanted to attend a rally. Something about women's rights."

"I thought I saw a bit of excitement down there," said Lucinda, looking towards the cathedral. "So your little Rosa has taken up a cause, has she?"

"She met someone who persuaded her to go. I don't know what it will achieve."

"Why don't we go and have some coffee in Mercers?" suggested Lucinda, then, without waiting for an answer, she led the way to the nearby department store.

Ben felt a little buzz of excitement as he followed them. Lucinda walked briskly, and he fell in behind, wondering whether he should be doing this.

When they arrived in the tearoom, Lucinda ushered them to a table by the window and summoned the waiter with her gloved hand. Coffee was brought, and Ben sat holding his cup, not saying anything as Lucinda spoke about the war, how she was so glad it was over, what a dreadful business it all was and how awful rationing had been.

"I've not been able to have any dinner parties, and we haven't bought any new clothes for ages, have we, darling?" She looked at Sapphire, who shrugged and shook her head. "That's why we're here today," she added.

Ben hardly followed her chatter, just stared at her, all the while recalling their liaison and feeling as if he had been set adrift from his present life. He put his cup down and tried to pull himself together. "How's Lionel?" he asked when he could get a word in.

Lucinda told him that she and Sapphire were expecting to see Lionel soon and that he had been to the palace to receive his award for gallantry from the king. She went on to gush about how they were all so proud of him. "He was so brave, and many of his men owe their lives to him. I am so relieved he survived. I have been so desperately worried about him."

Sapphire yawned, looking distractedly round the room at the other customers.

"And how is Charles?" asked Lucinda.

"He's been working in a hospital in Portsmouth for most of the war," Ben replied. "He's just commenced his studies at medical school and will hopefully qualify as a doctor next year."

"Oh, Ben, you must be pleased. A son who is a doctor!" She clasped her hands together, looking genuinely impressed.

Sapphire told her mother she wanted to go and look at the hats. "I'll see you there," she said, and saying a quick goodbye to Ben, she left.

Lucinda was the first to speak once they were alone, suddenly looking serious. "Ours has been a strange friendship, Ben."

Ben looked intently at her. "Yes, it has."

"I expect you wish it never happened," she went on. "But we share something good—Lionel."

"You know I love that boy, don't you?"

"Yes, and I know you loved me once."

"Lucinda…" he began.

Before he could continue, she put on her gloves and picked up her bag. "I'd better go and find that errant daughter of mine," she said quickly, rising to go. "Can you get this?" She gestured at the coffee cups on the table.

"Yes, of course," said Ben, getting up.

"Goodbye, Ben," she said as she turned to go.

"Goodbye, Lucinda."

He watched her slim, attractive figure move between the tables as she left. She didn't look back, but he could smell her lingering perfume.

Ben felt inside his jacket for his wallet. Fortunately, Sophie had given him some money from the jar on the dresser to purchase a few items for her sewing while he was in Exeter. He hoped he would have enough left for these. Mercers wasn't a place he would normally go, although he had taken Sophie there once or twice in the past, when he'd had more money.

He paid the bill and left, making his way to the haberdashery department. Able to buy all the items Sophie had asked for except one, he would have to tell her it was out of stock.

He had kept enough money for a beer or two, so he made his way to the nearest public house. As he walked along, he felt very churned up, knowing it would have been better not to have bumped into them but feeling glad he had. He wondered whether to tell Sophie when he got back. It would probably be better to do so. If he didn't, she might find out and start blaming him again. He spent the afternoon staring into his beer, thinking about the past.

At three o'clock, he returned to the cathedral, where he found Rosa and Agnes waiting for him. His daughter appeared very animated.

"We marched down the road and attracted a lot of attention," she told him excitedly. "Some people cheered, but we heard some young men shouting at us. I won't tell you what they said." She glanced at Agnes, who looked embarrassed.

"I was afraid you might come up against some hecklers," said Ben. He turned to his niece. "What did you think of it?"

"It was quite exciting," Agnes replied. "But I don't think I shall be going again."

"Why's that?"

"All the women were shouting slogans, and some were getting angry. It was a bit overwhelming."

Rosa laughed. "I thought it was great fun!" she said, linking her arm through her cousin's as they walked back to the station. "Thanks for coming, Agnes. I won't make you come next time!"

Back at home, Rosa excitedly talked about women's rights for the rest of the evening. She went on and on about how women should be given the vote and allowed to have more freedom, sparing Ben from having to tell Sophie about spending time with Lucinda.

When they finally retired to bed, he told Sophie, "I met someone when I was in Exeter. It was Lucinda, and she was with her daughter."

"So you've met Sapphire?" Sophie replied.

"Yes, she looks very like her mother."

"How was Lucinda?"

"Just the same, a little older. They were out shopping."

"Fancy bumping into them," remarked Sophie.

"I told them why I was there."

"Did she say anything about Lionel?"

"Yes, he's been to the palace to receive an award for gallantry."

Sophie did not respond for a few moments, then she said, "Did you tell her about Charles? How *he* spent the war mending broken bodies?"

"Yes, as a matter of fact, I did."

"He didn't get a medal."

"Why do you say that? Aren't you pleased Lionel got an award for bravery?"

"I feel it isn't right that the brave deeds of war are commemorated and the healing side is not," stated Sophie.

"Lionel is a soldier, and his job is to protect our country with his life. Doesn't that deserve a medal?"

"I just think the doctors and nurses deserve the same recognition."

"It's not quite the same, is it?"

"I don't see why not."

"There are times when I really don't understand you," said Ben as he turned over to go to sleep.

When Rosa returned to work at the hospital, she found that several patients had moved on and others had arrived. One or two of the new patients were ex-servicemen who needed more nursing care before they could be discharged.

On her rounds, she came upon a young serviceman called Danny who had been gassed, leaving him partially sighted. He told her he came from Plymouth, where he lived with his widowed mother.

"Just before the war, she remarried," he explained. "Her husband has two boys, so there won't be much room for me at home now. So here I am, a piece of flotsam waiting to be washed up somewhere by the great tide of life!"

How unfair that he has been injured like this at such a young age, Rosa thought. She spent extra time with him, as she thought it must be boring for him lying in bed all day, not able to see. She found him cheerful despite his problems and would often stop and talk to him as she carried out her duties on the ward. Her training meant that she should not single out patients for special attention, and she hoped Matron would not notice.

Danny's right eye was quite badly damaged, but despite this, Rosa could see he was a good-looking chap. She enjoyed helping him wash and shave and comb his hair. He told her she had "nice hands."

"Are you getting me ready to take you out later?" he would joke.

In the evenings, after her shift had ended, she would read to him. She had borrowed a few of her mother's books, and *Moby Dick* seemed an appropriate story to interest him.

The hospital had arranged for Danny to be moved to a retraining unit in Taunton to help rehabilitate him for civilian life, now that he had left the army. Matron asked Rosa to help get him ready. On the day of his departure, she emptied his bedside cupboard of his few belongings and packed them into his kit bag.

"I'm sorry we didn't get to finish *Moby Dick*," she said.

"Thanks for reading it to me," he replied. "It was a good story. Maybe I'll get to hear the finish one day."

"I hope so."

"I'd like to keep in touch, Nurse Browne. Maybe they'll make something of me at this place I'm going to. I hear they'll be teaching me Braille, so I could write to you."

"That would be good. I would love to hear how you're getting on. We shall all miss you here." She wrote down the address of Forge Cottage for him and put the folded the paper into his hand.

He stuffed it into his pocket, then said goodbye.

"Goodbye, Danny, and good luck!" Rosa watched as the porter pushed Danny's wheelchair down the corridor.

When he reached the door, Danny turned and waved.

Rosa felt herself welling up and put her hand to her mouth to quell her tears. Would she ever see him again? She told herself she was foolish, getting overfond of a patient, something that was deemed unprofessional. She turned to survey the empty bed in front of her and began to strip it down.

Presently, one of the other nurses came over and informed her, "Matron wants to see you, Nurse Browne. You go, and I'll finish this."

As Matron had charge of the whole hospital, Rosa wondered why she had been summoned. She looked up as Rosa entered her office, then began to gather some papers together on her desk.

"Ah, Nurse Browne! I need to speak to you," she said briskly. "This won't take long. I don't know if you're aware, but the recent Nurses Registration Act requires all nurses to be registered, which means you cannot work here as a nurse anymore. You need to be qualified, and that means you will have to train at a hospital for two years."

Rosa stood wide-eyed, not knowing what to say or do next. Why would she have to retrain if she had been nursing for the past few years? She clasped her hands behind her back and listened carefully to what she was being told.

"The war has created a lot of volunteer nurses like yourself, who have learnt about nursing on the job. Now the government wants them all to be trained properly at nursing schools and accredited. Of course, you will have to discuss this with your parents. When you decide what to do, come and see me, and I will help you submit your application."

"Can I ask where I would be able to train?"

"The nearest hospital would be in Exeter."

She told the matron she would let her know her decision, then returned to her ward.

She wondered what it would entail besides living away from home. Did she want to do that? It could be exciting going to nursing school. She would meet other applicants and make new friends. By the end of her shift that day, she had decided she did want to apply and would ask her parents at the weekend if they agreed.

She arrived home on Friday evening, eager to tell Ben and Sophie all the happenings at the hospital, but she began by describing what the matron had told her.

"It will be a lot of hard work, all that studying," said her father. "Are you sure you want to do that for two years? You're young, and you should be enjoying life."

"I love nursing, Pa. It's all I want to do."

"Where will you be living?" asked her mother.

"I'll be in the nurses' accommodation," Rosa replied. "I think I shall be well looked after."

"How do you feel about living away from home?" asked Ben.

"I'm quite excited. I expect there'll be a group of us away from home at the same time. I'll be able to come back here when I have leave, and the two years will go by quickly, I'm sure."

Sophie and Ben looked at each other, a look that meant they were mutually in agreement.

"You give it a go, my clever girl!" said her father. "We'll do whatever we can to support you, won't we, Sophie?"

"Yes, of course. We're very proud of what you're doing."

Rosa felt she had made some headway in allaying her parent's fears and was relieved when they finally said they were happy for her to go.

She spent a pleasant weekend at home, helping with the cyclists' teas. Anthea turned up with her group of chums again, and Rosa was astounded at her attire—knickerbockers and a belted jumper, together with a beret.

"Hello, Rosa!" she called out. "When are you coming to one of our meetings?"

Rosa put down the tray of teacups she was collecting. "I'm sorry, Anthea, but I'm having to go away for retraining."

"Where's that, then?" her friend asked.

"Probably a hospital in Exeter."

"I'll put you in touch with the group there."

"Thanks, that would be good, but I'll have to see how much time off I get." She finished clearing the tables with a feeling of anticipation. Life in Exeter sounded exciting.

On Monday morning, she went to see Matron to tell her of her decision to accept, and to get further details.

Matron expressed her approval. "We shall miss you, Nurse Browne, but you have made the right choice. The nursing profession needs nurses like you."

Rosa could feel herself filling with pride.

Matron gave her a handful of forms to fill in. "Let me know if you want any help with these," she said.

Rosa returned to her ward to begin her work for the day. She decided to ask her mother's help in completing the paperwork when she went home.

She continued carrying out her duties on the ward that week, helping with a new group of casualties who had arrived. She would miss the camaraderie they shared with her.

That weekend, Sophie and Rosa spread the sheets of paper out on the parlour table and began studying them. They peered at each form in turn, reading out each question carefully and writing out the answer.

When they had finished, Rosa stood up and stretched. "Thank goodness that's done. They want to know everything!"

"Nursing's a very responsible vocation," replied Sophie. "They need to make sure they have the right people." She took off her spectacles and looked at her daughter. "You're quite sure about this?" she asked. "You'll be away from home for several weeks at a time, and it will mean some hard studying."

"I would like to become as independent as I can be, Ma. I feel it's time to move on, and I do want to get qualified as a nurse."

"Your father and I will miss you," said Sophie, "but we want what's best for you and for you to be happy."

Rosa gave her mother a kiss and went to find her father. He was in the garden, tidying up the flower beds. The sun was shining, and spring was well on with blossom on the apple trees in the orchard. Rosa stopped to look round, breathing in the fresh air.

"All done?" asked Ben.

"Yes, thank goodness!"

"You're still sure about it, then?"

Rosa laughed. "Ma just asked me that! Yes, I'm sure."

Ben put down his hoe, and they strolled round the garden together, arm in arm, enjoying the fresh air. Rosa paused and looked back at the cottage. A thin trail of smoke was coming out of one of the tall chimneys.

"I love this place, Pa. It's so peaceful. I shall miss it."

"And your old ma and pa," said Ben, patting her arm.

"Yes, of course."

"Have you heard from that young man of yours at the hospital?" he asked.

"He's not *my* young man, but no, I haven't yet. I suppose it will take a little while for him to learn Braille."

They paused in the orchard to admire the trees. The apple blossom was in full bloom, and bees were buzzing round, busily burrowing into the flowers.

"Should be a good crop this year," remarked Ben, looking up.

Rosa leant towards her father and put her head on his shoulder. "Thanks for being such a wonderful pa," she said. "I'll miss you and Ma when I'm away. I know I will."

"You'll be all right, old girl," said Ben, hugging her.

They went back inside just as Sophie was getting the tea ready. She was busy buttering slices of bread.

"Best meal of the day!" said Ben, rubbing his hands together.

"You'd better wash before you come to the table," said his wife, eyeing him.

Ben grinned. "Yes, ma'am," he answered, heading for the scullery.

Rosa smiled at them both. Ma had always insisted on certain standards.

On Monday morning, Rosa took her bundle of papers back to the hospital and presented them to Matron.

"Well done, Nurse Browne. I hope you will be successful in your application. I don't see any reason why not. You've been an excellent nurse here, and I'll be sorry to lose you. Perhaps you'll come back to us when you've qualified?"

"Two years is a long time," replied Rosa. "I'm afraid I have no idea what I'll do afterwards."

"Well, the one thing you can't do is get married. You do know that, don't you?"

Rosa nodded and smiled. "I don't have any plans to marry," she replied.

CHAPTER FOUR
BILLY PROPOSES

WORKING IN THE KITCHEN ONE morning, Sophie heard a roaring noise and ran outside to see what it could be.

A man was coming up the lane on a motorbike, heading for the cottage. He stopped just before the gate, placed one leg on the ground, and raised his goggles.

"What do you think?" he asked.

"Billy!" exclaimed Sophie. "What a surprise!"

Having also heard the noise, Ben came out of the workshop.

"It's Billy!" Sophie called out to him.

"Well, I never! It's lovely to see you. We never expected to see you arrive like this!" Ben walked round the machine, peering down now and then to examine it more closely.

"When did you get back?" asked Sophie.

"About a week ago." He smiled broadly at his uncle's interest in the machine. "Hop on, Ben. I'll take you for a spin."

Before Sophie could protest, Ben was on the back. Billy turned the motorbike round and, with a twist of the throttle, sped off up the lane. After about five minutes, he returned with Ben smiling broadly over his shoulder.

"That was pretty amazing!" said Ben, looking excited.

Billy looked at his aunt. "Would you like a ride too?" he asked.

Sophie shook her head vehemently. "I know who will, though," she said. "Your mother."

"She's already had one," replied Billy, grinning. "And Harry."

"What about Tom?" Sophie asked.

"He wouldn't come out," said Billy. "I'm really worried about him. We haven't been getting along too well."

Sophie frowned slightly but made no comment.

Ben was admiring the shiny, new motorcycle. "I must get into these. I can see them becoming very popular," he told Billy.

"They had them in the war, Uncle, and I promised myself one if I managed to survive."

"You deserve it, then," said Sophie. "Can you stay for a bit? I can make some tea if you like."

"Yes, I'd love to." Billy leant his machine against the wall of the cottage and took off his gauntlets, hat, and goggles. Following Sophie inside, he sat down and began to chuckle. "Your face when I arrived, Aunt Sophie!"

"I'm not used to young men arriving on motorcycles," she answered. "We live a very quiet life here."

"Sorry if I frightened you."

"That's all right. We're so glad to see you. Tell us what you're planning to do. Have you left the army?"

"Yes, I stayed on for a while to requisition what horses I could save and bring back to England. The army was going to destroy them. I'm glad I joined the Royal Army Veterinary Corps, but now I want to start up my own practice."

Ben nodded in approval. "We wish you every success. And Dorothy?"

"I need to go and see her, Uncle Ben. We have a lot of plans to make."

While Billy seemed to enjoy chatting and reminiscing about when he lived at Forge Cottage before his mother married, he was reluctant to talk about his time serving in France.

"It was horrible, Aunt Sophie," was all he wanted to say. "I never want to go through anything like that again in my life."

Billy said his goodbyes and headed over to the village of Modbury, where his fiancée lived and where her father, Dr. Bailey, had his practice. Her mother, Caroline, was Donald's second wife and Aunt Sophie's friend.

Billy had known Dorothy since they were children. Before the war, they had met at Forge Cottage, where Dorothy kept her pony, and they had gone riding together. Billy had proposed before he left to join the army, and now they were at last to get married.

He turned the throttle a little more and sped down the lane, anxious to see her at long last.

As he entered the village where she lived, he slowed down considerably to manoeuvre round a sharp bend and then ascend the steep High Street to Acacia House, past his grandmother's house, where Aunt Sophie used to drop him off on her way to see Caroline. His grandmother had died just as the war had begun, and he had a feeling of sadness as he passed by. He was grateful she had paid for his private school fees, which had enabled him to go on to veterinary college.

He reached the top of the hill and stopped outside the imposing Georgian house that also served as a surgery. Wisteria clung to the walls, but the blooms were now faded, as it was late June.

Parking the motorcycle nearby, he rang the bell pull and waited. A surge of excitement rushed through him. He hadn't seen Dorothy for over a year.

He was shown in and found Dorothy with her parents, sitting quietly with her hands in her lap, in the conservatory at the back of the house.

Dr. Bailey got up and shook Billy's hand warmly. "Welcome, young man! We're so very relieved to have you back safe and sound."

"How are you, Billy?" asked Caroline. "We've been longing to see you, haven't we, Dorothy?" She turned to her daughter.

Dorothy managed a choked, "Yes," and Billy could see she was near to tears.

Feeling overwhelmed at seeing her again, he just wanted to take her in his arms. Instead, he went over and kissed her gently on her cheek.

"Hello, Dorothy. I *have* missed you," he said quietly.

She smiled up at him, the same sweet smile he remembered.

He turned to Dorothy's mother. "I'm well, thank you, Mrs. Bailey. Very glad to be here!"

He was relieved when she announced she had to go and see to the luncheon. As she got up, she glanced over to her husband, which prompted him to stand up too.

He gave a slight cough. "If you'll excuse me, I just need to go and close up the surgery," he said quickly, also making an exit.

As soon as they had gone, Billy embraced Dorothy in his arms. Holding her tightly, he said, "We can get married now."

"At long last," she responded. "Oh, Billy, I can hardly believe it!"

"I've never stopped thinking of you all through my time in France. I would get out the photo of you, and when I looked at it, I just knew I had to keep going." He reached into his pocket and drew out the crumpled photograph. "See! I still have it!"

Dorothy laughed, her eyes shining.

He stood back, holding her at arms' length and looking at her intently. "How about you, Dorothy? How has life been for you all this time?"

"Not too bad. I've had my piano pupils, and I've kept busy helping Daddy in his pharmacy. This war has seemed so long. We lost several men in the village, men Daddy knew as patients. It's been very hard to see the poor wives and mothers of the soldiers coping. Mummy and some of her church friends have been organising help for them."

"I think every village in Britain has been affected. This war will never be forgotten."

"What plans do you have for us, my love?" asked Dorothy. "I think Daddy wants to speak to you about them."

Before Billy could reply, Caroline returned and announced that the luncheon was ready.

As they entered the dining room, he suddenly said, "I forgot to tell you, I am now the proud owner of a motorbike."

"Did you come on it today?" asked Dr. Bailey as he joined them.

"Yes, and I got here so quickly. I called in to Uncle Ben's first to tell them I was back."

"What did Sophie think of it?" asked Caroline.

"I don't think she was very impressed, but Ben loved it."

"Now, young man," said Dr. Bailey, sitting down to enjoy the lunch his wife had prepared. "When do you intend to marry my daughter, and what are your plans?"

Feeling apprehensive, Billy thought, *I know he is going to ask me about money and my prospects.*

"We want to get married as soon as possible," he answered, turning to Dorothy beside him and taking her hand.

"I don't see any reason why that should not be so, but have you thought about where you would live?"

"I want to find a property in Kingsbridge, sir, that I can adapt into a surgery for the veterinary practice I want to set up."

"That will take time."

"Yes, unfortunately." Billy could feel his cheerfulness ebbing away.

"We would like to make a suggestion," interrupted Caroline. "Donald and I can offer you both accommodation here. It's a large house, and it would be such a shame if you can't get married straight away after waiting so long. Perhaps you would like to think it over."

Billy smiled broadly and looked at Dorothy. "Thank you for such a kind offer. If Dorothy agrees, then yes."

Dorothy nodded at him.

"My grandmother left me some money," Billy added. "It should be enough to cover the purchase price of the building and any alterations."

"Caroline and I would like to give you a gift of money too," said Donald.

"Thank you very much. That's very generous of you."

Donald picked up the bottle of wine on the table and poured everyone a glass. Holding his up, he said, "I'd like to propose a toast. Caroline and I wish you both every happiness and success in your new venture."

They raised their glasses in agreement.

Billy visited his uncle and aunt again, walking over from Millie and Harry's cottage. He told Sophie that he and Dorothy were now planning their wedding and would be living at Acacia House for the time being.

Sophie gave him a warm hug and told him how pleased she was that they could finally get married. "You've waited a long time. Ben and I wish you every happiness," she said affectionally.

"Thank you, Aunt Sophie. You and Ben have been so good to me." He kissed his aunt affectionally on the cheek. "Is Tom here?" he asked. "I want to ask him something."

"You'll find him in the workshop."

Billy made his way there and found Tom inside on his own. "Hello, Tom!" he said cheerfully. "I came over to tell you that Dorothy and I have set a date for our wedding at last. It's to be at the end of June, and I wanted to ask you to be my best man."

"I don't think so, Billy," replied Tom curtly.

Billy looked stunned. "What's wrong? I thought you'd be pleased to be asked."

Tom continued working at the bench.

Billy waited a few moments for a response. When none came, he said, "Well, I'm sorry you have declined, Tom. I hope you'll come anyway." He turned to go and walked slowly back to the cottage, where he told Sophie about Tom's response.

"I am sorry," said Sophie, putting down her sewing. "He seems to be set against you just now, doesn't he?"

"I don't understand it. It must be something to do with this damned war. It's had some strange effects on people. I know he had a rough time of it."

"Give him time to heal inside, Billy. He still seems very bitter."

Billy sighed. "Those poor boys, how they must have suffered."

"Ben has found him some work. They're building a bicycle together."

"I'm glad he has something to do. There's so much unemployment now, his chances of getting a job are bleak. Uncle Ben has been good to him."

Billy got up to go. "I'm going to write to Charles and ask him if he would be my best man," he said as he left. "I hope he agrees."

Soon after Billy sent out his letter, Charles replied that he would love to accept, much to his cousin's relief.

Billy had, however, another dilemma to deal with. He had not seen much of his birth father, Jonathan, over the past few years. He was now a vicar in a village in the next county. Dorothy and her family knew all about Billy's parentage and were willing to invite Jonathan to the wedding.

His father politely declined, saying that, regretfully, it was too far to come and he would have to get back to take the Sunday services at his church. He wished his son and soon-to-be daughter-in-law every happiness and hoped to visit them sometime in the future. Billy realised it was a diplomatic refusal and was relieved. His birth father's presence would have been a distraction and might cause some embarrassment to his mother.

A letter arrived from Caroline, asking Sophie to come and discuss Dorothy's wedding dress.

Sophie had not seen her friend for some time. Before the war, she'd been happy to take the horse and trap over to her friend's house, but now she was too nervous to travel through the lanes, as they had become busy with motorised vehicles. Ben said he would take her, so they set off one afternoon.

The journey was slow. The horse was getting old, and Ben had to keep pulling over to give him frequent rests. He broached the subject of getting a motor, telling Sophie that he could purchase a secondhand vehicle and get Tom to help him do it up. Sophie had to agree, as she was not inclined to drive the trap on her own anymore and could see the horse needed to retire. It would use up all their savings, but they needed some kind of transport.

When they arrived at Acacia House, Caroline welcomed her friend with enthusiasm. After lunch, they spent the afternoon measuring Dorothy and discussing ideas for her dress.

Before they left, Caroline gave Sophie invitations for her and the family to attend the wedding. Billy and Dorothy were to be married in the local church, and the reception of about thirty guests would be held at Acacia House. Caroline was full of excitement about the wedding.

"It won't be a sit-down meal," she explained. "Our dining room is simply not big enough. We shall have a buffet. It's the new way of doing these things, I'm told. I think it's better for the guests to move round and meet each other."

Florrie came home for her cousin's wedding but told her parents she would have to return to college to finish her course. She had completed almost two terms at her teacher training college since Christmas and would be returning to Forge Cottage to apply for a teaching position in a local school. Her brother also returned home, having obtained leave from his hospital.

Sophie and her daughters were very excited at the prospect of a wedding. They spent a lot of time deciding on their outfits and hats after spending an enjoyable morning shopping in Kingsbridge.

On the morning of the wedding, they all squeezed into the trap, the three women in the back and Charles sitting beside his father up front.

After a slow journey, they arrived and met family and friends at the little church at the top of the hill in Modbury. Millie and Harry were already there, together with Agnes and Tom, who was standing impassively beside them.

They settled into their respective pews in the front, and the organ began playing the "Wedding March." Dorothy had asked her sister Harriette's little girls to be bridesmaids, and they trotted behind, holding their little posies as the radiant bride made her way up the aisle, on the arm of her proud father.

After the service, to the sound of cheering, Billy helped Dorothy into the decorated horse and trap that had been prepared for them. They waved as they were showered with rose petals thrown by Sophie and Caroline.

Dorothy threw her bouquet into the crowd, and it landed in front of Charles. He looked round in panic and allowed Florrie to pick it up. She clutched it to her and gave Rosa a beaming smile.

CHAPTER FIVE

FLORRIE BECOMES A TEACHER

IN THE SECOND WEEK OF July, Ben met Florrie at Kingsbridge railway station and helped her load her trunk and bags into the back of the trap. He put his arm round her and kissed her.

"Welcome home, my love," he said. "Are you glad your course has finished?"

"It's been quite a struggle," she replied. "The college is very short of lecturers. They have lost a few of them, sadly. They had to bring in some women, who were heads of schools, to train us."

Ben drove carefully out of the station yard and then turned to go up the hill towards Clayden village. A motor car came veering towards them, just missing as it passed by. The horse tossed its head and shied to one side.

"Steady!" ordered Ben, pulling back on the reins.

"Those motorists should be more careful," exclaimed Florrie, gripping the side of the trap. "These motorcars are horrible, noisy things!"

Ben grinned. "I'm considering getting one myself," he said.

Florrie gave him a surprised look.

"But not just yet," he added quickly. "They're very expensive. I would have to get a secondhand one, and I think I can get a loan from the bank."

"Have you told Ma?"

"Yes, but she doesn't like them much either. She thinks there's too much rushing about these days. She says she prefers the times gone by when she could drive round at a leisurely pace in the horse and trap. Uncle Harry wants to get a van for the shop and is even talking about selling petrol."

They continued their journey home, along the narrow lanes with their high banks covered in summer flowers, cow parsley, and daisies buzzing with insects.

Upon reaching Forge Cottage, Florrie jumped down from her seat and ran to her mother, who was waiting at the gate. They hugged each other, then went inside, arm in arm.

Florrie asked if there was any post for her. Sophie said there was and went to the dresser, taking down a letter she had carefully tucked behind one of the plates.

"I think I know what this is," exclaimed Florrie excitedly, ripping open the envelope. "I didn't expect to hear so soon." Reading it quickly, she announced that it was her results, and she had passed. "I'm a qualified teacher!" She waved the letter in the air.

"I'm so proud of you," said Sophie, peering over her shoulder at the piece of paper.

Florrie beamed with a glow of pride.

"Well done, old girl," said Ben, giving her a kiss.

"All I need now is a job," she said.

"Do you know of any vacancies?" asked her father.

"Yes, there's one at the British School in Kingsbridge that I thought of applying for."

"You could easily get there from here," stated Ben. "I'll fix you up with a bicycle."

"Thank you, Pa!" She put her arms round his neck.

Florrie had never felt so happy. She lost no time writing her letter of application to the school in Kingsbridge. A week later, she received a reply inviting her to an interview the following week. She felt very excited that everything seemed to be falling into place after her difficult journey to complete her college course. She wondered how many other applicants there were.

There was also something else to consider, so she asked her mother what she should wear.

"Something you feel comfortable in," advised Sophie.

Florrie searched through her wardrobe, unable to decide. All her clothes were old and well worn, having not been replaced since before the war, except for her recent wedding outfit, which she felt was too formal.

"I haven't got *anything*," she said to herself as she surveyed her clothes spread out on the bed. "I need to buy something."

She and her mother drove to Kingsbridge and went to the dress shop on Fore Street. Florrie tried on a striped dress with a drop waist that suited her perfectly.

Surveying herself in the full-length mirror, she decided she liked herself in it. Suddenly, it occurred to her that she was an attractive young woman. She kept her fair hair long and wore it pinned up at the back.

Her mother came and peeked behind the curtain in the changing room. "Oh, that *is* nice!" she said.

Florrie smiled, knowing she would feel confident wearing it.

The shop sales assistant joined them. "Would you like to look at the hats?" she asked.

Sophie and Florrie looked at each other and laughed as Florrie nodded vigorously.

On the day of the interview, Ben declared his approval when Florrie came downstairs, wearing her new outfit. "Would madam care to enter her carriage?" he asked, giving a small bow.

Florrie was feeling very nervous but knew her father was trying to make her laugh. Sophie wished her every success and waved them both off.

When they arrived outside the school, Ben said he hoped it would go well. "Whatever you do, don't tell them your pa was a blacksmith," he said.

With a smile, she gave him a playful slap on the arm and then got down from the trap.

Ben drove away, leaving her looking up at the imposing façade of the high stone wall surrounding the school grounds. She took a deep breath and walked tentatively through the arched entrance, where she mounted some steps.

Florrie could be forgiven for thinking she was approaching a grand house rather than a school. The stone building was two stories high and looked somewhat austere. The windows were large, made of small panes of glass, and were placed deliberately high up to prevent the children from staring out of them during lessons. The school was built into the hillside, which was terraced, so Florrie had to go round the side of the school and climb up more steps leading to the schoolhouse behind, where the interview was to be held. Between the school and the house was a small yard that served as a playground.

Entering, Florrie was shown into a gloomy room where she came face to face with three gentlemen sitting behind a polished wooden table. She sat, waiting silently, clutching her handbag tightly in her lap, while the man in the middle examined his notes.

Finally, he looked up at her. "Miss Browne, welcome! I am Mr. Darkins, the local education officer, and this gentleman on my left is Mr. Fraser, the chairman of governors, and this is Mr. Faircross, the head-master." He indicated the other man to his right.

Florrie acknowledged them all with a "How do you do?" then waited for them to begin.

Mr. Fraser didn't start with any questions but began telling her about the school. "Our school is a British school, so called as it was not set up by the Church but founded in 1853. It was originally for the poorer classes, both adults and children, but it now serves as an elementary school for children up to the age of fourteen. Mr. Faircross will tell you about the methods employed here."

Florrie nodded to show she understood what had been said.

Mr. Faircross then spoke. "Before I do that, Miss Browne, can you tell us a little about yourself?" He leant forward, looking interested.

Florrie began by explaining about her interrupted training and what she had been doing in the war, then added, "I was born in Clayden village at Forge Cottage. My father comes from a family of blacksmiths, but he now builds bicycles. I was educated at a Quaker school, and I consider myself one, which is why I volunteered to nurse soldiers in the war." She stopped, wondering if she had said enough.

Mr. Faircross said, "Thank you." Smiling again, he asked, "What do you think you could bring to the school?"

"As I have grown up in the area, I would hope to give the children an interest in and awareness of their local history and environment so they could feel proud of their heritage and appreciate their surround-ings." Florrie paused, unsure if she had given the correct response to the question.

Again, Mr. Faircross thanked her for her answer. Then he said, "I hope that, as a new teacher, you will be able to bring some new ideas to our school. Up until now, teaching has been very much by rote, 'chalk and talk,' using monitors to teach the younger children. This system is being phased out, as it has proved unproductive for the monitors them-selves, who are often our older, more able pupils. The curriculum in British schools is mainly the three *Rs*—reading, writing, and arithme-tic—but there is also nature study, singing, craftwork, and physical fit-ness, which takes place outside when possible. I consider that literature and poetry are also important."

"Yes, I do too," replied Florrie, leaning forward. "My mother read poetry to me when I was a child." She began to relax, feeling that she understood the needs of the school and would fit in well.

The interview went on awhile longer, then finally concluded with a thank you from each of the three gentlemen.

"We'll be in touch with our decision soon," Mr. Darkins told her.

As she rose to go, Mr. Faircross gave her a friendly smile.

Florrie walked slowly down the hill to the quayside and sat on the harbour wall, listening to the waves lapping below while she waited for her father to collect her. She felt surprisingly tired.

Mr. Faircross looked pleasant enough, she mused. *I wonder if he's married.*

Ben arrived after a short wait and asked how the interview had gone.

"I think it went well," she replied. "They have more candidates to see, so they'll let me know the result by post."

They walked arm in arm up Fore Street to where the horse was teth-ered. Florrie stroked his muzzle as he looked dolefully at her. "Poor old thing," she said. "I think you need to get that motor soon, Pa."

Back home, Florrie waited impatiently for the letter that would fore-tell her future. Every day, she watched for Agnes to arrive with the post, often going outside and looking down the lane for her.

When Rosa arrived home that weekend, she was thrilled to hear that her sister had an interview and reassured her that she had every chance of success.

Florrie thanked her and offered her the trunk she had recently brought home. "I hope I won't need it, as I'll be working in a school locally," she told her. She still worried, anxious to know what her future would be. *What if I can't get a job? Will it mean having to leave home again?*

"I'm looking forward to going away," Rosa told her enthusiastically. "I've enrolled for my nursing course at the beginning of September."

"When do you leave the hospital?" asked her sister.

"Next week. The nurses are putting on a little going-away celebration after work on my last day. I shall be sorry to leave. Matron has been very supportive, and I think she hopes I will come back when I'm qualified."

"Will you?"

"Who knows, but I think it might be best to move on."

Agnes arrived the next morning with a letter addressed to Miss F. Browne.

Florrie opened the envelope with shaking hands. When she saw what the letter said, her eyes opened wide and she let out a yell. "I have the job! I've been appointed! I can't believe it!" She danced round the kitchen, making Agnes and her mother laugh so much that Ben came in to find out what was happening.

"What on earth is all this commotion?" he asked. As soon as he saw the letter in Florrie's hand, he gave her a big smile. "Well done, Florrie. I knew you would be the best one there!"

"What does it say?" asked Sophie.

Florrie examined the letter again. "It's from Mr. Faircross."

Sophie and Ben exchanged admiring glances.

"It says Mr. Faircross welcomes me to the staff of the school." She scrutinised the letter in her hand. "He wants me to come in at the end of the holidays to get my classroom ready, and I am to teach the class of six- and seven-year-olds." She looked up with an expression of pleasure.

"That's a lovely age to teach," said her mother, smiling with satisfaction.

Florrie hugged everyone, and Agnes waved goodbye and hopped onto her bicycle to continue her rounds.

Florrie was pleased when her father told her that he was going to take "his girls" out to celebrate. When Rosa returned the following weekend, having finished at the hospital, Florrie joined her mother and sister, and Ben drove them into Kingsbridge for some shopping and afternoon tea at a local hotel.

"I was with your mother, buying her wedding things here, when she was younger than both of you," said Ben over his shoulder as he and Sophie strolled past the shops.

Walking arm in arm behind their father, Florrie and Rosa looked at him and giggled.

CHAPTER SIX

ROSA RESCUES DANNY

Helping Rosa pack her trunk, Florrie handed her the carefully folded clothes and wrapped up her sister's spare pair of shoes.

"I don't know when I will be able to wear these," said Rosa as she packed them in. "We shall be in uniform most of the time."

"You'll be going to dances and socials," said Florrie.

"I hope so, but I don't think we'll be getting a lot of time off. The course is very intense." Rosa finished adding her few possessions and closed the lid.

Her mother came in with a tin. "A cake for you. Will it fit in?"

"There's always room for your cake, Ma!" Her daughter laughed.

First thing next morning, Ben took the trunk downstairs for Rosa's departure. It was an emotional time, and Rosa could see how upset her mother was as she stood at the door, looking sorrowful. Rosa kissed her and Florrie goodbye.

"You will write and tell us how you're getting on?" said Sophie. "Have you got everything? Did you pick up your purse? I hope the train isn't late." She continued fussing as Rosa and Ben went outside.

"Yes, Ma, and if the train is late, I'll just have to wait!"

Rosa had told her mother about her friend Danny and asked her to forward any post to her at the nurses' home. She had only heard from him twice since he'd left. Both letters had been brief, the first stating that he was learning Braille and trying out a variety of occupations to see which one suited him. In the second letter, he told her that he really had no idea what he wanted to do. Someone had transcribed each letter for him.

Rosa had replied each time and thought she would hear from him when she wrote about her nurses' course in Exeter. She had even suggested she could visit him, but she'd heard nothing back. She overcame her disappointment by concentrating on her new life.

When she arrived at the hospital in Exeter, she paid the taxi and dragged her trunk into the entrance. A hospital porter helped her by carrying it round to the nurses' accommodation, an austere-looking building at the side of the main hospital.

Here she met other young women who were also retraining. They chatted excitedly together, finding their room numbers and settling in.

Rosa was a little taken aback to find the rooms were very basic, with only two single beds with iron bedsteads, two chairs, and a chest of drawers placed between the beds. In the other two corners were small desks, each with a desk lamp with a green metal shade. Unfamiliar with electricity, Rosa was intrigued to find that the lamp lit up when she turned on the switch.

A young woman came through the door, heaving a large suitcase. She had dark hair in two plaits, which were tied up over her head. "Hello!" she said cheerily. "I'm Betty."

Rosa introduced herself.

"Nice to meet you, Rosa! Looks as if we're sharing. It's all going to be great fun!"

As they got to know each other, Betty told her she had a boyfriend and was determined to see him somehow. "Even if I have to climb out of the window," she added.

Rosa stared at her. *Fancy doing that! Whatever was her young man like?* she wondered.

"Have you got a boyfriend?" her new friend asked.

"Not really," answered Rosa. "I have a friend called Danny who I met when I was nursing. He's not my boyfriend."

Betty gave her a puzzled look, then said, "Come on, let's see what the others are doing."

Several of the girls had met up in one of the bedrooms, and Rosa and Betty joined them. The new recruits had found there were many rules to remember, and Rosa was surprised how strictly her life was to be regulated.

"You will be instantly dismissed if a man is found in your bedroom," said one of the girls. "And we need passes if we want to go out."

"I would never smuggle a man into my room!" Rosa protested, then felt embarrassed when the other girls laughed at her.

Listening to their chatter and banter, Rosa realised she had lived a very sheltered life. She was now twenty-three. Matron had kept a strict eye on her and the other nurses at her hospital, and she would never have done anything to make her parents ashamed.

Rosa had taken her mother's cake to share. Several of the others had also brought food, so everyone was enjoying treats and snacks while chatting away excitedly about being on their own, away from home.

Rosa heard a clink of glasses and was offered some cider.

"Is alcohol allowed?" she asked.

Again, the girls laughed, but Rosa felt it was all good natured. She sat on the bed, sipping her drink, wondering what her mother would think. She left the party before anyone else, heading back to her room for a good night's sleep so she'd be ready for the day ahead.

Rosa found that her course kept her very busy. When she wasn't on the wards, she was attending lectures and studying. She remembered how her parents had warned her that she would have to work hard.

She wrote home, describing her new surroundings and her room-mate, Betty. Her mother wrote back, and after reading her letter, Rosa felt rather homesick. Life in Exeter was proving to be challenging.

At home, Florrie was setting off for school at the beginning of the new term, full of anticipation. She had already gone in earlier that week to prepare her classroom and attend a staff meeting held in the same gloomy room where she'd had her interview. The other teachers welcomed her and appeared very friendly.

One of the older ones offered to give her any help she might need. "Despite all your training, this is where you start learning to be a teacher," she advised.

Florrie was looking forward to meeting her class and hoped she would be able to learn all their names quickly.

On arrival, she hung up her coat on the back of the classroom door and went over to her desk. Just as she did so, Mr. Faircross looked in.

"Good luck!" he called, leaning through the doorway.

Florrie smiled and thanked him.

The day went well, and the lessons she had carefully prepared seemed popular with the children. She ended the day by reading a story all the children enjoyed, before they were dismissed.

As she cycled home, she wondered how her sister was getting on.

It was several weeks before Rosa managed to obtain a pass to go to one of the women's socialist meetings Anthea had told her about. She caught the bus and arrived at her destination, which was a hall near the centre of Exeter.

She entered the building nervously and opened a door inside. She could see a large room full of women, young and old, and it was very noisy, everyone seemingly talking at once.

A confident young woman came up and looked straight at Rosa, saying somewhat briskly, "Hello, haven't seen you before. How did you hear about us?"

"I was told about your group by Anthea Smith," replied Rosa in a small voice.

"Oh yes, Anthea! I know her." The young woman relaxed a little.

"I met her at the cycle club," added Rosa.

"Welcome to our group. What's your name? I'll introduce you to some of our members."

Rosa told her and followed her into the room. It hadn't occurred to her that she should have to join the group to become a member.

"Sorry about the inquisition," said the young woman. "We do get infiltrated, so we have to be careful about who we let in."

Rosa was slightly alarmed when she heard this, and she wondered whatever could be going on.

There wasn't time to get to know any of the other women, as everyone was taking their seats for the meeting to begin.

The speaker who mounted the platform was a woman in her forties, dressed unconventionally in a loose-fitting, plain dress and flat lace-up shoes. She often raised her voice and put her arm in the air to make her point. Rosa thought that her views were very idealistic and rather aggressive. She seemed to be against all forms of government by an elite and kept talking about "the people." She rallied her audience to do more to promote their cause.

"We must get out there and show the world who we are!" she cried. "Waving banners is not enough. We must fight for our cause. Fight!"

There were murmurs of support round Rosa as she sat listening.

The woman continued, suggesting some antisocial actions that Rosa thought were quite shocking. She didn't agree with smashing windows or painting slogans onto public buildings, and she began to feel uncomfortable.

At the end of the speech, several members stood up and argued with the speaker about some of the points she had raised. Rosa could see that they could not agree with one another.

Rosa felt, as a nurse, she shouldn't be supporting events that might end up with people getting injured. She was relieved to leave the meeting early so she could get back to her hall of residence in time and not get reported by the warden for being late.

As she travelled back on the bus, she decided not to go to any more of the meetings. She had felt very out of her depth. She agreed with the basic ideals of female equality and the desire to make a more just society, but she didn't like the methods she had heard they were willing to use in achieving them. She felt the teachings of love and peace from her education at a Quaker school were the only right way.

Rosa wrote to her mother regularly but was selective in what she told her, having no wish to worry her. She had been surprised at what some of the girls got up to. They managed to smuggle in alcohol regularly, and

Betty somehow managed to see her boyfriend. Passes were limited, so some girls doubled up to give others their passes, and in general, they were up to all sorts of tricks to get round the rulebook.

Rosa wrote to her brother, asking how he was getting on and telling him about her experiences at the women's socialist meeting. She even asked him if he had a girlfriend yet.

Charles's letter arrived shortly afterwards, and Rosa sat on her bed, reading it after her lectures had finished for the day.

Dear Rosa,

It was lovely hearing from you, and I'm glad your training course is going well. You sound as if you have settled in now and are making friends.

Now that I'm back at medical school, I'm kept very busy. Like you, we work on the wards as well as attend lectures. I sometimes carry out quite serious procedures needing a lot of concentration. I have also been assisting in theatre from time to time. It's all very interesting work, but I'm absolutely exhausted at the end of the day, and then I must write up my notes. Not much time for girlfriends!

I think you should be careful getting involved with the group you mentioned. They sound like communists, and while their ideals could be said to be commendable, their way of achieving them is not. You could easily get injured at their protest rallies, which, I believe, often end in violence. Please be careful.

I don't suppose we shall see each other until Christmas. I shall look forward to your letters. Ma has written to me and lets me know all the news at home.

Your loving brother,

Charles

Rosa folded his letter and put it away, deciding to heed her big brother's advice about the socialists.

The weeks went by very quickly, and Rosa became resigned to the fact that she was going to find only her family's letters in her pigeonhole in the entrance hall.

Soon it was November, and Rosa was looking forward to her leave at Christmas, when it suddenly occurred to her that she could ask Danny to spend Christmas with her family. She wrote to ask her parents, and Sophie wrote back straight away that she and Ben would be very pleased to have him to stay.

Before Rosa could send her invitation to Danny, a letter arrived. It was not from her mother or brother, and she did not recognise the writing on the envelope. On opening it, she found it was from the superintendent of Danny's retraining unit. He informed her that Danny had attempted to take his own life and was now in the sick bay. He assured her that no action would be taken against him, and he requested that she exercise discretion. He explained that, having only found her correspondence and having no other records of family for Danny, he'd decided she should be informed.

Rosa was stunned and immediately felt sick to her stomach. *Poor Danny! Why did he do such a thing? What led him to this? He must be feeling desperate.* Many such thoughts tumbled about in her head as she tried to take it in. She sat on her bed, holding the letter in her hand, staring at it. *What should I do?* she wondered.

When she felt sufficiently recovered, she went straight to her tutor's office and showed her the letter, explaining that Danny was blind.

"He's a friend, a patient I met at the hospital back home," she explained. "I was about to ask him to come and stay with us for Christmas."

"Has he no family?" asked Miss Howells as she removed her spectacles after reading the letter.

"He told me his mother had remarried and lives at his old home in Plymouth. Apparently, he didn't get on with his stepfather or two stepbrothers, so he's never been back. I'm not sure his family even knows about his war injuries."

Miss Howells nodded and looked at Rosa seriously. "You must take compassionate leave straight away," she instructed. "This young man obviously needs emotional support, and you can provide that, Nurse Browne. You can easily catch up on lectures, and I will arrange cover for you on the ward. I know this is a confidential matter, and it will remain so."

Rosa thanked her for being so understanding, then hurried back to her room to gather her things for the trip home. She hurried to the railway station as fast as her legs would carry her and caught the first train home.

She finally arrived at Forge Cottage and burst through the door in the early evening, as her family sat round the table in the kitchen after their evening meal.

"Rosa! Whatever is the matter?" exclaimed Sophie. She stood up quickly and grasped Ben by the shoulder.

Rosa handed her mother the letter and then turned to her father. "Pa, would you pay the cabbie for me? I'm sorry, but I don't have enough money."

Ben went over to the jar on the dresser, where they kept a supply of cash, and went out to pay the driver. When he returned, Sophie read out the letter to him.

They all sat in silence for several moments at the news. Florrie took her sister's hand to comfort her.

Ben spoke first. "I take it you want to go there tomorrow?"

"Oh yes, Pa! Will you go with me?"

"Yes, of course."

"Whatever made him do it?" Sophie asked, shaking her head. "He must be very unhappy."

"I wish he'd written to me," said Rosa.

"I don't think he was able to," remarked Ben. "He must have got very low."

"We need to keep this to ourselves. It's a criminal offence to try to take your own life," Rosa stated sombrely. She shuddered to think of it.

"Do you think Tom should come too?" asked Sophie. "He's about the same age and has been through the war too. Danny could do with a friend."

They agreed that he should be told and invited to come with them to see Danny. Ben offered to go over to Harry's and see him that evening.

When he returned, he reported that Tom had said he did want to go with them.

The following morning, the three of them set off early, remaining silent for most of the journey. They travelled by train to Exeter and then changed to get to the town where Danny's retraining unit was located. Rosa felt the journey to be never ending, in her impatience to see Danny.

They walked along the High Street and asked someone to direct them to the retraining unit.

"You mean Tonbridge House. Just carry along here, and it's on the left."

Thanking the man, they hurried along until they came to the large mansion just outside the town. The building had tall stone pillars along the front, with steps leading to a wide entrance. They entered a spacious hall with a high ceiling and a wide curving stone staircase to one side.

A man coming down the stairs stopped and asked how he could help them. Ben explained why they had come, and they were shown to the superintendent's office.

When they entered, a thin, nervous man stood up and shook Ben's hand.

"Thank you for coming so promptly," he said. He wanted to know the relationship each of them had with Danny, then explained that Danny had downed most of a bottle of whisky and tried to drown himself in the bath. Fortunately, he had been found by a member of staff before he was successful.

Rosa felt sick all over again.

"We have been concerned about him for some time," he went on. "He has shown little interest in the training projects and sits by himself a great deal, not speaking."

Rosa thought that did not sound like the Danny she remembered. "Did he swallow much water?" she asked anxiously.

"He's had a thorough medical examination, and we're sure his lungs are clear, thank goodness," replied the superintendent.

Rosa breathed a sigh of relief.

"How is he in himself now?" asked Ben.

"Very quiet."

Rosa was relieved when the superintendent suggested she go in to see Danny first, and then Tom would come in a little later.

As she entered Danny's room, she looked round at the white walls and noticed the blinds pulled down over a small window.

She sat down quietly beside him on the bed and took his hand. "Hello, Danny. It's Rosa."

He stirred but said nothing.

"How are you?"

"Rosa, thank you for coming, but there is nothing you can do here. You'd better go home."

Her heart sank. "Please don't send me away, Danny. I've travelled all this way just to be with you."

He squeezed her hand gently. "I want to get out of here," he said. "They have been very good to me, but I feel controlled. There's nothing here for me. I want to make my own choices. I'm sorry for what I did. It was stupid. I'm sorry I've upset you."

"I'm so glad you're safe," she replied.

"Are you my girl?" he suddenly asked.

She laughed nervously. "Yes, I'm your girl, Danny." She felt a glow of pleasure at the thought that perhaps he did have feelings for her after all. She squeezed his hand, then continued, "I've brought my cousin Tom to see you. He's your age, and he was wounded in the war too. He's been at home recovering. Can he come in?"

Danny nodded.

Rosa got up to ask Tom to come in.

"Hello, mate," Tom said, approaching Danny's bed. "You've got yourself in a bit of a pickle, haven't you?"

"You could say that, Tom."

"Have you decided what you want to do?"

"I want to get out of here. I've tried to make a go of it, but it's not what I want to do. All they've offered me are repetitive tasks working machinery. I don't want to do that all my life."

"What *do* you want to do, mate?"

"I've no idea." Danny looked dejected.

Rosa held his hand a little tighter.

"I was like that," replied Tom. "You feel useless, don't you?"

Danny nodded.

"I ran away, and my pa and Uncle Ben, Rosa's pa, came after me. They gave me a right talking to."

Danny managed a brief laugh.

"Uncle Ben has given me work in his workshop, building bicycles. I think it's something you could do too, mate. Why don't you come home with us and give it a try? I've really enjoyed the work."

Before Danny could respond, Rosa said, "I was just about to write to you, Danny, to ask you to spend Christmas with us."

"I've got nothing else to do," he replied, shrugging.

Rosa let go of his hand. "I'm just going to ask my father to come in, Danny," she said quietly.

When she returned with Ben, they approached the bed.

"Danny, this is my pa, Mr. Browne. Would you like him to arrange your discharge?"

Ben shook his hand.

Danny nodded. "Yes, please, Mr. Browne," he said without hesitation.

While Ben went to speak to the superintendent, Rosa began collecting Danny's few belongings. Ben reappeared after a short while.

"I've signed all the necessary papers," he said. "You're now free to leave with us, Danny, if you're sure that's what you want to do."

"Yes, Mr. Browne. Thank you all for coming to help me."

Ben and Tom helped Danny get dressed, while Rosa waited outside. When he was ready, they took him to the superintendent's office, where he said goodbye.

"I wish you every success, Danny," said the superintendent, shaking his hand. "I'm so sorry we couldn't help you here."

The four of them then proceeded down the passage and out into the fresh air.

"Can you manage the walk to the station?" asked Ben.

"Yes, I think so," Danny replied, taking a deep breath. "It feels so good to be leaving."

CHAPTER SEVEN

THE DANCE

W HEN THEY ARRIVED BACK AT Forge Cottage, Rosa apologised about the smallness of the rooms, but Danny said it made it much easier to move round.

Sophie had cooked a special dinner that seemed to revive him, and with a genuine smile, he told her he had thoroughly enjoyed it.

Tom came over with Digger the next day and found Danny sitting in the kitchen, having just finished his breakfast. Sophie welcomed him in as she cleared the dishes.

Danny was aware of Digger's presence, hearing the animal panting as it pulled on its lead.

"What's that you have there, Tom?" he asked.

"This is my dog, Digger," said Tom, bringing the dog over to his new friend.

Danny reached down and fondled the dog, who responded by panting louder.

"I haven't had him long," added Tom. "He's still a bit wild."

Danny was enjoying stroking the animal. "You're lovely, aren't you, boy?" he exclaimed.

"What are you two planning to do today?" asked Sophie.

"I'm going to show Danny how to build a bicycle," said Tom.

He led Danny down to the workshop and guided him through the workshop door, then round the benches and objects in order, telling him what everything was as Danny ran his fingertips over each item. Ben kept a very tidy shop, so all his tools were on hooks and shelves.

"There's a lot here," said Danny after they had finished going round. "You'll have your work cut out showing me what to do. I have a lot to learn."

"It's not boring work," commented Tom. "There're so many different parts to each bicycle. Uncle Ben does all the welding work, and I usually fit all the pieces together."

Tom and Danny worked on the project all that morning and the days that followed, and soon the bicycle began to take shape.

Ben would sometimes let the two boys off early, and they would go for walks with Digger or catch the bus and go fishing off Kingsbridge quay. He told them he wanted to build a tandem so they could go for rides together, and that would be their next project.

At the beginning of December, Rosa arrived home for Christmas, and she was impatient to see Danny again.

"How's he getting on?" she asked her mother as they sat in the kitchen.

"I hardly see any of them, only for meals," Sophie told her. "They spend all their time in the workshop."

Rosa wandered down there to see what they were doing. They greeted her cheerfully but quickly returned to their work, too busy to chat. She sat and watched for a short time as Ben welded the frame on one side of the shop, and on the other side, Danny and Tom worked on fixing the pedals.

"We're making a tandem for the boys," Ben told her.

"I must see that when it's finished," she said. "As long as you don't expect me to ride it."

With that, she returned to the cottage to help her mother with the Christmas preparations.

Ben followed her soon after, leaving the two lads to clear up.

After he had gone, Tom asked his friend, "What do you think of our Rosa?"

"She was very kind to me when I was at the hospital," Danny replied.

"I reckon she's a bit taken with you. Is she your sweetheart?"

Danny said nothing, continuing his work on the tandem.

"I don't have a girl," Tom confided. "Rosa offered to take me to a Valentine's dance last February, but I said I didn't want to go. I think she was hoping I'd find one there."

"You should have gone," advised Danny. "At least you can see if the girls are good-looking."

They continued to tidy up and then went to the cottage for lunch.

In the afternoon, they helped Ben fill the woodstore, and he suggested the two young men go for a drink after supper.

"It will be my treat," he said.

At the Two Foxes, the publican wouldn't take payment, as he knew they were both ex-servicemen, so they enjoyed some free drinks. They found a quiet corner and sat themselves down.

Danny began asking Tom about Billy. They had been talking about their families when they worked together, and Tom had revealed his feelings about his brother.

"Why don't you like him?" asked Danny.

Tom frowned and put down his beer. "I haven't told you all about him," he began. "My ma had Billy when she was fifteen. She was seduced by the rector's son, and his family refused to help her and sent their son away. Uncle Ben was furious. He waited until Jonathan returned on a visit and lay in wait for him. When he confronted him, Jonathan denied everything, so Uncle Ben beat him up."

"Wow!" exclaimed Danny, clearly shocked. "I can't imagine Mr. Browne doing anything like that."

"It was a long time ago," Tom assured him. "Uncle Ben helped my mum raise him, and then she married Aunt Sophie's cousin. He died, and then she married my pa and had me and Agnes. So he's not my real brother."

"He is if you have the same mother," pointed out Danny.

Tom stared into his drink resentfully, thinking how unfair it was that Billy had come through the war unscathed and had inherited money from Jonathan's mother. He had nothing and felt he had no hope of being employed.

Suddenly thinking of poor Danny's plight, Tom roused himself. "I'm so glad we're pals," he said, looking up. "You're a good mate, Danny."

Rosa often went to the workshop to see Danny and Tom at work. She surveyed the parts of the unfinished tandem, spread over the bench and floor.

"Do you think you'll ever get it going?" she asked.

"Uncle Ben seems to think so!" Tom replied. "We're hoping to ride it on Christmas Day, aren't we, Danny?"

"Listen, you two," said Rosa. "Speaking of Christmas, there's a dance in Kingsbridge next Saturday. I saw a poster advertising it at the shop. I want to have some fun, so you are *both* going to take me there."

The young men looked at each other.

"I can't dance," said Tom.

"Neither can I," added Danny, wiping his hands on a rag.

"You two are hopeless," said Rosa. "After supper, I'll give you some lessons in the parlour." With that, she spun on her heel and, with her head in the air, left them before either could object.

The dance lessons continued all week, and the following Saturday, Rosa wore her best frock and put some long rows of beads round her neck. She had tried to persuade Florrie to join them, but she had declined.

"I don't think the parents want to see one of their teachers jigging about," she said.

Rosa replied, "Oh, for goodness' sake! You must get out and enjoy yourself, Florrie."

Florrie still refused, convinced she was right.

In his van, Harry took Rosa, Tom, and Danny to the church hall in Kingsbridge and arranged to collect them at ten o'clock. They paid for their tickets at the door and went in.

"Where's the bar?" asked Tom.

"There's no alcohol," said Rosa. "It's a church event. There's only juice."

It was quite crowded, but eventually, they found a table and three empty chairs.

"Shall I get the cocktails?" asked Tom in a posh voice, making Danny laugh.

Rolling her eyes at Tom, Rosa said, "I do hope you are not going to be silly all evening."

Tom grinned at her, then left her and Danny alone at the table.

While they waited, Rosa described their surroundings to Danny. "We're in a big hall," she began. "There's some decorations hung across the ceiling, twists of crepe paper with balloons tied either side."

"I can hear it's big. The sounds echo."

A small band on the stage at the end of the hall was playing a lively dance tune. Danny looked happy and tapped his foot to the beat.

Tom soon returned with glasses of juice for each of them. Sitting, he strained his neck to look round for girls.

Ignoring her cousin, Rosa suggested to Danny that they dance.

Danny stopped smiling, suddenly looking uncomfortable. "I don't really think I can. I—"

"No excuses. You'll be fine," said Rosa reassuringly, taking him by the hand and leading him carefully onto the dance floor.

Once there, they found themselves being jostled by other couples.

"There's not much room," said Rosa. "We'll just go round once or twice and then go back."

Danny nodded and held on to Rosa, squeezing her hand tightly and placing his arm round her waist. They shuffled round, and gradually, Danny began to remember his steps and respond to Rosa's. As they both relaxed, their movements became easier, and they glided round the floor to the waltz music the band was playing.

"This is easier than I thought!" Danny exclaimed, and he held Rosa a little closer.

Rosa closed her eyes, feeling a glow of pleasure from having her Danny so near to her.

At the end of the dance, they returned to their table, where they found Tom looking doleful.

"Your turn now, pal," said Danny, letting go of Rosa's hand.

"We'll have a couple of dances to get you started, then you're on your own," Rosa said as Tom stood up.

After they had moved round the floor a few times, Tom appeared to be managing well, and Rosa told him she was impressed.

"Have you and Danny been secretly practising together?" she asked, laughing.

"I'm just a natural," replied Tom.

"I want to see you dancing with some of these girls," said Rosa, making it clear she wanted to just dance with Danny.

"I can't ask them all. Some will have to be bitterly disappointed."

Rosa gave him a playful slap. "You old charmer. I must say, you do look very smart."

Tom had slicked his dark hair down with some oil he'd borrowed from his father. He wasn't as tall as Harry but was of slim build, and his limp had all but gone.

The music came to an end, and they returned to their table to find Danny wasn't there.

"Do you think he's walked out?" Rosa said anxiously.

Tom looked round a moment and then pointed him out, on the dancefloor with a girl.

"How did he manage that?" he asked Rosa.

Within minutes, Danny was led back by a young woman who thanked him and then left.

"I didn't expect that," he said. "I was just sitting here, and someone asked me if I would dance with his sister, so I did."

Tom and Rosa looked at each other in astonishment.

When the band began playing again, Tom scanned the room, determined to not let Danny get one over on him. He got up and strolled towards an attractive young lady, but a young man got there before him. Rosa told Danny, and he laughed.

Tom returned looking peeved. "Stop laughing, Danny," he said.

Tom eventually found a partner, and they disappeared among the couples on the floor. Danny and Rosa joined in a few more dances and then sat and chatted for the rest of the evening.

Eventually, the final dance was announced and then Tom reappeared, looking animated.

"Have you had a good time?" asked Rosa.

Tom nodded. "I'll say!"

After collecting their coats, they found Harry waiting for them outside and clambered into his van.

"Did you enjoy yourselves?" he asked.

They agreed they had, despite there being no beer. Tom said he would be going to the next one because he had met some great girls.

Rosa smiled to herself.

CHAPTER EIGHT

A NEW VENTURE

FLORRIE SIGHED CONTENTEDLY AS THE last child left through the classroom door, clutching one of the paper Christmas trees she had made with them that afternoon.

She tidied away her books and locked her desk. Picking up the small gift Mr. Faircross had given her at lunchtime, together with the other teachers, she placed it in her school bag and took her coat down from the hook behind the door. She had decided to put her present under the tree at home and open it on Christmas morning after church.

As she passed Mr. Faircross's office, he came out and wished her Happy Christmas. "Your first term's over, Miss Browne," he said, smiling. "I think you've made a very promising start."

Florrie blushed slightly. "Thank you, Mr. Faircross."

"Will you be spending Christmas with your family?" he enquired.

"Yes, both my sister and brother will be home." After a pause, she said, "Are you staying here?"

"Heavens, no! I shall be going home to my parents in Plymouth."

She wished him goodbye and then went to get her bicycle out of the school shed.

Sophie loved Christmas. All three of her children would be home once again to celebrate the festive season.

Rosa arrived home first and, together with her sister, began helping their mother with the preparations. Charles joined them a day or two later and brought with him a bag full of books he hoped to study for his exams. Sophie had written to tell him that Danny was with them but that she had arranged for him to stay at Tom's so Charles could have his own room for studying.

Ben brought home a small fir tree, which he put in the parlour. On Christmas Eve morning, Sophie and the girls set about decorating the tree from the box of decorations they had acquired over the years. Some looked decidedly worn, but when their mother suggested they buy some new ones, Florrie and Rosa insisted they should be kept.

"We've always had these," protested Rosa.

"I could make a few more," suggested her sister. "I did some at school with the children."

Ben came in with logs. "My, that's looking good," he said, nodding towards their handiwork. He dumped the wood by the fire. "What's next?" he asked, knowing there was a lot of jobs to be done.

"You can go to the farm and fetch the turkey," Sophie instructed. "I ordered it last week, so it should be ready."

"Yes, ma'am," answered Ben, giving a mock salute that made the girls laugh.

That evening when all the preparations had been completed, the family gathered in the parlour, round the fire.

Sophie looked round at the faces of her children, illuminated by the burning logs. *How much longer will I have my family together?* she thought as they happily chattered together.

Millie and Harry came over on Christmas morning together with Tom, Danny, and Agnes. The parlour at Forge Cottage had never been so crowded.

After Christmas dinner, Ben ushered his family along to the workshop. They stood outside while he swung open the two wide doors and wheeled out the finished tandem. Everyone clapped and cheered, Tom and Danny looking very pleased with themselves.

Tom guided Danny to the machine, and he climbed on the back. Then Tom hopped on the front, and pushing with his foot on the ground, they set off down the lane. The two of them wobbled unsteadily from side to side, causing Rosa and Florrie to burst out laughing. Eventually, they steadied themselves and rode away round the bend.

"Well!" said Sophie. "I think that's a wonderful achievement, Ben!"

Millie and Harry agreed, saying what a talented man they thought Ben was.

Ben beamed, putting his arm round his wife's waist. "I couldn't have done it without those two lads," he said modestly.

Sophie knew he could have, and she felt proud of him for sharing the praise.

A short time later, the riders reappeared, puffing slightly as they drew to a halt outside the workshop.

"Oh, Mr. Browne!" exclaimed Danny. "Tom was pedalling so fast, and I felt the wind on my face as we went along. It was wonderful!"

"She goes like a dream, Uncle Ben," Tom said.

Immediately after Christmas, there was a cold spell, and Charles and Rosa returned to their courses.

One day, Ben came back from the stable, looking sombre. "He's gone," he said.

Their faithful servant had succumbed to old age, and Ben had found him collapsed in his stall. He went over to the farm to arrange for the removal of the carcase, and when it was over, he joined Sophie in the kitchen.

"It feels like the end of an era," he said as he sat down in his chair by the range. He glanced warily at Sophie. "I think it's time to look for that motor."

"Can we afford it?" she asked anxiously.

"We'll have to. I'll sell the bicycle I made. The boys have their tandem now. And I'll try and get a loan from the bank. I don't really want to use up all our savings."

Sophie told him she thought that was a good idea. "I bet you're glad that awful Mr. Wilmott-Smith isn't there anymore," she said, and they both recalled the time Ben had gone to the bank to get a loan for the cottage extension many years before. He had got short shrift from the manager, since the man had been Sophie's employer when she was a governess at his home and she had walked out on him.

Florrie was sitting with them at the kitchen table, peeling potatoes for supper. "It would be lovely to have a motor car," she said. "You could take me to school. I don't think I can cycle there through the winter, it's so cold."

Her mother nodded in agreement.

Given permission to purchase a motor, Ben acquired a loan at the bank and then went to enquire at several garages for a secondhand vehicle.

One of them offered him an old Ford Model T that had been involved in an accident and was badly dented. It was an open-top vehicle with a roof that folded down at the back. The windscreen was cracked, and the metalwork on the side was crumpled and battered. It had four-spoke wheels with rubber tyres.

After giving it a good look over, Ben decided he could repair it, so he made an offer. It was accepted, and he said he would come for it the next day. He planned to ask Harry if he would tow it back for him with his van.

Ben and Harry collected the motor the next morning. Tom and Danny were outside with Digger, and when they drew up outside the workshop, dragging the motor behind Harry's van, Tom stopped playing with the dog and stared at the wreck in wide-eyed wonder.

"It's an old banger," Tom said, sounding incredulous. "It's all beaten up."

"It's just the bodywork. The engine's fine."

Tom peered underneath. "It's a bit rusty, Uncle Ben."

"Yes, yes, I know," replied Ben testily. "All that can be rubbed down."

After a week of hard work, Ben decided to take the motor for a short test drive. Harry came over and gave him some instructions on how to drive. Harry cranked up the engine by turning a handle at the front, and the motor spluttered into life and then made a satisfying roaring sound as Ben put his foot on the pedal and tentatively drove up the lane.

Sophie and Florrie had joined Harry and the boys to see him off, and they cheered as Ben drove away. *This is going to change our lives*, thought Ben as he manoeuvred the motor through the narrow lane.

At supper that night, Ben talked of all the places they could go now they had some transport. "We'll need to see how she goes," he added cautiously. "I don't want to break down miles from home."

He looked at Sophie, thinking she did not look convinced. He turned to Danny. "I've had an idea that I want to talk to you and Tom about tomorrow," he said. "Now that work on the motor is finished, we need something else to do."

The following day, when Tom arrived for work, Ben put his proposition to them both. "When I was scouting round the garages, one of them had some old ex-army motorcycles round the back," he began. "The owner told me he had picked them up cheaply but hadn't the time to repair them. I told him I was interested, and he said I could have them for what he paid for them. There's three altogether. Now, this is what I propose. We buy these machines and do them up. I think we could make a tidy profit, and if we do, we could go into business servicing motorcycles. They're very popular right now."

"But I don't know anything about motor bicycles, Uncle Ben," said Tom.

"Billy has asked me to service his for him," replied Ben. "I'm sure they're not that complicated. He's coming over later, and we can look at his machine. I'm sure we can figure it out."

Tom sat silently for a while, thinking about what his uncle had said. "What do you think, Danny?"

"Sounds like a great idea to me, Tom. Let's do it."

"I do think there's a future in this enterprise," said Ben reassuringly as the three men shook hands.

CHAPTER NINE
CHARLES ACCEPTS AN OFFER

SOPHIE HUMMED HAPPILY AS SHE hulled gooseberries to make jam. The bushes in the garden had produced a good crop, as they did every June. She thought back to when she'd first come to live in Forge Cottage. The pantry had been full of old jars of preserves, some of them from Ben's mother's time. She had cleared them out but kept the jars, meaning to make her own in the years to come. This she had managed to do, owing to Harry tending the kitchen garden, something Ben had never bothered with.

She remembered the gentle kiss goodbye Harry had given her one evening after he finished his work, and how angry Ben had been about it. A smile spread across her lips as she recalled how she had reacted to his accusations.

She heard the gate click and suddenly realised the men were coming in for their afternoon tea break and she had forgotten to put the kettle on the range. She jumped up and busied herself getting the tea ready. While Ben and the boys disappeared to the scullery to wash their hands, Sophie placed her homemade fruitcake on the table.

"Ooh! That looks good, Aunt Sophie!" exclaimed Tom, drying his hands. He told Danny what was waiting for him.

They sat down, and Ben cut them all a slice.

"We've had two new jobs come in today," he said, his mouth full of cake. "Word is certainly getting round about our repair business."

Ben and the two boys had worked hard over the past few months, rebuilding the motorcycles Ben had purchased, and they had sold them for a good price. It seemed they were well on their way to successfully building up a motorcycle-repair business.

To begin with, money had been tight after the expense of Ben's secondhand Ford and the three motorcycles. When Ben had set up his bicycle-repair business, he had opened a bank account at the bank in Kingsbridge, but it had dwindled to almost nothing. The jar on the dresser had very little in it at one time, and Sophie had had to ask Millie for her provisions "on account" one week at the shop.

Gradually, things improved, and Ben was even able to offer the two boys a small wage. Danny declined, saying that, as he was living rent-free, he would prefer to forgo his.

Ben and Sophie were looking forward to their son's return after he finished his finals. Danny was to stay with Millie and Harry again so Charles could have his old room back.

Ben went to Kingsbridge station to meet him, and he put his son's cases in the back of the motor, then cranked up the engine. After a few false starts, they set off up the road.

"How has Ma taken to motor travel?" asked Charles as they drove along.

"Your mother is still a bit nervous of it," admitted Ben. "She keeps thinking we're going to break down."

Sophie came out of the kitchen and flung her arms round her son as soon as he walked through the door. "Charles, welcome home!"

"Glad to be home," Charles said when she held him back at arm's length.

She studied the tall figure in front of her. "Well?" she asked.

Charles laughed. "I've passed," he said. "I even got some commendations!"

Sophie's face lit up. "Oh, Charles!" was all she managed to say.

Ben put a strong arm round his son's shoulders. "Well done, my boy," he said. "All those years of study, and you've made it!" He went into the parlour to fetch glasses and a bottle he had kept specially for this occasion.

"Shouldn't we wait for Florrie?" asked Sophie.

Before anyone could answer, Florrie came through the door, breathless after her bicycle ride home. "Hello, Charles! I guess you've passed?" she said, eyeing the bottle on the table and the glasses Ben was setting down beside it.

Charles nodded, looking pleased with himself.

"Congratulations are called for!" announced Ben as he popped the cork and poured them each a drink.

Shortly after Charles returned home, Agnes brought a letter addressed to him. It was from Dr. Bailey, asking to see him.

I wonder want he wants, thought Charles, intrigued.

Upon replying, he received an invitation for him and his parents to come to lunch.

On the appointed day, Ben drove them to Modbury, and Sophie expressed her amazement at how quickly they got there. The motor even managed to climb the steep hill up to Acacia House.

They were shown into the conservatory, and Charles was congratulated by his hosts. After they had tea, Charles accompanied Dr. Bailey into his surgery.

"We can talk undisturbed here," said the doctor as he offered Charles a seat. "Now, young man, I expect you're very relieved it's all over with."

"Yes, indeed, sir."

"And how were the finals? And the viva?"

Charles explained about his oral interview. "I think I gave the right answers," he added, then he described the nature of some of them.

The doctor nodded wisely. "Yes, yes, they always ask *that*," he said. "Of course, mine was a long time ago, and medicine has changed a lot since my day." He leant forward. "It's why I asked to speak to you, Charles. I want to make you a proposition."

Charles sat forward, excited to hear what Dr. Bailey was about to say.

"I'm getting old, and I'm planning to retire. When, I'm not sure yet. I need an assistant for now, and I would like to offer the job to you. You would work with me and get to know my patients. When the time is right, I may be able to offer you a partnership."

Charles felt his spirits rise, then fall just as rapidly. "Before we go any further, Dr. Bailey, I must tell you that I simply do not have the funds to buy into your practice if you were to offer me this opportunity."

The doctor smiled. "Let's not worry about that at this stage. As I said, I'm looking for an assistant at this time. Billy and Dorothy have moved into their new home in Kingsbridge, so we can offer you board and lodging with us, and we can settle on a salary later."

Charles could not believe what he had been offered. This was just what he wanted to do, and the chance to work with someone he knew and respected was a great opportunity.

Without hesitation he replied, "I would very much like to accept your offer, sir. Thank you so much for considering me."

"Excellent!" said the doctor, leaning back with satisfaction and rubbing his hands together. "I'm so glad you've accepted."

They returned to the conservatory to join the others, and Dr. Bailey took Charles by the arm and said, "May I introduce my new assistant!"

Charles looked round at everyone as they offered him their congratulations. He had never felt so happy. He just hoped his training would enable him to do the job well, though he was encouraged by the thought that Dr. Bailey would be there.

Charles decided to relocate to the Acacia House straight away, much to Sophie's consternation. She tried to persuade him to stay home until the end of June, but he felt he had outgrown his home and wanted to start work as soon as possible. He began to pack away his books and clothes and the few other items he had, and everything went into his large suitcase.

Despite his eagerness to begin his new career, he felt something was lacking. Deep down, he had a feeling of loneliness and isolation.

He couldn't understand why he felt that way with such a loving family round him. He hoped that his work and living with the Baileys would make him feel more secure.

Sophie fussed round him, making him promise to come and see them often. "We were so looking forward to you coming home," she said. "And now you're off again!"

Two weeks later, Charles came home for the weekend to assure his parents that he had settled into his new home happily. He was pleased that both villages were on omnibus routes, even though it meant he had to change at Kingsbridge.

"Mrs. Bailey is looking after me very well," he told his mother. "She sends her love."

The following day, he was happily settled in the parlour when he heard the noise of a motor outside. He put his book down and got up to see who it was.

An open-top motor drew up outside the cottage and hooted loudly. Ben had gone outside, followed by Sophie. Charles stood in the doorway, peering over his mother's shoulder to see who it was.

"Papa! Hello!" the driver called out, taking off his goggles. It was Lionel. He was wearing a wide, flat cap and a white scarf wound round his neck. He jumped out and embraced his father.

Sophie and Charles stopped at the gate, watching as Lionel helped a young lady out of the passenger side of the motor.

"You've met my sister," Lionel said, turning towards Sapphire, who was removing her headscarf.

"Yes, not so long ago," Ben replied, smiling at her.

Sophie and Charles joined him.

Lionel greeted them enthusiastically. He kissed Sophie lightly on her cheek and shook Charles's hand.

"It's wonderful to see you after all this time," Charles responded, returning the handshake. He regarded his half-brother with admiration and some awe, as he had always looked up to him. Lionel had the confidence and joie de vivre Charles felt himself lacking. He was shaking his half-brother's hand, but his attention was on Sapphire. "How lovely to meet you," he said, looking intently at her.

She gave him a bright smile, and he felt unable to take his eyes off her. She walked past him to greet Sophie.

He suddenly became aware of his father enthusing about Lionel's motor and turned his attention towards them.

"Not mine, I'm afraid," said Lionel. "A Vauxhall Tourer, my father's new toy."

The motorcar was a work of art, with its shining metalwork and the clean, smooth lines of the design.

Ben ran his hand over the side and up and along the front. "She's beautiful!" he said, his eyes gleaming.

As Ben and Lionel walked round the motor, Charles stole another glance at Sapphire. She had a very pretty face, and her hair was cut fashionably short. Her long scarf was draped round her neck and shoulders. He thought she looked very elegant, very stylish.

"Charles."

Someone calling him caught his attention, and he turned towards the voice. His mother told him they were all going into the cottage, so he followed them inside.

Everyone took a seat in the parlour, Charles sitting down beside Sapphire.

Ben went to the cupboard to find drinks. He took out a bottle and some glasses.

Lionel shook his head. "No, thank you, Papa. I'm driving a valuable vehicle, remember! A cup of tea would be wonderful, though."

As they drank their tea, Lionel told them about himself. "I'm still in the army. They've asked me to stay on in my regiment, as there's a lot of sorting out still to do since conscription ended last year. I've been busy demobbing soldiers and reorganising things. It's mostly administrative work, although I do have to travel round the country sometimes."

Ben regarded him proudly. "You've done very well, receiving that medal, Lionel. We were all very impressed. Many congratulations."

"Thank you, Pa. It's been a privilege to serve my country."

"Charles has been doing well," Sophie stated.

Her son smiled and gave a little shrug.

"He's a qualified doctor now," she added.

"Well done, old man!" exclaimed Lionel. "I do admire your tenacity, sticking to all that studying. What are you going to do now?"

"I'm working in a general practice. Ma's friend's husband is a doctor in a village near here, and he invited me to be his assistant."

"You're well on your way, then, which is what we should be doing." He turned to his sister. "Ready?"

Sapphire smiled sweetly and stood up.

"Thank you for the tea, Mrs. Browne," she said, addressing Sophie. "I hope you didn't mind us dropping in on you like this. Lionel was *so* keen to see you all again after we told him we'd bumped into Mr. Browne that time, but he's been *so* busy, haven't you?" She put a hand on her brother's shoulder.

"I'm sorry I've left it so long to come and see you." Lionel gave his father a kind smile.

They went outside, and Charles opened the car door for Sapphire. She settled herself into her seat.

"Goodbye, Charles," she said coyly as she wrapped her scarf round her hair.

"Goodbye, Sapphire," he said, leaning towards her with one hand on the door. "I hope I have the pleasure of seeing you again."

She gave him a smile and a knowing look as they sped away.

Lionel was pleased about seeing his father and Charles again. He had been immersed in his work in the army for over five years and had missed them.

As a captain, he enjoyed the privileges of his rank and was popular with his men and his commanding officer. He would often be found in the officers' mess, unwinding after a strenuous day, drinking with his fellow officers.

His work was demanding, reestablishing a somewhat decimated army that needed to train new recruits and reequip its units after the devastating war. There was much to be done, and he often had to travel round the country. He liked his work but found it had taken over his life and left him little time for family or courting.

Deciding he needed to make more time for himself, Lionel applied for some much-needed leave one weekend and took a young lady out, the two enjoying a pleasant meal together at a smart restaurant in London's West End. Later that evening, he escorted her to a taxicab and then, deciding to spend the night at his mother's flat in London, made his way there.

He arrived at about eleven thirty and put his key in the lock. As soon as he opened the door, he saw a light on and heard voices.

"Hello?" he called as he entered. Walking straight through to the sitting room, he was surprised to see his half-brother sitting on the sofa. "Charles!" he exclaimed. "Fancy seeing you here!"

Startled, Charles jumped up and greeted Lionel with a hasty handshake.

At that moment, Sapphire came out of the bedroom, wearing nothing but a silk robe.

"Hello, Lionel," she said coolly. "This is unexpected. How lovely to see you! Charles has come up to town to sightsee for the weekend, so I said he could stay here." She gave Lionel a brimming smile and then went over to a side table and poured him a drink.

Lionel stayed standing, not quite sure what to think.

"Do sit down, darling. Here you are," she said as she passed Lionel a tumbler of whisky.

Lionel took it from her and sat down, quickly deciding to pretend he believed his sister's explanation to spare his brother's feelings. "Well, Charles, here's to your very good health," he said, then downed his drink. "It's good that you get some time off. How's it all going?"

"Very well. I'm told the patients like me. I'm finding the work very interesting and sometimes challenging, but Dr. Bailey gives me a lot of support."

"That's good, old man. Glad to hear it."

"Have you got some leave?" asked Charles, wondering why his half-brother had suddenly turned up.

"Yes, I'm going to catch a train home tomorrow."

After he had finished his drink, Sapphire poured him another.

"Where am I sleeping?" he asked, putting his empty glass down.

"In the spare bedroom," replied Sapphire, opening her eyes wide and smiling sweetly. "Charles can sleep on the sofa. You don't mind, do you, Charles?"

"No, of course not," replied Charles, looking nervously at Sapphire.

Lionel bid them both good night and went to his room, closing the door behind him.

He lay in bed, thinking, *What on earth is Charles letting himself in for?* He knew his sister had little regard for the feelings of young men, and he was afraid that Charles was going to get hurt.

Still, he pondered, *they are adults and have every right to do what they want.* He was very fond of his brother and had always realised that Charles looked up to him. *Should I interfere?* he asked himself. *Should I tell him what my sister is like with men?* It was difficult interfering with someone else's love life. He decided to leave well enough alone and see how the relationship progressed.

After a restless night, he left early the next morning, noticing on his way out that the sofa was unoccupied.

On his way home, he thought about his own relationships and decided he would not again ask out the young lady he had shared a meal with.

All the women I meet are the same, rather boring and too well off, he thought. Why couldn't they do something with their lives, like his cousins? Then they might be able to engage in an interesting conversation. He was beginning to despair of ever meeting anyone to whom he could form a real attachment.

CHAPTER TEN

TOM AND DANNY MAKE PLANS

ONE MORNING, AFTER THE POST had been delivered, Ben came into the kitchen and found Sophie reading a newspaper.

"Where's that from?" he asked.

"Millie and Harry have started to deliver newspapers with the post, for those who have ordered them. Agnes asked if we would like to have one."

"That sounds a good idea. It will certainly keep us informed, especially about what this government is up to. I believe David Lloyd George seems to be doing a fair job."

"I could read some of the articles to Danny after work," she added. "I'm sure he would be interested in what's going on in the rest of the world."

Tom and Danny had made a habit of going to the Two Foxes after work every Friday. The late June evenings were getting lighter, and they would share a few beers, often sitting outside, deciding what to do with themselves at the weekend.

One evening, after they'd made their plans, Tom told Danny he wanted to ask him something.

"What's that, then?" Danny looked intrigued.

"I was reading Ma's newspaper the other day and saw an advertisement. It said young men are wanted to go and work in America. They especially need motor mechanics." He paused to see Danny's reaction.

"What are you suggesting?" asked Danny.

"We could go, mate. You and me! We've had lots of experience doing up motorcycles and Bens's old motor. What do you think?"

Danny leant back in his chair. "I don't think they'll want me," he replied.

"Why not? You've proved you can do the work. You told me you've got partial vision in one eye."

"I don't know," began Danny tentatively. "What about Mr. Browne? We'd be letting him down if we went, after all he's done for us."

"I don't know about you, but I want a decent wage. Uncle Ben's given us a good start. I think he'll encourage us."

"What about the money for the passage over there?"

"My pa said he'd give us the money. The shop's been doing very well. And we may be given some assistance if I answer this advertisement."

"You asked your pa, then?"

"Yes, he thinks it's a good idea, but not my ma. I think she'll go spare. I'll have to talk her round."

"We'd come back, though?"

"Depends whether we have work to come back to. I'm hoping we'll do very well over there."

Danny revolved his glass of beer round slowly between his two hands while he thought it all over. Finally, he said firmly, "I'll go with you, Tom. You're right, there's no future for us here."

Tom looked delighted and gave his friend a hearty slap on the back.

"I'm so glad you've agreed! You won't regret it! It will be such an adventure!"

When Tom and Danny appeared for work on Monday morning and Ben began allocating their jobs for that day, Tom said, "Uncle Ben, Danny and I have something to tell you."

Ben put his pencil behind his ear and attended to what his nephew had to say.

"We've decided to go to America. I read something in the newspaper about how they need mechanics over there. Everyone's getting motors and motorcycles, and I think we would find work very easily. Pa has given me some money, so we're going to book our crossing soon."

Stunned, Ben stood staring at the two young men. Finally, he said, "Is your father happy about this?"

"Oh yes, we talked it over. Ma's a bit upset."

"I should think she is." He shook his head in amazement.

"We're very grateful for all you have done for us, Mr. Browne," added Danny hastily.

"Yes, well, I've done what I could. It's only right you should be thinking of moving on. To be honest, there isn't enough work coming in for all of us, and you boys want to get on rebuilding your lives. I think you may well be doing the right thing."

"Thanks, Uncle, for being so understanding," said Tom. "I thought you'd be angry with us."

"I'm not angry, Tom, just surprised. I must say, I admire you boys for your enterprise."

After lunch, Ben let the two boys off to discuss their plans and sat himself in his chair.

"What's wrong?" asked Sophie as she cleared the table. "You've been very quiet."

"Tom and Danny have just told me they're leaving to go to work in America."

Sophie put down the dishes and came and stood beside Ben. "Whatever made them decide that?" she asked.

"They read it in the newspaper, apparently."

"What will Millie and Harry do? With Tom going so far away, it will be like losing a son."

"I expect they want to see him happy and settled. It's a great opportunity."

"Yes, I know, but poor Millie! I wouldn't want our Charles to go away like that."

"It may not be for long. Perhaps they can make a bit of money and come back."

"And what about Rosa? She'll be heartbroken if Danny goes. She's very fond of him."

Ben told her he would go over and see Millie and Harry that afternoon.

When he arrived, he asked his brother-in-law what he thought about it.

"There's no stopping them," said Harry. "They really want to go, and do you know, I think they will make a success of it."

"Will they be coming back?" asked Ben.

"Who knows? If they do well, they could apply for citizenship, I suppose."

"Young people today!" muttered Ben. He looked at his sister, sitting across from him and being very quiet. "They'll do all right," he reassured her, reaching out and holding her hand. "If not, they'll be back!"

Millie was near to tears.

Agnes put an arm round her mother and said, "I'll be here, Ma. I'm not going anywhere."

Millie patted her daughter's hand. "It's such a shock. I never thought he would go away like this. Your father and I hoped he would take over running the shop, but he's shown no interest in it."

"I think he might have done but for the war," Ben observed. "It's unsettled a lot of young men. There isn't much for him here, and he needs a regular job that pays well."

"I hope young Danny can make a go of it," said Harry. "We know he's a good mechanic, but I don't know how he will fare over in America. Only time will tell."

Ben gave his sister a heartfelt hug. "We must support them," he said, "and hope they make a go of it."

Harry smiled resignedly and nodded as he showed his brother-in-law out. Ben strode back to Forge Cottage, feeling a little better and wondering what was for supper.

When Florrie came home from school, she looked astounded upon being told the news. "Who's going to tell Rosa?" she asked.

Sophie looked at Ben, who was due to collect her the next day from the station.

His own worries set aside and not wanting to upset Sophie, he replied, "She's busy with her own life for now. I'm sure she'll be happy for him."

Ben arrived early and parked his Ford in the station forecourt. He sat, waiting, in the motor, watching the people coming and going, but his mind was troubled. How was his daughter going to take the news?

In the end, he thought it best to wait until they got home before telling her that Danny was leaving. Sophie would be there, and she would know what to say if Rosa became upset.

He looked up and saw Rosa come out of the station building, looking anxiously round.

He jumped out quickly and waved. "Over here!" he called.

She came over, smiling broadly. "Hello, Pa. I've so looked forward to coming home!"

Ben kissed her and took her suitcase. "It's lovely having you back, my love," he said.

When they arrived home, Sophie made tea, and they all sat round the table.

"We've something to tell you," Sophie said.

Ben explained about Danny and Tom's new venture, and Rosa listened attentively. "We haven't known very long," he said.

Rosa sat silently, all her cheerfulness gone. "Thank you for telling me," she said, and then she picked up her bag and went upstairs.

Ben got up to follow her, but Sophie put a restraining hand on his arm. "Leave her for a bit," she said. "She wants some time to herself."

Ben nodded and sat down again.

He went up to see her a little later, and when he came down, he told Sophie she was inconsolable. "All I could do was tell her we both have faith in her that she will be able to get over this."

Rosa came down for her meal, her eyes still red from crying.

She looked at her parents resolutely. "I've told myself that I'm very lucky to have a wonderful family and a career I love, so I'll just have to carry on as best I can," she said, managing a faint smile.

She kept her distance from Danny over the next few days, saying she had some studying to do. At mealtimes, Danny and Rosa didn't speak much, and Danny would get up from the table to go over to Tom's house straight after supper.

"I wish they'd talk it over," said Sophie as she and Ben lay in bed, discussing the situation. "He needs to say *something* to her."

"We'd better not interfere," said Ben. "Let them sort it out."

When Rosa's two weeks of leave came to an end, she came downstairs with her case packed, ready for her father to take her to the station.

As Rosa kissed her mother goodbye, Sophie held her for a few moments. "Be brave, darling," she said.

Rosa tossed her head. "Danny has every right to do what he thinks best," she said. "He's never made any promises to me." She quickly went out to the motor and was silent for the journey to the station.

Ben gave her a hug as the train drew in. "Goodbye, my best girl," he said. "Remember your old pa is always here for you."

"Oh, Pa!" she said, clinging to him. "I feel my life is never going to be the same again. I thought I meant something to him!"

"He's a young man who wants to make a life for himself, my love. Give him time. Who knows, he may come back for you when he does."

She shook her head. "I don't think so."

The guard blew his whistle, so Rosa quickly boarded her train. "Goodbye, Pa! Don't worry. I'll be all right!" She waved as the train pulled away.

Ben was left standing on the platform, feeling helpless as he watched it disappear down the tracks.

At the beginning of July, Tom and Danny sailed for New York.

Ben and Sophie joined Millie and Harry to see them off from Southampton docks. The boys were excited and waved madly as the liner pulled slowly away from the harbour. Millie clutched a handkerchief to her face to stifle her tears.

CHAPTER ELEVEN

FLORRIE HAS A DATE

H ER FIRST YEAR OF TEACHING was nearly over, and Florrie told her parents that someone from "the office" was coming to observe her and speak to her headmaster about her progress. She was nervous, but the other teachers assured her that she was certain to pass the inspection.

It was two weeks before the end of term when the official arrived. Mr. Faircross brought the inspector into her classroom and introduced him to Florrie. Turning to leave, Mr. Faircross gave her an encouraging smile.

Florrie went about her day as the man observed, then he studied the children's exercise books at the end of the day. He also examined her wall displays, making notes in his notepad before he left, having barely said a word to her all day.

Florrie sat down at her desk to do her marking, anxious about when she would hear the results. She desperately hoped that she had done well.

Mr. Faircross returned sooner than she had expected, striding into her classroom with a wide smile. "Congratulations, Miss Browne. You passed with flying colours!"

Florrie smiled broadly.

"I had absolutely no worries about you," he said. "But I expect you're relieved."

"It's good to get it over with," she agreed.

"You need to celebrate." Mr. Faircross walked over to look out of the window, then came back and stood before her. "I…er…wondered if you would like to go to the picture house that has just opened. We could go to the early showing so you wouldn't be too late getting home."

It was the first time Florrie had seen her headmaster visibly nervous, which took her by surprise.

"I've never been to a picture house before," she said.

"I was going to suggest this Friday, after school."

"Can I let you know?" Florrie asked.

"Yes, yes, of course." Mr. Faircross began to leave but turned before he got to the door. "It's good to have you join our staff," he said cheerfully.

"Thank you, Mr. Faircross," replied Florrie.

Once she got home, Florrie told her parents that she was now officially a teacher. Ben suggested a celebration.

"I am going to celebrate, Pa. Mr. Faircross has asked me to go out with him." Florrie could feel her cheeks reddening slightly as she spoke. Whatever would her father think?

Ben and Sophie looked at each other in astonishment.

"He's offered to take me to the picture house in Kingsbridge on Friday."

"Have you accepted?" asked her mother.

"No, I told him I would let him know. Are picture houses suitable places to go?"

"I'm sure it will be quite all right," Ben told her. "You may get one or two rough folk there, but on the whole, it will be families or couples, like yourself."

Florrie was relieved. "I think I will go. I was so surprised when he asked me, I really didn't know what to say."

"You go and enjoy yourself," encouraged Sophie.

Deciding to accept Mr. Faircross's invitation, Florrie tentatively knocked on his office door after school the following day.

He looked up as she opened the door and stood in the doorway. "Ah, Miss Browne. Off home?"

"I would like to go to the picture house with you on Friday, Mr. Faircross. Thank you for asking me."

Her headmaster looked pleased and, getting up, came round his desk to face her. "Not at all," he replied. "I hope you enjoy the moving picture. I think it's a good one this week."

As she went out, he followed her and helped to get her bicycle out of the shed in the playground. He stood at the top of the steps and gave a wave as she rode away.

On Friday afternoon, she tidied her classroom, prepared her work for the following week, and then went up to the schoolhouse and knocked on the door. Mr. Faircross answered quickly, and they set off down the hill for the five-thirty showing.

The picture house was a plain-looking building on the corner. When they entered the small foyer, he paid for their tickets at a small opening in the wall, where the attendant sat. While she waited, Florrie looked at the posters on the walls, advertising the picture.

When they entered the dark, smoky auditorium and found their seats, Florrie could see that they were in the better raised ones at the back of the hall, and she could hear a pianist playing at the side of the stage.

Suddenly, there was a whirring sound, and a bright shaft of light shone through the darkness from a small opening at the back of the hall, and Florrie could see movement on the screen. She gave a surprised gasp as the moving objects became people. Every few minutes, large writing appeared, telling the audience what the actors were saying to each other.

Overcome, Florrie clasped the headmaster's hand in her excitement. "Oh, Mr. Faircross! This is wonderful!" she blurted out.

"Please, call me Stephen," he whispered, leaning towards her. "But Mr. Faircross at school, of course," he added, smiling.

Florrie wasn't sure about calling him by his Christian name—he was her headmaster, after all.

He held her hand for the rest of the showing, and when they emerged into the daylight, he asked her if she had enjoyed the film.

"Yes, very much," she replied. "It's all so…so unbelievable!"

He took her arm as they strolled back to the schoolhouse. "I'm glad you liked it," he said.

Florrie thought he was a pleasant-looking man, and he had behaved very differently outside of school. He was relaxed and seemed to enjoy her company. She'd had no idea he was attracted to her, since he had always been quite formal with her up until then.

When they arrived back at the school, Stephen got her bicycle out for her again.

"Have a safe journey," he said as she set off.

Florrie felt strangely elated as she pedalled back to Forge Cottage. *I've been too fond of staying in at home*, she thought. *I do hope he asks me out again.*

She was pleased when he did ask her.

He came into her classroom after school and suggested they go on a day cruise in the holidays. He told her how paddle steamers took passengers round the estuary in July and August, leaving from the quayside. Florrie thought it sounded an enjoyable trip, so she accepted, and they arranged a time for the following week, when the term had ended. She said she would bring a picnic.

On the appointed day, she set off to Kingsbridge on her bicycle and arrived at the schoolhouse in good time. Stephen had made coffee to have while they waited for the tide.

Florrie noticed the garden needed some attention as they sat outside in the sunshine.

"Have you lived here long, Stephen?" she asked.

"About six years," he replied. "I came here with my wife. She was a teacher, but of course, she had to give it up when we married. She died three years ago."

"I'm sorry to hear that, Stephen," said Florrie. "It must have been a difficult time for you."

"It hasn't been easy," he replied. "The children have been a great help, and I do enjoy what I do."

They sat silently for a while, and then Florrie said, "My first year has gone by quickly, and I have enjoyed it too."

He looked at her and gave a kind smile.

They finished their drinks and started off for the Crab Inn to catch the boat.

As they walked down the hill, Florrie realised she was feeling more comfortable in Mr. Faircross's—Stephen's—company. He carried the picnic basket she had prepared, and she was looking forward to the day ahead, when they could share the meal together and perhaps get to know each other a little more.

They waited a short while on the quayside until the small vessel came alongside. They boarded and found their seats on deck. Smoke came out of the funnel as it chugged away down the inlet. Florrie looked round at the view of the coastline, feeling sure it was going to be an enjoyable day.

At the end of the afternoon, they returned to the schoolhouse, feeling their faces glowing from the sun and wind. As they walked back up the hill, Stephen told Florrie that he would be going away in the summer holidays.

"I always visit my parents then," he said. "They live just outside Plymouth. I'm taking them on holiday to the Isles of Scilly. We must arrange another outing when I get back."

Florrie's heart sank. She had been looking forward to spending some of her summer holiday with him. Now she would have to wait a few weeks. She felt hard done by. First, he takes her out, and then he leaves her for a while.

When Stephen handed her bicycle to her, he leant towards her and kissed her gently on her cheek. "Thank you for a lovely day," he said.

Florrie's heart fluttered. She had never been kissed by a man before. She wanted him to embrace her and kiss her some more, but he drew back, looking awkward.

"Thank you for suggesting it," she replied matter-of-factly, overcoming her emotions.

"See you on Monday, then," he said. "Only one more week to go."

During the last week of term, the weather was wet, and Florrie stayed late at school to do her marking rather than carry the books home in the heavy rain. Throwing the last book on the pile, she looked out of the window. It was still raining.

Sighing, she put on her coat and hat and got her bicycle out. Head down, she cycled along as fast as she could against the wind and rain. When she reached home, she left her bike in the shed and hurried inside to the warm and cosy kitchen.

"You're soaked, darling!" exclaimed Sophie, looking up from sewing.

Shivering, Florrie stood dripping on the floor.

The table was strewn with dress material and sewing items. Plunging a pin into her large pincushion, Sophie got up quickly to help her daughter out of her wet things. She went to get towels and then rushed off to get the tin bath out. She placed it on the floor in front of the range and soon had it filled using the kettle and some saucepans full of hot water.

When she was dry and changed, Florrie sat down at the kitchen table and drank a welcome cup of hot tea.

"Why didn't Pa think to come and fetch me?" she asked, feeling disgruntled. Her father had promised to collect her anytime it rained.

Sophie tried to cheer her up. "Never mind, darling. The term's nearly finished now. Are you going on any more dates with Mr. Faircross?"

Sophie's words hit a nerve, and Florrie glowered. "Chance would be a fine thing! He's asked me out twice now and then he tells me he's going away for the summer holidays to see his parents. They're going to the Isles of Scilly. I don't see why he couldn't have included me," she said truculently. "I thought he would be wanting to see more of me in the holidays."

"I don't think it's appropriate for you to go, darling," began Sophie. "You're not engaged. You don't want to rush things. Be patient and let your friendship grow slowly before you decide what your life is to be."

"Except my life isn't worth living if I'm left on my own for the next few weeks."

"Perhaps we ought to have a holiday," said Sophie. "I'll ask your father about it."

When Ben came in later and found out Florrie had got soaking wet on her way home, he was full of apologies and promised to take her in and collect her for the rest of the week.

"Thank you, Pa," said Florrie, cheering up.

After supper, Sophie made her suggestion about a holiday. They decided on a seaside venue, and Sophie said she would send off for places to stay in Cornwall.

When Florrie went upstairs to bed, she thought about Stephen, and a few doubts began to creep into her mind. Was he serious or did he just want a friend to go out with? Would he always be going off without thinking about her?

Her thoughts ran on as she fell into an uneasy sleep.

CHAPTER TWELVE

CHARLES IN LOVE

T THE END OF JULY, Caroline wrote to Sophie and Ben to say she and Donald had some concerns about Charles. He had been with them for nearly six weeks now and had made a good start. Donald was very pleased with his reliability and knowledge. He had shown himself to be good with the patients, and they liked their new doctor. Recently, though, he had seemed preoccupied. She said her husband was wondering if he was, after all, suited to general practice work.

Sophie replied, saying that she and Ben thought it could be a reaction from his years of intensive training and work during the war. She asked them to give Charles a little more time to settle in and suggested he take a break and come home for a short while so they could then talk to him and find out if anything was bothering him.

Caroline wrote back, saying that Charles had been taking time off— hadn't he been coming home? She said that Donald would lighten his duties, though he didn't think they had been too arduous.

Sophie and Ben decided to wait and see if things improved.

Lionel was keen to keep in touch with his father and Sophie. He wrote to them, asking about Charles, as he hadn't heard from him, and Sophie answered straight away.

"My friend Caroline has written to me about him," she wrote. "She says he is very quiet and withdrawn. She and Dr. Bailey are concerned for him." She went on to ask Lionel if he knew what the matter might be. She also shared that she and Ben had decided to arrange a holiday in Cornwall, and they hoped that Charles would be able to come.

When Lionel read her letter, he realised what the trouble probably was. Sapphire was messing Charles about.

He sighed deeply, wondering what he could do. He arranged some more leave, and the following weekend, he travelled home to Exeter and went to speak with Sapphire straight away.

She was sitting on the sofa, flipping through the pages of a magazine as Lionel entered. She looked up. "Hello, Lionel. Wasn't expecting you."

"I got some more leave," he replied. "I wanted to see you, as it happens."

"Why me?" She returned her attention to the magazine.

"I think you know, Sapphire. It's about Charles." He sat down next to her on the sofa.

"Oh, don't worry. I'm not seeing him anymore," she said, not bothering to look up. "He's too serious for me. He keeps bothering me, but I've told him it's over."

Angry with her, Lionel thought, *How dare she treat a man's feelings like that?*

With a final glare before he stormed out, he said, "You are the limit!"

When he'd calmed down, Lionel went to find his stepfather, who happened to be home. He found him in the lobby, sorting out his golf bag.

"Pa, can I ask a favour? I need to see Charles. Can I borrow the motor?"

"Of course, dear boy! Don't drive too fast!" he added, grinning at his son.

As he drove down to Modbury, Lionel wondered if he was doing the right thing. He arrived in the afternoon, hoping Charles would be in.

Caroline took Lionel through to the conservatory, where Charles was sitting alone, holding his head in his hands, and deep in thought. When he saw Lionel, he stood up, pushing his hair back nervously.

"Hello, Charles," Lionel said quietly. "Can we talk in here?"

Charles nodded and sat down again. "I know why you're here, Lionel," he said. "She's dumped me, you know. She said she didn't want to see me anymore." He looked at Lionel in despair. "She doesn't answer my letters, and I can't get to see her. I thought she loved me!" Bending over, he covered his face with his hands.

Lionel sat beside him and put an arm round his shoulders. "I know she's my sister, but I'm afraid this's what she's like. You're not the first, and you won't be the last. You'll come to realise you can do better, believe me. You'll have to try and get over this, old man."

Uncovering his face and staring at the floor, Charles said nothing.

"You work too hard, and you need some time off. How about I arrange some leave and we go on a walking trip together?"

"My parents have already asked me to go away with them and my sisters. I told Ma that it would be difficult to get the time off at present," Charles told him dolefully.

"Wait here," said Lionel.

He went to find Dr. Bailey to explain the situation. When he returned, he told Charles that the doctor had agreed to let him have a week off.

"It's all settled," he said. "Dr. Bailey thinks you probably need a holiday too."

"Thank you, Lionel. I'm very grateful for your concern." Charles looked up, his eyes filled with sadness. "Does anyone else know?"

"We can keep all this quiet," he said quickly. "I told the doctor you were getting over a love affair and needed a break. He was very understanding. I've asked him to keep it confidential." Lionel didn't want Ben and Sophie hearing about it. "I'll have a word with my sister as well." Lionel suggested they explore the Coast Path in Cornwall. "We could meet up with your family one of the days," he suggested.

Charles brightened. "I'd like that," he said.

"Can you write to your ma, asking her to book two extra places at the guest house for one of the nights during their stay?"

Charles readily agreed, and Lionel got up to go.

"Try and forget her," he said as he left. "My sister's still very young, and she's thoughtless. It was obviously never going to work out."

Charles nodded, his expression now cheerful.

Lionel was pleased his visit had done some good. "You'll need a good pair of walking boots!" he called out over his shoulder.

CHAPTER THIRTEEN

HOLIDAYS

IT WAS AUGUST, AND TWO young men could be seen walking in a southwesterly direction along the cliff path of southern Cornwall, making their way towards the cove where Sophie and her family were on holiday. There were quite a few miles to go, and in three days, they hoped to be almost there.

They travelled light, with just a change of clothes and a few personal belongings in a rucksack. Lionel had insisted on bringing his box Brownie camera, hoping to take some photographs of the stunning coastal scenery.

The path was rugged and twined round the top of the cliff, often precariously near to the edge. Lionel and Charles had equipped themselves with walking poles and strode along happily, finding much to talk about as the sea beat against the rocks below them.

On the fourth day, they were approaching the cove. Sophie's family were unaware that the brothers would be joining them. Lionel had asked her to arrange for them to be on the beach that day.

From their vantage point, Charles could see his sister Florrie enjoying herself immensely as she roamed the beach, her bare arms and legs warmed by the sun, and her fair hair blowing freely in the sea breeze. Her sister, too, was lost in another world, scanning the rock pools for sea life, her short, dark hair flopping over her forehead as she bent down to examine each crevice in the rocks. His mother was sitting on a rug with her book on her lap, where it lay unread.

Ben had been for a swim, and as he returned to fetch his towel, he spotted Lionel and Charles weaving their way down the cliff path. He waved vigorously, shouting, "Sophie, look who's here!"

Sophie and the girls quickly joined him and there was a great deal of excitement and laughter when the two men reached the beach.

"You were so surprised at seeing us!" exclaimed Charles, his face beaming. He gave his father a hug, even though he stood there dripping wet from his dip in the sea.

"I had no idea you were in Cornwall too," Ben replied, looking at his wife suspiciously.

Sophie admitted she and Lionel had planned meeting up as a surprise.

Lionel came and put his arm round Sophie, who he gave a conspiratorial smile.

Ben embraced him and then stood back, proudly regarding his two sons standing side by side, their radiant faces glowing from their open-air trek.

Charles turned to his two sisters as they excitedly waited their turn to greet their brothers.

"This is such a lovely surprise!" exclaimed Florrie. She turned to Lionel. "You're both looking very well," she remarked, looking at her handsome tanned brother.

Rosa took hold of Charles's hand. "Come on!" she beckoned. "We're going for a paddle."

Charles and Lionel took off their boots and socks and joined their sisters.

Sophie and Ben sat by the rocks, kept amused by the antics of Lionel chasing Rosa with a piece of wet seaweed and Florrie splashing Charles as they entered the sea. Rosa shrieked, and Charles yelled. The years seemed to roll away as the four of them ran excitedly round like children again.

The remainder of the morning was spent by the girls looking for shells and the young men building sandcastles with mock seriousness.

Rosa whispered something to Florrie, and they crept up on their two brothers and tried to sabotage their efforts.

Finally, after many protestations and bantering, Sophie called a truce, and they all came together for their picnic lunch. Their landlady had made them sandwiches, filled some flasks with tea, and packed up some slices of fruitcake, creating a picnic feast that Ben spread out on an old blanket. Charles flopped down next to his mother and helped her pass round the cups of tea she had poured out. Rosa snuggled down next to her pa, who gave her a warm smile. Florrie was showing Lionel her collection of shells and asking him if he knew what some of them were.

The sandwiches and cake were eaten quickly, and everyone then settled down for an after-lunch nap while Sophie packed everything away.

The afternoon passed by with quiet conversations and walks along the beach. The tide rolled steadily in, and Sophie announced that they should be getting back to the guest house in time for supper at six o'clock. Their landlady had given strict instructions for them not to be late.

Ben rolled up the wet towels and stuffed them into his canvas bag. Sophie remembered that bag. It had held their picnics when they were courting. She picked up the picnic basket, which Lionel came and took from her, carrying it up the cliff path together with his rucksack. Charles followed with the girls, and finally, Sophie came behind. She had lingered back, wanting to remember a wonderful day out with her family.

The guesthouse was a short walk away once they reached the top of the cliff path. The wind was fresher up there, and Rosa shivered as they reached the top.

Ben put his strong arm round her shoulders. "Have you enjoyed your day?" he asked.

"Oh yes!" she replied, her face lighting up. "I hope we can do this again!"

Back at their lodgings, everyone disappeared into their rooms for hot baths and rests before the dinner gong sounded in the hall.

After dinner, the family adjourned to the communal lounge with the other few guests and got out board and card games to play. After a day in the fresh air, bedtime was early.

The following day, Sophie, Ben, and the girls waved goodbye to Lionel and Charles as the men trudged off down the road to commence their walk along the cliff path.

Refreshed from her seaside holiday, Florrie began her new term at the school, ready to welcome her new class that morning.

She was just entering the names of the children into the register when Stephen came in to greet her and ask if she had enjoyed her holiday.

She answered him coolly.

He suggested they go for a picnic the following weekend, but she told him she was busy.

"I have to help my mother with the cycle club teas," she said.

Stephen turned to go, but before he reached the door he said, "Florrie, have I done something to upset you?"

He really has no idea what he has done wrong, thought Florrie. "If you must know, yes," she replied.

He came back over to her desk. "Can you tell me what is bothering you?" he asked gently. "What is it I've done?"

"I don't want to discuss it now," she replied tersely. "I have to get on."

Stephen went away with a perplexed look on his face.

This conversation made Florrie feel out of sorts, and she didn't enjoy her first day back at school. She missed her old class, though she got to see them in assembly with their next teacher. The children in her new class were strange to her, and she had to learn their names. Everything they did bothered her, and she snapped at the children a few times, which was unlike her. They regarded her warily, and she and they were glad when the end of the day came and they disappeared through the door.

She cycled home, feeling upset that she had not been able to share her holiday with Stephen, upset with his lack of awareness, upset how she had spoken to him, and upset with herself for being a bad-tempered teacher with her new class.

When she got home, she pushed her bicycle roughly into the shed and banged the door shut. Entering the kitchen with a disgruntled look on her face, she closed the door with a bang.

Sophie looked up as her daughter came into the kitchen. "Hello, Florrie, whatever is the matter?"

Florrie sat down at the kitchen table and started crying.

Sophie sat down next to her daughter and placed a comforting hand on her back. "Is it anything to do with Stephen?"

"Yes," she replied between sobs.

"Has he finished with you?"

She took a deep breath and began collecting herself as she replied, "No, but I think I upset him today. I was a bit short with him."

"Whatever's wrong? Is it because he went away without you?" asked Sophie.

"Partly. It's just that I feel he takes me for granted, that it's convenient to go on our little dates, but it doesn't seem to be going anywhere."

"Are you in love with him?"

"I don't know. I'm attracted to him, and I like his company, but sometimes I wish he could be a bit more—well, you know, what is the word?—ardent. Show he really cares for me."

"Perhaps you could show your feelings towards him a bit more so he will then know it's all right to show his. Don't forget, he lost his wife not so very long ago."

"That's another thing. I sometimes feel I'm filling her shoes."

"That's bound to happen when a man has been married before. There's nothing wrong in him wanting someone in his life."

Florrie wiped her eyes and hugged her mother. "Thank you, Ma. You've been a real help. Can I invite Stephen over here to meet you all sometime?"

"I think that would be a very good idea, but wait until the teas have died down."

When Florrie arrived at school the next morning, she was surprised to find a bunch of flowers on her desk. This gave her an excuse to go and see Stephen. She went to his small office, but the door was closed, which meant he had a parent with him and she would have to wait until school finished for the day.

She made a real effort to be good natured with her class all day, praising them for their work.

After school, she made her way to Stephen's classroom, finding him wiping the blackboard clean of the day's arithmetic.

"Thank you so much for the flowers, Stephen."

He turned round. "I think I know why you feel annoyed with me," he said. "I have really neglected you over the summer holidays, and I'm sorry. The thing is, I was supposed to go on holiday with my parents for just two weeks and then come back here, but my father has been very ill. He's had a heart attack, and I should have written to let you know. I've been so busy taking my mother to the hospital for visits."

"Stephen, I'm so very sorry. How is he?"

"He's back home now and seems to be recovering."

"I'm so glad. It must have been a very worrying time for you."

"Yes, but I think he'll be all right for now."

Remembering what her mother had said, Florrie gave him a hug.

He responded, pulling her closer to him and holding her. "I was so looking forward to coming back to you," he said.

"Where shall we go for that picnic?" she asked.

CHAPTER FOURTEEN

LIONEL FALLS IN LOVE

ETURNING FROM HIS WALKING HOLIDAY with Charles, Lionel arrived at Paddington Station and was walking along the platform, deep in thought. Much relieved that Charles seemed to have gotten over his first love affair, he reflected on how much they'd enjoyed their walking holiday together.

A local train pulled in, spurting steam and screeching its brakes as if in pain. As Lionel passed by, carriage doors flew open and people began emerging, all of them in a hurry. Just in front of him, a young woman stepped out but suddenly lost her footing and began to fall. He put his arm out to try and catch her, and she managed to grab it, twisting round as she did so and ending up sitting on the ground.

"Are you all right?" Lionel asked.

"I…I don't know," the young woman replied, rubbing her leg. "I think I may have twisted my ankle."

"Allow me to help you up," said Lionel, reaching down to offer his hand.

She had dropped her art portfolio, and what looked like line drawings had spilled out. A passer-by retrieved the sheets of paper and handed them to Lionel, thinking he was with the young lady.

Lionel helped her to stand, and she winced in pain. "Can I suggest I help you over to the station buffet and you can rest for a while?" he asked.

She nodded and limped painfully beside him, holding on to his shoulder.

They passed through the ticket barrier, and he guided her through the entrance to the buffet. He found her a seat, and she sank into it. Lionel could see she was in a state of shock, and she looked rather pale.

"I'll get you some tea." He quickly returned with two steaming cups of tea and placed them on the table. "Here we are, good old railway tea. Not quite tea at the Ritz, I'm afraid," he quipped, trying to make her relax.

"I wouldn't know," she said, giving a slight smile. "I've never had tea at the Ritz."

"Every young lady should have tea at the Ritz," Lionel replied, and for the first time, they regarded each other.

She had an open, pleasant face, and despite the pain she was in, she was trying to smile. Her blue eyes were bright and alert, and he felt quite mesmerised by them. Her auburn hair, which had been pinned up, had come loose and partly fallen over her forehead. Lionel thought it made her look very attractive.

He introduced himself, "Captain Lionel Wells, at your service, as they say." He hoped his being in uniform would reassure the young lady that he was a gentleman.

"Miss Craig, Amanda Craig, and yes, you have been of service, thank you very much." She bent down and rubbed her ankle. "I think it's swollen," she said. "I shall have to go back home. Could I ask you to see when the next train leaves? I live in Richmond."

Lionel went to look at a railway timetable and then came back and told her there wasn't one for another half an hour. He was pleased by this delay, as it gave him time to get to know this charming girl a little better.

He sat down beside her, and they sipped their tea for a few minutes, watching the hustle and bustle of the station.

She said, "Please don't let me delay you. I'm sure I can manage now."

"I insist on staying. You'll need assistance to board your train. Is there anyone who can collect you at the other end?"

"I'll get a taxicab, thank you," she replied, looking at him gratefully.

"Can I ask where you were trying to get to today?" he asked, glancing at her portfolio.

"I was going to do some sketching at the British Museum. I'm hoping to apply to art school, and I'm preparing my portfolio."

How interesting, thought Lionel. He wasn't used to young ladies doing anything.

"What kinds of things do you draw?" he asked.

"Oh, just about anything that appeals to me, the shape or texture of an object."

"So you live in Richmond?"

"Yes, my father works in stained glass and has a studio there."

"Is that what you hope to do as well?"

"No, I hate the sound of cutting glass. Makes me shiver!"

They both laughed and looked at each other again. He liked her naturalness and easy-going manner.

"Are you returning to your regiment?" she asked.

"Yes, I've just been on holiday, but I live in Devon, near Exeter. My father is a lawyer and works here in London."

She nodded, then looked up at the large station clock on the wall. "I think my train must be here soon," she said.

Lionel suddenly felt disappointed that the time had gone so quickly. He stood up, helped her to her feet, and, picking up her portfolio, held her arm as she limped painfully beside him.

"You must rest that foot when you get home," he said.

"Yes, I will."

When they reached her train, he helped her into a first-class carriage and made sure she was settled comfortably. She began to protest, saying she always went second class.

"Here's your ticket," he said, placing it in her hand. "I bought it when I went to find out the times."

She got out her purse. "Here," she said, holding out a few coins in the palm of her hand. "Please take what I owe you."

"No, I insist," he said. "I hope you have a safe journey home."

"Thank you, Captain Wells. Thank you so much." She replaced the money in her purse and leant towards him. "Do you like art?" she asked.

"Yes. Yes, I do." Lionel looked puzzled and put his head to one side, waiting to hear more.

"There's an exhibition I want to go to at the National Gallery at the end of next month," she said eagerly, her eyes bright. "I shall probably be there on the Saturday afternoon."

The engine began to pump steam, ready to depart.

Lionel opened the carriage door and, as he got out, said, "I'll be there."

The train began moving, and he waved goodbye until she disappeared from his sight. He stood on the platform as the carriages went past, feeling as if he was in a dream.

When he came to, he suddenly realised she had asked him out on a date. He felt elated, realising this chance encounter had given him the opportunity to get to know a very attractive young woman. Forgetting all about Charles, his mind was full of her as he returned to his barracks.

Back in his rooms, Lionel had an idea. He had been asked to chair a meeting of officers to commission a memorial for those in his regiment who had lost their lives in the war, to be put in the regimental chapel. He thought that a stained-glass window would be just the thing and wondered if Miss Craig's father would be interested. When they heard his suggestion, the Memorial Committee were very enthusiastic and appointed him to ask Miss Craig's father to submit some designs.

On the day of the exhibition, Lionel set off to see if he could meet Miss Craig. He was sure he had the right day and place, but would she be there?

The gallery was busy, as it was a Saturday. He bought his ticket and set off towards the exhibition hall, scanning to the left and right for any sight of her, hardly noticing the paintings on the walls. Finally, he saw her sitting quietly on an upholstered bench in one of the galleries, contemplating a large painting.

He went over and said, "Hello again, Miss Craig."

She looked round quickly and smiled broadly. "Captain Wells! How lovely to see you!"

He sat down, and she turned her attention back to the painting.

"I love this piece," she said. "The way the colours lie together and form such beautiful shapes!"

Lionel looked for a moment and then nodded his agreement, feeling a little speechless in her presence. He loved the way she had done her hair, two coils of plaits on each side of her head.

"What do you think of the other works?" she asked.

Lionel hadn't really noticed them since he'd been too busy looking for her. "I think I shall need your expert opinion to guide me," he said diplomatically.

"Of course," she replied pleasantly.

They spent an hour strolling round as Miss Craig talked about the pictures. Lionel listened attentively to her elucidating descriptions. When they finally came to the end of the exhibits, he asked if she would like some tea, if she had time.

"I'd love some, as long as I don't get back too late," she replied.

He escorted her outside, and she held on to his arm as they descended the steps and walked across the square, then up towards Piccadilly Circus.

"Where are we going?" asked Miss Craig.

"We're going to take tea at the Ritz," Lionel replied, giving a self-satisfied smile.

"But that's so extravagant!" she exclaimed.

"As I said before, every young lady should have tea at the Ritz at least once." Lionel felt rather pleased with himself that he had impressed her.

"That's very generous of you, Captain Wells. I would have happily settled for Lyons' Corner House! Thank you very much."

At the entrance to the Ritz tearoom, they were met by a waiter and shown to their seats. Miss Craig gasped, staring at the opulence round her. The white-and-gold ornate pillars and arches supported a huge atrium, and large potted palms gave the room a continental feel. Above her, a huge gilded candelabra hung down from the glass ceiling, flooding the room with light.

"I'm sorry I don't have a posh frock on," she said as she slid off her light coat.

"What you have will do very well," said Lionel. "And you look lovely in it."

"What a beautiful room," said Miss Craig, still looking round with genuine awe, her eyes showing her amazement. "This is so kind of you," she said, turning to look at him.

"It's not easy getting reservations," he explained. "They give preference to their own guests, but as I'm an officer in uniform, they made an exception."

The waiter came and placed a silver teapot, milk jug, and sugar bowl on the immaculate white tablecloth. He returned with a cake stand full of dainty sandwiches and cakes.

"Those are a work of art!" she exclaimed.

After Lionel had ordered a special blend of tea, the waiter returned with the teapot and proceeded to fill the elegant cups. When he left, Miss Craig passed the silver milk jug to Lionel.

"Do you think we could go on to our Christian names now?" she asked as she used silver tongs to take a cube of sugar from the bowl.

Lionel readily agreed, and they chatted amicably together.

When she asked about his work in the military, he told her about his efforts to create a memorial and described the commission he was thinking of asking her father about.

"I'm sure he would be very interested, Lionel," she answered, sipping her tea. "He never turns down any work."

Lionel took a sheet of paper from his pocket and gave it to her. "Here's the brief," he said, "and the budget we have allocated."

She looked at it, her eyes opening wide. "That's a very generous amount," she said. "Is it a very big window?"

"The dimensions are on there," replied Lionel. "But if he wants to visit the chapel to take a look, he would be very welcome."

"Why don't you discuss it with my father? Come to lunch, any day will be fine. I think he would like to meet you." She wrote her address on a piece of paper. "I think you should be able to find us quite easily," she said, handing it to him. "We're not far from the station."

Lionel folded it carefully and put it into his pocket. "Thank you, I would like that very much, Amanda. I can come Thursday if that's all right?"

She said it would be.

They finished their tea, and Lionel paid, then he helped Amanda get her coat on. As they went out, she gave one last admiring look round.

Outside, Lionel hailed a taxicab to take them to the station. He sat with her until her train was due and then said goodbye at the ticket barrier.

"Until Thursday, then. Goodbye, Amanda."

"Goodbye," she replied. She began walking towards her train but then turned and waved.

Lionel waved back and felt a surge of happiness as he turned to return home.

He counted the days until Thursday came, and then he arrived promptly at Richmond just before twelve o'clock, finding the modestly sized brick Victorian villa at the end of a row of similar ones.

Amanda answered the door, and as he entered, he stopped to look at the paintings hung on the walls either side of the hallway.

"Hello, Amanda," he said, bending down slightly to embrace her. "Are these all yours?" he asked.

"Some of them," she replied. "Some are my mother's."

They went into a small comfortably furnished room with sculptures and houseplants and some art books on a table.

"I'll go and get Daddy," she said.

She soon returned with her father, who was wearing what looked like overalls and had the same laughing eyes as his daughter. She introduced him to Captain Wells.

"Hello, young man!" he said, shaking Lionel's hand. "I hear my daughter fell into your arms, so to speak." His manner was one of gentle teasing.

"I wish I could have prevented her getting hurt, sir."

"Oh, don't do all that 'sir' business. I'm not the lord of the manor. Just 'Mr. Craig' will do for now."

"Please call me Lionel," he replied. "We won't bother with the 'Captain' business either."

He was invited to sit down, and Amanda excused herself to finish getting the lunch ready.

Her father asked him about his journey, and by the time he'd replied, Amanda pulled a draped curtain aside and asked them through.

They went to the back of the house, into a small room that looked out onto a small courtyard garden. A round table was laid with some stoneware plates and glass goblets, and there was a small vase of flowers in the centre. Amanda had prepared a chicken salad with homemade bread, after which they had fresh raspberries and cream.

When they finished, she brought in a jug of fresh coffee and then excused herself so Lionel and her father could discuss the commission.

Mr. Craig said he would like to see where the window would be in the chapel, and Lionel assured him that could be arranged.

"Come and see my studio," he then said and led Lionel outside and through the courtyard, into a small single-story building at the end. Inside, he showed him some samples of his work and a sketchbook of designs.

Lionel was fascinated as he listened intently to Mr. Craig describing the process of making a stained-glass window. "I can see you have to cut each piece very accurately," observed Lionel as he peered down at the partially finished window. "It obviously takes great skill."

"Years of practice," replied Mr. Craig. He set his glass-cutting tool down and regarded Lionel seriously. "Amanda is only just nineteen," he began. "She lost her mother at quite a young age, and I have brought her up on my own. She has always wanted to go to art school, and I would like her to have the opportunity. She needs her freedom, so it is important that I allow her to have that. I want to ask you if you would also let her have that freedom. She's too young to have a serious relationship, but I know she's very taken with you. She talks of little else."

Taken aback, Lionel had no idea what to say.

"You are, I imagine, quite a lot older than her?" Mr. Craig asked.

"I'm nearly twenty-seven." Lionel had never felt he was too old to be attracted to Amanda. *What exactly is her father getting at?* he wondered.

"I have nothing against you, Lionel. I can see you're a fine young man, but you've come along too soon. I will always put my daughter's interests first, and she needs to be free to go to art school and develop her potential."

Lionel could feel a surge of anxiety rising inside him. "What would you have me do, Mr. Craig?"

"Wait. At least for a year, wait, and then she will be that much older and know what path she wants to take."

Lionel felt deflated, realising he didn't really have an option. "Have you spoken to Amanda about this?" he asked.

"She knows my thoughts on the matter."

"I see." Lionel was beginning to feel that Mr. Craig was trying to see him off.

Just then, Amanda came in. "Would you like to take a walk round our courtyard garden?" she asked.

They went outside, and she showed him some of the plants. At the side, beside an acer tree, was a bench, so they sat down.

"Has Daddy been talking to you?" she asked, looking at him warily.

"Yes."

"What did he say?"

Lionel told her what her father had asked him to do.

Amanda looked upset.

"Amanda, I can't go against his wishes. He is right, wanting you to concentrate on your studies, and I am willing to help with that until we can be together again." He placed his hand gently on her knee.

She put her head down. "Oh, Lionel!" she said desperately.

He took her hand and held it. "He didn't say we couldn't write to each other."

She looked up suddenly. "Oh, Lionel, I would love to hear what you're doing!"

"A year will go by very quickly," he said, trying to reassure her. "I promise, faithfully, I will be waiting for you."

She nodded.

"Can I ask you one thing?"

She nodded again.

"Can I have one quick kiss before we say goodbye today?"

She glanced nervously towards her father's workshop and then whispered, "Yes."

He pulled her gently towards him and held her in the kiss until she finally pulled away from him.

"That wasn't a quick kiss, Captain Wells!" she exclaimed, her eyes shining.

"It has to last me a long time," he replied, grinning at her.

They got up, and he held her hand as they went back to the house.

Inside, Mr. Craig gave Lionel a disapproving look as they came in, hand in hand.

"Ah! There you are. I'll be in touch about the commission, Mr. Wells. Perhaps you would be so kind as to leave your address."

Lionel scribbled it down. "I'll look forward to hearing from you, Mr. Craig." They eyed each other for a second, then Lionel said, "I wish you good day." He turned to Amanda. "Thank you for the delicious lunch. Goodbye, Amanda." He squeezed her hand and smiled confidently at her as he left.

CHAPTER FIFTEEN

LIONEL DECIDES HIS FUTURE

IN THE MIDDLE OF SEPTEMBER, Lionel heard from Mr. Craig, who apologised for the delay in getting in touch and explained he had been finishing another commission. He asked if he could come later that week to view the site in the chapel where the memorial window was to be fitted.

Lionel wrote back, confirming he'd arranged their visit accordingly.

Three days later, he met Mr. Craig at the station and they got a taxicab to the barracks. After the usual pleasantries, Lionel asked after Amanda.

"She has her place at art school," Mr. Craig replied. "It's for a year, at present, and then she needs to apply for the main course."

What would that mean for me? Lionel asked himself. *Is he saying I might have to wait even longer?* Lionel expressed his best wishes for her success.

When they arrived at the barracks, he took Mr. Craig through to the chapel. It was a simple brick building situated a short way from the men's quarters. The windows on each side were pointed, and most had clear glass. The memorial window was to be at the end, near to the altar.

Mr. Craig looked round as they entered. Inside, there were rows of wooden pews, and the lower part of the walls was panelled and displayed coats of arms and insignia, making the chapel colourful. Two large crossed-over flags flanked the wall, one a Union Jack, and the other, the regimental colours.

Mr. Craig spent some time taking measurements and making a few quick sketches. When he'd finished, Lionel escorted his guest to the buffet lunch he'd arranged in the officers' mess, with the rest of the committee present, as well, to meet Mr. Craig. In the afternoon, he showed him round the barracks and then it was time for him to leave.

As Lionel hailed a taxicab to take his guest to the station, Mr. Craig promised he would submit some designs as quickly as he could. Then he said, "I consider it a great honour, Captain Wells, being given this commission, and I shall give it my best shot." After a short pause, he added, "As regards Amanda, thank you for agreeing to my request. I hope there are no hard feelings."

"None at all, Mr. Craig. I quite understand, but it hasn't been easy."

"Well, perhaps you could write to her," he said, relenting slightly.

"Thank you, I'll do that," said Lionel, smiling inside.

"But not too often," said Mr. Craig as he got into his taxicab. "Goodbye, and thank you for your kind hospitality. I've enjoyed my day."

When he'd gone, Lionel sighed heavily and returned to his rooms. He felt surprisingly tired after the day's events. He filled a glass of whisky and sat down to think things over. He had already penned one letter to Amanda and hoped it had reached her. He was still waiting for a reply.

After a while, he got up to replenish his glass and found the bottle was nearly empty. He went to a small cupboard nearby to get out another, checking that he had several bottles left.

While he drank his whisky, he wrote to Charles. If he couldn't see Amanda, he would have plenty of spare time at weekends. He saw this as an opportunity to invite his half-brother to come and stay.

Charles sat comfortably in Lionel's small sitting room at his quarters, having arrived that morning. Lionel was describing his visit to Amanda's home and what her father had said about waiting a year before they could date.

"That's a bit much, isn't it?" responded Charles, taking the drink that was handed to him.

Lionel drained his glass and got up to refill it. "What can I do? She's not yet twenty-one, and her father still holds parental control. I believe he's paying for her to go to art school. I think he has her best interests at heart."

"Do you think you can wait a year?"

"I'll have to. I've waited all this time to meet someone like her." He swallowed down his whisky. "Well, Charles, what shall we do this weekend?" he said, changing the subject. "Let me show you the sights."

After a brief discussion, Lionel went out to arrange an extra place at the officers' table for dinner that evening.

When he'd gone, Charles got up and opened the small fitted cupboard from which Lionel had been getting the bottle to pour his drinks, under a narrow bookshelf. Inside were about half a dozen bottles of whisky. He closed it quickly and sat down again.

Just what I suspected—he's started drinking, thought Charles. He knew Lionel liked a drink, but several a day were not good for him. He wondered if it could be as much as a bottle, having seen so many in the cupboard.

Lionel returned and poured himself another drink. Charles said nothing.

The next morning was spent exploring London, ending up in Trafalgar Square.

Charles glanced over to the National Gallery. "Have we time to go in?" he asked.

"No, not really," replied Lionel. "Let's find somewhere to have a drink."

Charles followed Lionel to a bar, where Lionel downed several more whiskies.

When they returned to Lionel's rooms, Charles said, "Can I ask how much you drink in a day?"

"Oh, not a lot. No need to worry yourself, old man," his brother answered evasively.

"I'm a bit concerned about you, Lionel. Is something bothering you? You do seem to be drinking quite a lot."

Without answering, Lionel stood with his hands in his pockets, avoiding Charles's gaze.

"If you are," Charles went on, "you need to deal with the cause. Something must be on your mind." He put a hand gently on his brother's shoulder.

"You don't miss much, do you?" muttered Lionel, looking at the floor.

"Can you tell me what's troubling you?"

Again, silence. After a few moments, Lionel paced the room, then sat down. "Just about everything," he replied eventually.

Charles sat down beside him. "I'm listening."

"I miss her so, and I don't think I can wait a year. Also, it may come as a surprise to you, but I've decided to leave the army. I've been thinking about it for quite a while now. It's a big step to take. I've done well and would probably get promoted if I stayed on. 'Why am I leaving?' I keep asking myself."

"Do you know what you want to do outside of the army?" asked Charles.

"I've talked it over with my stepfather. I know I don't want to do what he does, representing criminals in court, but I am interested in the law and think I would like to set up as a solicitor eventually. If I decided to go down that road, I would have to train for two years. I really don't know what to do."

Charles felt Lionel's pulse, then examined his eyes. "How long have you been drinking like this?"

"A few weeks, maybe longer."

"I'd like to help. You must stop drinking so much. I noticed you drink your whiskies neat. Try and drink less and add soda." He asked Lionel for a sheet of paper, then got out his fountain pen and began to scribble something down. "Here you are," he said, handing it to Lionel. "This is how to cut down gradually, over the next two weeks, by rationing yourself. No one's expecting you to stop drinking altogether, just drink less. I know you have a lot of concerns now, and I hope you sort something out when you leave the army. Make some decisions instead of worrying. If you concentrate on your career, the time will go by faster, and before you know it, you'll see Amanda again."

Lionel clasped his brother's hand. "Thanks, Charles. It's been a great help talking to you about things."

"When I get back home, I'll make something up for you to take and post it to you. It will help to calm you."

And he did so, sending off Lionel's sedative straight away.

After Charles's visit, Lionel sat in his room to compose a letter to Amanda. He wanted to tell her that one of his colleagues had told him his father had a solicitor's practice in Egham, so he had written to enquire if he would take him on. The solicitor had replied, offering him an interview the following week. He wrote about his plans, then added that he was keeping busy but still very much missing her.

He did not have to wait long for a letter back from Amanda. He saw it straight away in his in tray at work—an envelope with a beautifully inscribed name and address. With enormous relief, he opened it quickly. She, too, was missing him, and she told him a little about her experiences at the art school. She had even drawn some pictures in the margin to illustrate them.

Lionel folded the letter carefully and placed it in his inside pocket. He felt convinced of her commitment to him, now that she had written. He still longed for her, remembering their kiss in the garden.

The interview in Egham went very well, and Mr. Cartwright agreed to take him on.

When he told his commanding officer that he was going to leave the army, the man spent an hour trying to persuade him to stay, but Lionel had made up his mind.

Another letter arrived from Mr. Craig, saying that he had several designs to submit and asking when he could show them to the Memorial Committee. Lionel answered immediately and invited him to come the following week.

Mr. Craig arrived with his portfolio on the appointed day and gave a short presentation. After a lively discussion, one of the designs was chosen, and Mr. Craig left to begin work on the window. He didn't mention Amanda, and Lionel did not enquire.

After several weeks, a letter from Mr. Craig arrived, saying that he had completed the commission and would like Lionel to arrange for it to be collected.

Lionel travelled to Richmond in an army transport with some of his men and oversaw the removal of the glass window to the regimental chapel. Mr. Craig returned with them and watched as the window was carefully lifted into the opening and fastened in. Members of the committee were present, and it was a poignant occasion as everyone stood silently admiring the window after its installation.

Lionel could see that Mr. Craig had produced a beautiful work of art that was perfect for the memorial. The window depicted a standing soldier holding his rifle, looking up towards a dove hovering above him, and his other arm was reaching up as if he wanted to touch it. The background showed stark trees in a ravaged landscape beneath white clouds set against a blue sky. The writing along the bottom paid homage to the fallen and wounded of their regiment.

The committee congratulated Mr. Craig and voiced their admiration for such an impressive memorial. He responded by saying that it was a privilege to have been asked to carry out such a commission.

Lionel spoke to Mr. Craig, congratulating him on his work. The man listened in his quiet, modest way and thanked him. Mr. Craig was invited to the officers' mess for a celebratory lunch, and Lionel invited him to the service of dedication to be held the following week. Mr. Craig accepted and, thanking Lionel, left to return home. Again, no mention was made of Amanda.

At the end of an exciting day, Lionel returned to his quarters and immediately got out a bottle of whisky. His hand tightened round the neck as he struggled with himself. *Why don't I have the guts to face up to things rather than turn to drink?* he asked himself.

He put the bottle back and made himself some coffee.

CHAPTER SIXTEEN

A SURPRISE VISITOR

IT WAS THREE WEEKS SINCE their course had begun, and Rosa and Betty were sitting on their beds in their room at the nurses' home, opening their letters. Betty read hers quickly and then turned to Rosa.

"Who's yours from?" she asked.

"My ma. It's just news from home. Is yours from your mother?"

"Good Lord, no! I don't think she's written a letter in her life. It's from my boyfriend. He wants us to get married."

Rosa was just about to congratulate her when Betty said, "What does he think I'm doing here if I wanted to marry him?" She tossed the letter to one side.

Rosa could not help but feel sorry for the young man.

"Have you heard from your friend…Danny, was it?" Betty enquired.

Rosa reddened slightly. "No, he's gone to America with my cousin to look for work. They're motor mechanics."

"Is he coming back?"

"I really don't know. I doubt it."

Betty jumped up and went to her locker, where she produced a packet of cigarettes. She took one out and offered the packet to Rosa.

"No, thanks, I don't smoke."

"Do you mind if I do?"

Rosa did but said, "No, but perhaps you'd better sit by the window."

Betty went to open the window and perched on the windowsill, blowing puffs of smoke out. When she'd finished, she stubbed out the cigarette on the ledge and threw it out the window. "That's better!" she said, closing the window.

Rosa liked Betty despite her mildly reckless ways. She had shown her that young women could have boyfriends, without marrying, and be able to carry on with their careers.

"We're modern girls," she'd told Rosa.

Rosa thought she probably appeared rather old-fashioned to her friend. Betty had shown her how to wear makeup and had advised her on her wardrobe, telling her that her clothes were out of date. Rosa took it all in good heart, but she wondered what her mother would think.

"Sounds as if your Danny's dumped you," said Betty in her straightforward way. "I'll have to get you fixed up at the next dance."

Rosa didn't want to be "fixed up." She just wanted her Danny back.

Ben was busy clearing out rubbish from his workshop to make more room for the motorcycles. Later that day, he was sweeping up when he heard a vehicle coming up the lane.

A taxicab stopped outside, and the driver got out to open the passenger door.

Ben saw who it was immediately and exclaimed, "Danny!"

"Oh, Mr. Browne, you're there!"

The cabbie got his case out and, after refusing payment, drove off.

Ben held Danny's outstretched hand and guided him into the cottage. "Look who we have here, Sophie. The prodigal son!" he called out as they went in.

Sophie looked amazed as Danny came through the door, and she immediately hugged him. "Welcome back, Danny!" she said. "Is Tom here as well?"

"No, he's still in New York." Danny felt his way to a chair and sat down. "I'm glad you haven't moved the furniture round, Mrs. Browne!" he joked.

"What's happened?" asked Ben. "Why have you come back and not Tom?"

Danny began to explain.

"When we arrived, Tom found work straight away. He had a good job. No one wanted to employ a partially sighted man like me, though. You need to work very hard over there. If you can't keep up, they don't want you. Everything's moving so fast, and they can't afford to take any passengers. I felt I was holding Tom back. He wanted to help me find work, but I wouldn't let him give up his job, so we agreed I should come home. I hope you don't mind my turning up here."

"You know this is your home now, Danny," said Ben. "But how did you manage on the journey?"

"Tom found a family returning to Britain, and they helped me."

Sophie had made a pot of tea, and she offered Danny some of her fruitcake.

"Thank you, Mrs. Browne. I've missed your baking!" He munched his large slice happily. When he'd finished, he wiped his mouth and said, "How's Rosa?"

Sophie glanced at Ben. "She seems to be enjoying her training."
Danny nodded.

"She was very upset when you decided to go off like that," said Ben.

"I think it was a bit of a mistake. I let Tom talk me into it, and he didn't want to go on his own. Will she be coming home soon? I'd like to see her."

"I don't think so," replied Sophie. "She had time off to go on holiday with us, but I don't think she has any leave for a while."

Danny bit his lip and reached for his tea. Seeing him slumped in his chair, looking very tired, Sophie suggested he go up to bed.

When he'd gone upstairs, Ben and Sophie looked at each other in astonishment.

"Well, what a surprise!" said Ben. "I wonder how Rosa will feel about seeing him again?"

That evening, Danny woke refreshed, and while enjoying supper with Ben and Sophie, he described his adventure with Tom a little more.

"We had a good crossing, although travelling steerage is a bit basic. We had to share a cabin with two Irishmen who were also looking for work. When we arrived, we had to stand in long queues to be checked. The immigration man told us our visas only lasted for six months and we would have to obtain work permits. We could apply for citizenship later, if we wanted. We told him we were motorcycle mechanics, and he said skilled workers were very sought after, but he advised us to get into automobiles, as they call motors over there."

"Where did you live?" asked Sophie.

"We were directed to a men's hostel in New York, not far from the harbour. It was a bit rough, Mrs. Browne, so we decided to find somewhere else as soon as we found work."

"Did it take you long to find work?" asked Ben.

"No, we went round to some garage repair shops, and Tom found a job before the end of the first week, but they wouldn't take me on because of my eyesight. I told Tom to take it. The pay seemed very good. I tried to find work, and one place offered me a job sweeping up. I tried it for a while, but they fired me by the end of the week for not doing it properly. It was so boring. I got other deadbeat jobs, like emptying trash cans and clearing up horse muck from the roads. Before long I was thinking to myself, what sort of life is this? I told Tom I was going back home. I felt guilty, leaving him, but what else could I do?"

"I think you did the right thing, Danny. Tom can come home if he's unhappy," Sophie said gently, putting her hand on his arm.

Danny looked reassured.

"To be honest with you," said Ben, "I'm glad you're back. I could do with your skills. I'm planning to set up a motorcycle-repair business. What if you and I went into partnership? I think we could make it work."

With a huge grin, Danny replied, "That sounds great, Mr. Browne. Thanks!"

September was nearly over when Florrie invited Stephen to have tea at Forge Cottage, one day after school, and meet her family. She told him her father would collect them from school and take him back to the schoolhouse afterwards.

"I'd like that very much, Florrie. Thank you," he said, looking pleased.

A week later, Ben drove to the school to pick them up. They were waiting outside. Ben approached Mr. Faircross nervously, and Florrie introduced him.

As they shook hands, Stephen said, "I expect you're proud of your clever daughter, Mr. Browne."

Florrie looked embarrassed as Ben agreed. "She gets her brains from my wife, Mr. Faircross. Not me!"

Sophie had prepared one of her special teas in the parlour, but before they sat down together, Florrie showed Stephen round their small property, ending up at the workshop.

She introduced Danny, who was working there, and Stephen spent a while talking to him and asking him about his trip, which Florrie had told him about.

"New York's a crowded, noisy place, Mr. Faircross, but it was exciting. There's lots of opportunities, but you need to be strong or clever, so that left me out. I'm glad to be back, though."

As they walked back to the cottage, Stephen, who was interested in Danny's training, asked if he'd learnt Braille.

"Yes, but I don't really use it now," he replied.

After tea, Danny went back to the workshop to finish a piece he was working on.

When he'd gone, Stephen turned to Florrie and said, "I think I can help that young man. He needs a Braille typewriter, and I'm sure we can get him some reading material too."

"Rosa used to read to him when she was here," replied Florrie. "I suppose I should do it now."

"I'm sure he would appreciate that," said Stephen, smiling warmly at her. "I think he should be getting some sort of pension too. I'll look into it."

"That's very kind of you," she said.

Stephen also spoke to Ben about his new business, suggesting that his workshop premises might be a bit out of the way for motorcyclists to find. "You need to be nearer a main road so people see where you are," he said. "But I realise that's easier said than done."

"You're probably right, Mr. Faircross. I hadn't thought of that," Ben replied.

When it was time to go, Stephen thanked Sophie for the tea and then kissed Florrie on the cheek before he and Ben went out to the Ford.

After waving them off, Florrie returned to the kitchen, smiling broadly at her mother.

"He's a very likeable young man," said Sophie. "You've chosen well there."

"I think you could say he chose me!" joked Florrie, full of good spirits.

"Are things any better between the two of you?"

"Yes, much better. He's had some family problems. His father has been ill. I think I need to be patient. I do hope he can do something for Danny. He deserves it." She began helping her mother clear the tea table.

CHAPTER SEVENTEEN

DANNY'S OPERATION

FTER READING HER MOTHER'S LATEST letter in her room, Rosa put it down and looked out of the window, wondering whether she was glad Danny had come home. She was just getting over him, and here he was again. What did he feel about her now? She very much wanted to get together with him but was unsure about his feelings towards her. *I can't bear the thought of him not wanting me*, she thought.

She wrote back to her mother, saying she was glad that Danny had returned safely. Her mother had given some details about the trip, and Rosa wasn't surprised Danny had to come back. She was glad he had found some work with her pa.

Why couldn't she be like Betty and toss it all aside? Her painful memories had returned, how abandoned she had felt. She knew she didn't want to get hurt again.

Sitting in the kitchen, chatting to Sophie as she got supper ready, Danny asked her again if she knew any more about Rosa coming.

"I really don't know," replied Sophie. "She doesn't get a lot of time off. Her life seems to be at the hospital now." She put the potatoes on to boil and sat down at the kitchen table. "Tell me more about your time in America," she said.

Danny began describing his trip. "I owe Tom for my passage back, but he's making good money over there. Everyone seems to have a motorbike or automobile, and they aways need repairing. Tom was livid when I couldn't get work, but I told him to hang on to his job. I told a bit of a white lie, Mrs. Browne. I told him I was homesick."

"That was considerate of you, Danny."

Florrie arrived home from school, looking very excited. "Mr. Faircross has investigated your case, Danny," she blurted out. "And he thinks you should be getting an army pension. He wants to come over to see you."

"Will he be giving me lines?" joked Danny, remembering his time at school, when he had to write out the same sentence repeatedly as punishment for some wrongdoing.

She smiled. "No, he just wants a few details."

Florrie offered to read to Danny that evening. He mentioned that Rosa had begun reading *Moby Dick* when he was at the hospital, but he had left before she finished it. Florrie found the copy on the bookshelf in the parlour, and after supper, Danny settled down happily to hear the end of the story.

The next day, Millie came for her usual weekly visit, and she had a letter from Tom. "He's desperate to know if Danny got home safely," she said. "I'll answer straight away, but goodness knows how long it will take to reach him. He says that next year he wants Harry and me to go over there to see him. Imagine that, Sophie!"

"Do you think you'll go all that way?"

"I don't know. We're going to think about it. He says he will pay for our passage."

"It will be such an experience if you do go."

"Who would look after the shop? I'm sure Agnes would want to come too. It would take such a lot of organising." She looked wistful. "I do miss him."

"He sounds happy over there, Millie," said Sophie gently. "You've always wanted that for him. I think you and Harry should go."

Ben collected Stephen from the schoolhouse the following day so Stephen could get some details from Danny before submitting a claim for his pension. He said he couldn't understand why no one had sorted out his pension before now.

Danny didn't have much paperwork, but he gave details of where he had been stationed and, most importantly, his army serial number. Stephen also asked him about his family, and Danny told him he had lost touch with them after the war.

Stephen spoke to Florrie afterwards about something else that was on his mind. "Did you say that your brother was a doctor?" he asked her.

"Yes, he's in general practice in Modbury."

"I think Danny should see an eye specialist, Florrie. They're breaking new ground in treatments all the time. Nothing will be lost in trying."

Impressed with Stephen's interest in Danny, Florrie remarked, "That would be wonderful for him. How kind of you, Stephen, to care so much about him."

"It's because I never got to serve in the war," he replied. "I wasn't conscripted, as I was teaching at the time. I feel for all those young men who went in my place. I just hope I can help to improve the quality of Danny's life, one way or another."

"I'll write to my brother," offered Florrie.

When Ben left to take Stephen home, Florrie sat with Sophie to pen the letter to Charles.

"I hope something can be done for him," said Florrie.

When Charles replied, suggesting an appointment at the eye hospital, Sophie asked Danny what he would like to do.

Danny thought for a few minutes. "Can't do any harm," he replied. "I know I shouldn't get my hopes up. I think I've come to accept it now."

She sent a letter right away, and Charles responded by telling her that Plymouth Hospital had a good ophthalmology clinic and he would arrange for a consultation straight away.

Stephen, meanwhile, had submitted his claim, on behalf of Danny, to the army's pensions department and was waiting for a reply.

Florrie was working in her classroom after school sometime later, when Stephen came in, looking pleased and waving a sheet of paper excitedly.

"They've accepted my—or, rather, Danny's—claim," he said.

"That's wonderful!" answered Florrie, looking up from her marking.

"What's more," he went on, "it will be dated from when he was discharged. It could be a substantial amount of money."

"Well done!" she said. "Danny will be so grateful. Thank you so much, Stephen." She stood up and gave him a hug.

He held her and suddenly said, "I do love you."

It was the first time he had told her he loved her, and she had to contain her excitement as he waited for her reaction.

"You've made me very happy," she said simply.

He smiled at her, then returned to the matter at hand. He said, "I need to see Danny again. Could your father bring him to the schoolhouse tomorrow, after school?"

After saying she'd arrange it, Florrie pedalled home as fast as she could to give Danny the good news.

Danny was, as usual, chatting to Sophie in the kitchen.

"That's great! I can pay all my debts now, and I'm going to buy you all presents!" he exclaimed when she told him.

Ben took Danny over to the schoolhouse the next day, and they sat round the table while Stephen spread out the paperwork.

"Your pension will be paid every month, and you can collect it at the post office or a bank." He showed Danny how much it was to be together with the back payments. "I'd advise you to open a bank account. Perhaps Mr. Browne would go with you." He looked at Ben.

"I can take him into Kingsbridge," he said.

"As soon as you know the number of the account, let me know, and I can let the army pension people know where to send your money."

Danny sat up, making himself taller. "Fancy me having a bank account!" he declared proudly.

"It's quite a lot of money, Danny." Stephen put the sheets of paper into a folder. "I'll let you have all this when we've set up the account," he said.

"Thank you, Mr. Faircross. I'm so grateful for all you've done."

"I'm glad I've been able to help."

Ben and Danny wasted no time, and they were in the bank, waiting to be seen, the following day.

Ben got up to enquire at the counter about his business account. Danny heard every word, and it was evident there was very little left in it. Ben came back, looking desolate.

They completed their business and walked back to the motor.

"Well, Danny," said Ben, putting a hand on his shoulder. "What are you going to do with all that money?"

"I've been thinking about that, Mr. Browne," replied Danny seriously. "What would you say if I asked you to make me a partner, and we'd look for somewhere nearer the main road for the business, like Mr. Faircross suggested. I have enough to pay for it, I think."

Ben stopped in his tracks. "Danny, that's a very generous offer! Of course I'll make you a partner! I was beginning to wonder if my business would survive. There's more competition now, new garages are opening all the time, and I certainly can't afford to pay for any new premises without your help."

Later that week, they drove through the lanes as Ben looked for a suitable building. He finally drew up at the side of the road and parked up.

"This one might do, Danny," he said, turning the engine off. "It looks like a large barn." They got out and went through a gate, and Ben surveyed the building. "Looks like it's had cattle in it," he said, looking round on the ground at the mess.

"I can smell hay," said Danny, sniffing the air. "Will it be big enough?"

"Oh yes, I think so. Needs a lot of work, though."

After a short ride, they found the farm, farther down the lane, and the farmer outside, working in the yard. Ben introduced himself and Danny.

"I want to enquire about the barn up the road," he began. "Is it for sale?" He explained what his purpose was in asking.

The farmer appeared interested and asked them to come back the next day.

"I couldn't have done this without your help, Danny," replied Ben as they drove home. "Do you know, I think we're going to make a success of this!"

The farmer eventually agreed to sell, and Ben and Danny began to get the new premises ready. Ben ordered a huge sign to be made. He had decided to leave the bicycle stock in the old workshop, as all the cyclists were used to going there and Sophie could always open it up if any showed up in the week.

They had leaflets printed, and they distributed them in Kingsbridge and the local villages. Within a few weeks, there were some enquiries, and their new venture had begun.

Danny was given an appointment at the eye hospital in Plymouth, and Sophie and Ben took him there by train.

Danny sat quietly for most of the journey. Sophie reached out and held his hand. He grasped it thankfully, and they sat in silence.

She looked out of the window at the trees and the hedgerows in their autumnal colours. *It would be so wonderful if Danny could see such beauty*, she thought as they passed by.

At the hospital, they sat and waited. Eventually, they were ushered into the consultant's room, and he asked Danny a few questions.

"You say your eyes were damaged in the war?"

"Yes."

"Do you know what caused it?"

"Mustard gas."

An expression of pain showed on the doctor's face, and he frowned and pursed his lips. "I see."

He scribbled some notes down. Looking up, he said, "I've dealt with quite a few of these cases now, and some have been successful. I may be able to help you, as you have some partial vision in one eye. We are only just beginning to understand cases like yours, caused by exposure to gas. You'll have to be a guinea pig if you go along with any treatment I might be able to offer, and I can make no promises at this stage, you understand. I'd now like to examine you."

After a lengthy process, the doctor put his torch down on his desk. He went on to explain that Danny had some scar tissue that he would attempt to remove in an operation, then said he would write and arrange an admission date.

A week later, the hospital wrote to say that Danny's operation was scheduled for early November. After reading it to him, Sophie asked what he thought about it.

"I don't feel nervous anymore, just excited," he replied.

Sophie looked at him with a gentle expression on her face.

Ben and Sophie set off with Danny to the hospital on the day of the appointment. Danny was given a room to himself, and Sophie fussed round, putting his few clothes in the bedside cupboard and making sure he had everything at hand.

"Do you think I've made the right decision?" Danny asked anxiously as he lay on the bed.

"Definitely. The doctor seemed very optimistic. You have nothing to lose by going through with it," said Sophie encouragingly.

Danny nodded, but Sophie could see he was putting on a brave face. She put her arm round him. "Goodbye, Danny. We shall be back after the operation. Good luck!"

As she and Ben left, Sophie glanced back at the young man in the bed, who looked rather bewildered. *How alone he must feel when we've gone*, she thought.

When she got home, she wrote to Rosa, telling her about the consultation.

Sophie worried about Danny for the next few days until she heard, and when the letter did arrive, she hurried to find Ben before she opened it.

"Ben! A letter from the hospital!" she called to him.

Ben came out of the workshop and stood impatiently while his wife opened the envelope as fast as she could.

She scanned the letter. "The operation went well, and Danny is recovering," she told Ben. "The bandages are due to be removed next week, and we are invited to be there." Sophie's eyes were full of tears. "Oh, Ben, I'm so relieved!"

Ben put his arm round her. "We must let Rosa know," he said softly.

"And Stephen," added Sophie. "If it wasn't for him, Danny would not have had this chance to see again."

Sophie wrote to her daughter about the news, but no reply came before they left to see Danny.

She and Ben set off the following week and were shown into Danny's room. Sitting on the bed beside him, holding his hand, was Rosa. Sophie was so relieved to see her there.

Danny smiled and greeted Ben and Sophie cheerfully.

"How are you, Danny?" asked Ben.

"Excited," he replied. "I know I may be disappointed, but I prefer to be hopeful."

Sophie could feel the anticipation in the room and prayed that all would be well.

The doctor arrived, and the nurse proceeded to take off the dressings. She unwound the bandages carefully and slowly, and it seemed to take an age. Finally, they were all removed, and she carefully eased the pads of lint from Danny's eyes, then swabbed his eyes gently with saline solution. Sophie winced at the sight of Danny's red and swollen-closed eyes.

Very gradually, Danny opened his eyes as everyone in the room held their breath.

"What are you seeing?" asked the doctor.

Danny blinked and peered round at them all, trying to focus. "I can see something. Yes, I can see people, I think!"

Everyone waited.

"I can just about see you all," he went on. "You're a bit blurry."

He turned towards Rosa. "Is it you, Rosa? Is that you?"

"Yes, Danny, it's me."

Danny squinted at everyone round him. "I can see you all. I really can!" he exclaimed.

"I would like to do a more thorough examination, if you could wait outside," requested the doctor, addressing them all.

Sophie and Ben went into the corridor, followed by Rosa, and when the door closed behind her, she hugged her father and began weeping with relief.

"I'm so glad you came, Rosa," said Ben. "Either way it went, Danny needed you to be here."

"I asked my tutor for special leave. Remembering what had happened to Danny before, she allowed me to come."

Eventually, the nurse invited them back into Danny's room.

"I've done a full examination," said the doctor. "Danny has practically no vision in his left eye, but he now has some reasonable sight in the right eye, and it will compensate. His vision should improve slightly during the next week or so, but there is also a chance it could deteriorate, though I doubt that very much. Danny must be aware of what might happen. We are not out of the woods yet, as they say." He turned his attention to Rosa. "I understand you are a nurse, Miss Browne?"

"Yes, sir. I'm in my final year of training."

The doctor gave her instructions for Danny's care. "He'll need very careful nursing," he emphasised. He turned to Danny. "You can go home today, but no sudden movements or jolting," he said. "Take it very slowly to begin with." He gave a satisfied smile and left.

The nurse spoke to Rosa, giving her dressings and lotions.

Ben helped Danny dress while Sophie packed his things, then Ben went out to see about payment for the operation. He hoped Danny had enough left in his bank account to pay. When he returned, they made their way out.

Rosa put her arm through Danny's as he walked unsteadily to the door.

"You're prettier than I imagined," he said, looking at her intently. As they journeyed home, Danny said, "I really didn't think this operation would work. I'm so grateful to you all for your care and support. I'm a lucky fellow!"

When they got back home, Sophie and Ben gave Rosa and Danny some time together.

Rosa hugged him. "I'm so happy for you," she said, her eyes welling up with tears.

"Rosa, I would like you to be my girl, now that I feel more of a man. Before this, I always felt…well, inadequate."

"You should never have felt like that, Danny," replied Rosa. "You sacrificed your sight, fighting for your country. You have every reason to hold your head up and be proud of what you have done, and yes, I will be your girl."

As Rosa nursed him for the next week, Sophie and Ben watched them growing closer, and they were relieved their daughter was happy again.

Then Rosa had to return to her course, which was hard for her.

"I'll be thinking of you," she reassured him before she left. "I know Ma and Pa will take good care of you."

He pulled her towards him and kissed her gently. "Write to me," he said.

Danny's eyes healed surprisingly quickly, and he was keen to get back to work, but Ben insisted he recuperate properly. While continuing his recovery inside the cottage, Danny began telling Sophie about his home life before the war.

"My father died when I was thirteen, and I had to leave school and find work by the time I was fourteen," he began. "I worked in the dockyard for a while, and when I was seventeen, I enlisted in the army to fight in the war. Mum had remarried just before I went away, and now she had two stepsons. When I would go home on leave, I had to sleep on the settee. I didn't like my stepfather. He was a rough man, and we fell out. After that, I didn't return home."

"Danny, you ought to write to your mother to tell her your good news," said Sophie.

"That's what Rosa told me to do," replied Danny. "My mother doesn't know I was blinded in the war. I never told her."

"She'll be very worried about you. Would you like me to help you write a short letter, just to let her know you're all right?" offered Sophie.

Danny agreed, and Sophie went to find her writing pad and pen. He dictated the letter, and Sophie read it out to him when she had finished writing. They walked to the village store together to post it. They saw Millie as they were leaving the post office.

"Danny," she began, "Harry and I wondered if you could do us a favour? It's about Digger."

Danny peered down and saw the dog at his feet, eagerly wagging his tail.

"Tom made us promise we would keep him before you both left. We love him, but none of us has time to walk him or even play with him. He tends to get in the way all the time when we're working, because he wants company. We wondered if you would take him on?"

Danny knelt and fondled him. "Millie, I'd love to have him. Can I take him home now?"

Millie went to get the lead and gave Danny two tins of meat for Digger's supper.

The following day, Ben took Danny and Digger to the barn with him. As they drew up, Danny could see a huge sign outside.

BROWNE AND COLLINS
AUTO AND MOTORCYCLE REPAIRS

"Mr. Browne, that's really good!" said Danny as he stared up at it. "You've put my name up there too. I feel like a real partner. Can I come back to work now?"

CHAPTER EIGHTEEN

FLORRIE'S ENGAGEMENT

Florrie was surprised when Stephen invited her to his home for Christmas.

"Wouldn't it be too much for your parents to have another guest, with your father having been ill?" she asked.

"I've already asked my mother," he replied. "They would very much like to meet you."

"I'll have to speak to my parents," said Florrie. "If Rosa doesn't come home for Christmas, it would mean they would be on their own with just Danny. I know Charles will be on call again this year."

That evening, Florrie spoke to her mother about it. "I'm unsure whether to go," she said. "I do enjoy Christmas festivities at home, and I don't really want to leave you and Pa."

"I don't mind you going at all, my love," replied Sophie. "Stephen obviously wants you to meet his parents. Have a think about it."

Florrie decided to accept. She wanted to spend more time with him, and she was curious to know about his family.

The next day at school, he asked her what she had decided to do.

"I'd love to come and spend Christmas with you," she told him. "I shall look forward to it."

Florrie began thinking about their relationship, as it was becoming quite serious. She wondered what she would say if he asked her to marry him. It would mean she would have to give up teaching, but the alternative was to stay single. Did she want that? She wondered if he would be a good husband and asked herself if she loved him. It hadn't been an intense love affair, like in one of the romantic films he had taken her to see. But more importantly, Stephen was steady and had proved to be a good man. *Yes*, she decided. *I think I will accept if he asks.*

Just before Christmas, Florrie packed a bag, and she and Stephen set off for Plymouth. On the train journey, Stephen held her hand, and she could see he looked very happy.

Stephen's home in Plymouth was a modest terraced house. His mother, a slim, cheerful woman, opened the door when they arrived. She gave Florrie a look of admiration as she welcomed her inside. Florrie wondered what Stephen had told his parents about her.

His father was resting in their small sitting room, and he rose slowly to meet her. Florrie could see he wasn't well, though he greeted her cheerfully. Mrs. Faircross bustled about, getting the tea, which she put on a small round table near her husband's chair.

Stephen's father asked Florrie about her family. Florrie told him about Forge Cottage and described her father's move from blacksmithing to bicycles and now to motorcycles and cars.

She commented that he must be proud of Stephen's becoming a headmaster. His father laughed and said Stephen would never become rich, but yes, he was proud.

Florrie looked round the room, noticing that Stephen's mother had put up a few Christmas decorations but no tree. On the sideboard was a photograph of Stephen and his first wife. *She looks very pretty*, thought Florrie, realising that she, too, must have sat in that room, drinking tea, years before. *I wonder how I'm measuring up.*

Stephen asked his father how he was, and Mr. Faircross said he was much better. But Florrie saw Stephen's worried look and knew he was unconvinced.

Later, alone in her small bedroom, Florrie contemplated her present and future. She was now twenty-seven years old. It had been a struggle to complete her teacher training because of the war, and now she would have to give it up if she married Stephen. All that work for just two, maybe three, years of teaching. If they married, she would be living in the schoolhouse, and their little ones could be running round the playground one day. She smiled at the thought of Stephen teaching their children.

She fell into a contented sleep, to be woken by Stephen's mother coming in with a cup of tea the next morning.

After breakfast, Stephen said he had to go out, so Florrie took the opportunity to help Mrs. Faircross prepare the vegetables for the Christmas dinner the next day. When Stephen returned, he invited Florrie out for a meal that evening and said she could get dressed up.

Intrigued, Florrie asked where they would be going.

"I'm not telling you," he replied, giving her a mischievous look. "It's a surprise."

Early that evening, she went to her room to get ready. She was intrigued at what Stephen was up to.

She unpacked her new dress and hung it up on the wardrobe, ready to put on. It had been quite expensive, and she'd had to use up some of her savings. She had chosen a dark green silk dress with a cream collar and tassels round the hem. It came to just below her knees, and she had bought some cream-coloured shoes with small heels and bar straps together with matching stockings. She got dressed and put her hair up, then went downstairs.

She felt a glow of pleasure when Stephen looked at her admiringly and told her she looked lovely.

At seven o'clock, a taxicab arrived and took them to a local hotel, where they were shown into an elegant restaurant with a string quartet playing on a small stage in the corner. Florrie had never been to such a smart place before and wondered how Stephen could afford it.

Feeling confident in her appearance, she held Stephen's arm proudly as they were led to their table. As the waiter held out her chair for her to sit down, she looked round at the well-dressed couples and groups sitting at other tables. Their waiter then lit a candle in a silver holder beside a small vase of roses on their table. Florrie thought it all very romantic.

When Stephen picked up the wine menu and ordered some champagne, Florrie guessed what was coming. She had an excited feeling inside, and her hands were trembling. She hoped she would not spill her drink.

She clutched her evening bag tightly. The lady in the dress shop had advised her she would need one to match her dress, and she was glad of it. Inside was her handkerchief and her powder compact, and she thought she might burst into tears and need to dash to the ladies room to repair any damage to her looks.

The waiter returned, opened the bottle, carefully poured out some champagne, and then placed the bottle in the silver ice bucket.

As Florrie picked up her glass, she saw Stephen reach into his pocket and produce a small ring box.

With a nervous smile, he opened the box and presented it to her. "Florrie, I would like to ask you to be my wife," he said simply.

Florrie stared at the ring. It was set with three small diamonds, and they sparkled as they caught the light of the candle. Although she had suspected this was coming, she still felt overwhelmed with emotion.

She put down her glass and looked into his eyes. "Oh, Stephen, I would love to be your wife!"

He looked relieved and leant over and kissed her. She felt her love for him welling up inside her as he took the ring out of the box and placed it on her finger.

Stephen suggested they tell his parents during Christmas dinner the following day, and Florrie excitedly agreed. "Though they might know about our engagement by the smiles on our faces when we get back," he added.

They made their announcement the next day, and Mr. and Mrs. Faircross were delighted and offered their sincere congratulations. Stephen's mother gave her a kindly smile and a kiss. Florrie knew then that she was welcomed into their family.

CHAPTER NINETEEN

LIONEL PROPOSES

LIONEL HAD FOUND HIMSELF COMFORTABLE lodgings in Egham, nearby to the solicitor's office where he was to begin his training after Christmas.

The work he was assigned was proving to be quite intensive, and his weekends were spent studying. He was glad that he was feeling clear headed, having realised that drinking too many whiskies wouldn't help him to study. Charles's medication had certainly been welcome.

He arranged to meet up with Charles, and they enjoyed exploring London together or going to see a show. They stayed at Lionel's rooms at his barracks, not wanting to risk using his mother's flat and bumping into his sister.

Lionel noticed that Charles did not seem to have any girlfriends and wondered what he could do about it. They met some young women in a cocktail bar, and Charles was very shy and quiet, causing Lionel to suspect he was still hankering after Sapphire.

They were out for a meal, and he was surprised when Charles asked him about his sister.

"I don't really know what she gets up to. I know she has a job at Liberty department store on Regent Street. I sometimes see her when I go home, but to be honest, we don't get along too well."

"I was sorry it all ended," Charles spoke quietly, almost to himself, head down. "Did you fall out over our affair?" he asked, looking up at Lionel.

"Partly, I suppose, but before then, she was very flighty and always liked her own way." Lionel realised he probably saw his sister in a different light than Charles did, so he said no more.

Charles continued his dinner with a faraway look in his eyes.

Lionel scored out the date with his pen on a calendar he had on his desk at the office. It was the end of January, which meant there were six months left before Amanda finished her year at art school. He would try seeing her again then, but he had no idea what her father had in mind for her future and if she would continue with her studies.

Her letters always gave him a lift, and he looked forward to receiving one every few weeks. He enjoyed hearing about her life at the art school, and he told her about his work at the solicitor's, hoping it would be of interest to her.

He thought about her constantly, longing to hold her in his arms.

Just after Easter, a letter arrived from Amanda, which surprised him.

Dearest Lionel,

Thank you for your letter. I always enjoy reading what you have been doing. You sound as if you are working very hard.

We were sent to the British Museum to sketch the Elgin Marbles. They are stunningly carved, such exquisite movement and detail in the draperies. I had a wonderful time there.

Having said that, I really don't want another three years of studying art. I know what I do want to do, and that is set up a studio so I can sculpt in clay. I think I could make a go of it. I've talked it over with Daddy, and he's not against the idea. What do you think, Lionel? I feel quite excited about it.

I shall be leaving the art school in three months' time. Are we going to meet up again? I do hope so.

Your loving friend,

Amanda

Lionel could see that Amanda was planning her future and wondered if she would include him. She did ask when she might be seeing him, and her letters had drawn them closer together. She often wrote that she missed him. What plans did her father have?

He sighed. Time seemed to be passing so slowly.

Lionel carefully folded the letter and placed it with all her other letters in the top drawer of his desk. As he did so, he took out a clean sheet of writing paper and began composing a reply.

Lionel arrived early and waited in the foyer of the National Gallery, realising he had never felt so nervous, not even during the war.

It was the end of June, and the time had come round, at last, when he could see her again. He had written to ask Amanda to meet him there one Saturday, and she had agreed.

He felt he could hardly breathe as he waited. His eyes avidly scanned every young woman who walked through the revolving door, his heart missing a beat when he thought one of them was her. Thoughts raced through his mind. *How will she be after a whole year of separation? Why did I allow myself to agree to it?*

He was just getting out his handkerchief to wipe his forehead when she appeared, so he put it away quickly and tried to compose himself.

The first thing he noticed was that Amanda had changed her hairstyle to a short bob. She was still just as attractive as he remembered, and he felt a huge surge of relief.

They regarded each other slightly awkwardly until Lionel embraced her gently, kissing her cheek, and told her she looked lovely. Amanda stepped back and looked him up and down. Lionel was no longer in uniform. She laughed and told him he looked very different in civvies.

"Let's go for a walk," suggested Lionel, and Amanda looked up into his face with shining eyes as he took her arm.

As they strolled down towards the River Thames, Lionel asked her about her plan to open a studio.

"I would like to be a sculptor, making portrait heads or small statuettes."

"Where would your studio be?" he asked.

"I'd have to rent one," she replied. "Daddy said he would help me out."

Lionel swallowed hard, wondering where *he* fitted in, if at all.

He was silent for a while as they walked along the path, stopping to admire the river. It was a fine summer day, and the water sparkled in the sun, the waves lapping the sides of the embankment wall.

"Amanda, do you still want us to continue seeing each other?" he asked, wistfully looking over to the other side of the river.

"Oh yes, Lionel. Of course I do!"

He pulled her gently towards him and kissed her, then said, "I hope your plans work out. I have another year to go before I become a qualified solicitor, and I would like us to go on seeing each other as much as possible. I don't know about your father, but I will not have any more constraints put on my time with you."

"He hasn't mentioned you at all," admitted Amanda. "I think he hopes our friendship has petered out."

"You haven't broached the subject, then?"

"No." As she said this, she turned her head away and stared at the river.

I think she must choose between her father and me, thought Lionel. He told her, "I think you ought to speak to him about us."

"All right. I promise I will."

"Tell him you want to continue seeing me."

She nodded but looked uneasy.

They turned to walk back up to Trafalgar Square to find somewhere to have tea and decide when they would next meet.

The following week, as he sat at his desk in the solicitor's office, Lionel's heart was still singing. To his great relief and happiness, his reunion with Amanda had gone well after such a difficult past year.

He arranged some time off so he could take Amanda down to Devon to meet his family, and two weeks later, they set off early on the Exeter train. He planned to borrow his father's motor and take Amanda to Forge Cottage the following day.

Lionel had booked first-class tickets so they could have a little privacy, and the carriage was not crowded. He asked Amanda about her father.

"He still thinks I'm too young to have a serious relationship," she told him. "He suggested I wait while I set up my studio."

Did he indeed? thought Lionel. Taking her hand in his, he asked, "What do you want to do?"

"I want to stay with you," she said, putting her head on his shoulder and closing her eyes.

He looked down at her. *How wonderful it would be to wake up with her by my side every morning,* he thought.

After a while, she stirred, opened her eyes, and gave him a radiant smile.

"Amanda, will you marry me?" The words tumbled from his lips with no regret attached to the spontaneity of it.

She continued to hold his gaze, replying softly, "Yes."

He drew her nearer to him, holding her tightly, his whole body filled with happiness. "I fell in love with you when I helped you up from the platform," he said quietly. "I couldn't believe I'd met such a beautiful girl."

"Oh, Lionel. I'm sorry Daddy made you wait so long. I didn't want it to be that way."

"What does he want you to do?"

"He said he would like me to go back to art school, that I'm too young to leave home."

Not too young to stay at home and cook his meals, thought Lionel. Drawing her closer, he said, "Nothing's going to keep us apart now. Let's keep this to ourselves for a while, though. I haven't even got you a ring yet."

"When are we going to speak to Daddy?"

"As soon as we get back," he promised.

A taxicab took them to his parents' house, and Amanda emerged and stood waiting for Lionel to pay the cabbie and get their weekend cases out of the boot.

"I didn't know your house was going to be as grand as this," said Amanda, looking up at the fine Georgian mansion. The house was set amongst some huge elm trees, and crows were noisily flying round, screeching and calling to each other as they circled their nests.

Lucinda met them as they entered. "How lovely to meet you, Amanda. I do hope you had a good journey."

As his mother led them both into the drawing room, Lionel was amused by Amanda's awe of their surroundings. She continued staring round the room. Above a white marble fireplace was a large gold-framed portrait of Lucinda in a blue silk dress.

"What a beautiful picture," said Amanda, admiring it.

"Amanda knows all about art, Mother," explained Lionel. "She once took me on a very elucidating tour of the National Gallery."

Amanda beamed a smile at his compliment.

Lucinda looked impressed as she picked up the silver teapot that had been placed on an elegant antique side table. "Come and have some tea," she said, inviting them to sit down. "You must tell me how you two met." She poured Amanda's tea.

"It was at a railway station, Mrs. Wells. I fell onto the platform as I was getting out of my train, and your son picked me up."

Lucinda beamed a smile at Lionel.

"You have a beautiful home," observed Amanda, looking round.

"Thank you, dear. I'm very fortunate."

"Amanda's father makes stained-glass windows. He has a studio in Richmond," explained Lionel.

"How interesting. You're quite an artistic family, then. What does your mother do?"

"My mother died when I was twelve," Amanda replied. "But she liked to paint watercolours. My father brought me up."

"He sounds a very special man."

"Yes, he's always taken good care of me."

During this exchange between Amanda and his mother, Lionel drummed his fingers impatiently on the arm of his chair. "We actually met a year ago," he said. "Her father wanted Amanda and I to separate for a year until she finished her art studies. It's been hard on both of us."

Amanda looked at him a little reproachfully. "Daddy was only doing what he thought best for me."

How she worships that father of hers, thought Lionel.

When they'd finished their tea, Lionel excused himself to go wash and change.

Lucinda turned to Amanda. "I expect you would like to change, Amanda. Trains are so dirty, aren't they?"

"Yes, they can be."

She showed Amanda to her room upstairs. It was beautifully furnished, and she had her own bathroom with fluffy white towels hanging on a brass rail.

She was busy looking round when she heard a tap on the door. She opened it, and Lionel was standing there.

"Is everything all right, Amanda?" he asked. "Have you got all you need?"

"It's a lovely room, thank you. I'm sure I'll be very comfortable. I hadn't realised dinner would be so formal. I've nothing suitable to wear."

Lionel could see by her face she was concerned. He looked her up and down her for a moment. "Don't worry, I'll borrow something from my sister's wardrobe. She's about your size, I should say."

"Won't she mind?"

"I shouldn't think so." He hurried down the hallway.

Lionel returned with two cocktail dresses and laid them out on the bed. Amanda selected the pale green one and thanked him, then gave him a quick peck on the cheek before shooing him out of the room.

After her bath, she put the dress on, checked herself in the mirror, and went downstairs.

When Lionel saw her, he raised his eyebrows. "Splendid!" he said.

Amanda laughed at his reaction, then became serious. "Lionel," she whispered, "this is all very grand. I'm afraid I'm not used to it."

He put his arm round her. "Well, my father *is* a top London lawyer," he said quietly. "Don't expect this when we're married, though. A solicitor earns nothing like a lawyer!"

He ushered her into the drawing room, where Lucinda was sitting, waiting. Lionel proceeded to pour them all drinks.

"Are we expecting Father?" he asked his mother, wondering if he'd be coming home for the weekend, since it was Friday.

"Yes, he'll be here at about ten, but we won't wait dinner for him." She turned and looked at Amanda. "You look lovely, my dear," she said, smiling sweetly.

"Thank you," said Amanda. "I'm afraid I didn't pack an evening dress, but Lionel was kind enough to find me one of Sapphire's. I hope that's all right?"

"Perfectly," replied Lucinda. "I'm glad it fitted you so well. Sapphire has so many dresses!"

Amanda began to sip her drink, and Lionel came and sat beside her.

The maid announced dinner was served, and Lionel escorted Amanda and his mother through to the dining room. They crossed the wide hallway, and as she entered, Amanda was amazed to see another beautifully furnished room. A large oval dining table had been lain with a decorated porcelain dinner service. The cutlery was silver, and beside each place were cut-glass wine glasses sparkling as they caught the light from the candelabra in the centre of the table.

"This looks wonderful!" exclaimed Amanda as Lionel showed her to her seat.

"You've done us proud, Mother," added Lionel.

"It's lovely for me to have family to entertain."

When they were all seated, the maid began serving the entrée, and Amanda looked lost as she wondered which cutlery to choose from the various pieces either side of her plate. She looked up to see what Lionel was doing. He winked at her as he picked up a small knife and fork.

Over dinner, Lucinda asked Amanda about her art studies.

"We've been doing a lot of sketching and detailed drawing. I've also completed some watercolours and oils. What I really love is sculpting in clay."

"Amanda wants to set up her own studio, Mother," explained Lionel.

"How interesting! And what sort of subjects will you choose?" asked Lucinda enthusiastically.

"Portrait heads and small figurines. I'll have to get them cast in bronze."

"I wonder if I could sit for you," she suggested. "It would make a wonderful present for Samuel."

"There! You have your first commission," exclaimed Lionel.

Amanda beamed, replying that she would be delighted to take it on.

After dinner, they retired to the drawing room, and Lucinda showed Amanda some of her tapestry work.

Sometime later, Samuel arrived home and joined them. He went over and kissed his wife, then shook Lionel's hand warmly. As he turned to Amanda, Lionel introduced her.

"This is a pleasant surprise! How long have you and Lionel known each other?" Samuel asked.

Amanda looked at Lionel, not sure how to answer.

"We met last year. Amanda had to complete her studies at art school, so we've only just got back together again."

Samuel turned to Amanda. "I'm so glad Lionel's brought you here to see us, my dear, and I hope you enjoy your visit."

With a smile, Amanda replied, "Thank you, Mr. Wells. You have a lovely home."

"Thank you, I certainly work nearly all the hours God sends to pay for it!" He poured himself a drink.

Lucinda excused herself and went to arrange for his supper to be sent up. Samuel began talking to Lionel about his solicitor's training.

Amanda asked if she could retire to bed, as it was getting late, saying she had found the day exciting but exhausting.

The next morning, after they had finished breakfast, Lionel asked his stepfather if he could borrow his motor to take Amanda to Clayden village. Samuel readily agreed and asked Lionel to give his regards to Sophie and Ben.

Lionel went outside to check the Vauxhall Tourer before their journey, and while he was looking under the bonnet, a taxicab drew up alongside.

Sapphire emerged carrying several shopping bags and a small weekend case. "Hello, Lionel, be a darling! Can you take care of this?" She waved towards the driver, then hurried inside.

Lionel was very surprised his sister had arrived but not that she'd left him to pay the taxi driver. He sighed and got his wallet out.

When he went back inside, he found everyone in the drawing room just as Sapphire threw all her bags down onto the sofa.

"How lovely to see you," greeted Lucinda when she saw her daughter. "I'm glad you could make it at such short notice." She had sent Sapphire a telegram when she knew Lionel was bringing his girlfriend home, asking her if she could come too.

Samuel put down his newspaper. "Hello, darling!" he said.

Amanda entered behind Lionel, stopping to stand beside him.

"Amanda, come and meet my daughter, Sapphire," invited Lucinda.

Sapphire turned to their guest and extended her hand with a coy smile.

Amanda shook Sapphire's hand lightly. "Hello, Sapphire," she said somewhat shyly.

"Hello, Amanda. This is quite an honour. Lionel has never brought any of his girlfriends home before."

"That's enough, thank you, Sapphire," said Lionel firmly.

Samuel grinned and quickly hid behind his newspaper again.

Sapphire began showing her mother her purchases, bubbling on and on about her favourite items and gossiping about the salesgirls.

Lionel told Amanda it was time to go to Forge Cottage, so they said their goodbyes and left.

As they drove away down the drive, he said, "That's my family, Amanda. I hope you're not too overwhelmed."

"Your sister seems a very modern girl," she remarked. "I think I shall have to rethink my wardrobe!"

"I don't want you turning into a flapper, although you looked good in her dress last night."

"I have some more family to meet today," she said with a smile.

"Yes, and they couldn't be more different," answered Lionel.

Lionel had put the top down, and the air blew against their faces as the motor sped along the lanes.

"The countryside round here is very beautiful," commented Amanda along the way. "Richmond is pleasant but is getting very built up."

When they arrived, Ben was coming up the lane and waved at them.

"Oh, Lionel, you are so like your father!" gasped Amanda as Ben came nearer.

"Hello, Pa!" he said, getting out. "This is Amanda." He drew her forward.

"Hello, I'm Ben. It's lovely to meet you!" he said. "Let's go inside. Sophie is excited to meet you too."

As they entered the kitchen, Amanda remarked, "What a charming cottage," and Lionel noticed her looking round eagerly.

Sophie greeted Amanda warmly. "It is so nice to meet you, Amanda. Hello, Lionel. Always good to see you, dear."

Lionel sniffed the air. "That smells so good, Sophie. Brings back memories."

Smiling, Sophie replied, "I've just made a new batch of bread. We'll have some later."

Florrie came downstairs to greet the visitors, and they went into the parlour. Sophie brought in coffee and some homemade biscuits.

Amanda seemed much more comfortable with Florrie than she had been round Sapphire. The two young women seemed to get on well together. Lionel congratulated Florrie on her engagement and asked about Stephen while Amanda admired her ring.

Danny joined them for tea, and afterwards, Ben and Sophie invited Lionel and Amanda for a walk and showed them round the property. They ended up in the orchard, under the apple trees. Ben said they were doing well this year and picked an apple for Amanda to try, but then said it was wormy and threw it down.

"These trees are getting old," he remarked, "like me."

Sophie put her arm in his and stood close to him. As the others wandered away, she whispered, "What a lovely girl he has chosen, Ben."

After lunch, Lionel said he wanted to go and see Charles, but he promised to come again soon. They drove on to Modbury, and Charles was thrilled to see them, even though it was a short visit.

When they were alone for a few moments while Amanda freshened up, Lionel told Charles about his engagement. "We haven't told anyone else, so keep it to yourself, old man. I have yet to speak to her father. I shall be asking you to be my best man."

"I would be delighted," replied Charles.

When they left to return to Lionel's home, Amanda said how much she had enjoyed her visits.

"You have yet to meet my other half sister, Rosa," explained Lionel. "She's training to be a nurse in Exeter."

That evening after dinner, Sapphire came and sat next to Amanda on the sofa. She asked how she and Lionel had met, and Amanda told her about her accident at the station.

"How romantic!" exclaimed Sapphire. "I wish that would happen to me. Why did you have to split up for so long?"

Amanda explained.

"Your father sounds awfully strict. I wouldn't let my pa do that to me." She lowered her voice. "He's tried a few times to bring me in line, but it hasn't worked. He gives me an allowance, but I'm trying to be independent. Lionel thinks I'm an absolute air brain, but I have a good job at Liberty department store, and I love it."

"I'm sure Lionel doesn't really think that, Sapphire."

Sapphire laughed and whispered, "I had an affair with Charles, and he's never forgiven me. We don't really see eye to eye about things. For some reason, he thinks he can tell me what to do."

"I think older brothers are like that," said Amanda. "Not that I'd know."

Sapphire suddenly looked at Amanda in a different way and said, "I hope we shall be pals, Amanda. I think you're a great gal, but you must always stand up for yourself in this life."

Lionel and Samuel came into the sitting room just then, and Lionel looked over at them. "What's that sister of mine telling you?" he asked.

"Girl talk. Nothing to do with you," retorted Sapphire, standing up to leave. "I have some packing to do."

When she'd gone, Lionel sat down next to Amanda. "Be careful what you tell Sapphire," he said quietly. "Before you know it, it will be all round London."

"I like your sister, Lionel. I think she's going to be a good friend to me."

Lionel raised his eyebrows. "I have warned you," he replied.

Next day, after a lazy Sunday morning breakfast, Lionel suggested he and Amanda go for a walk so they could discuss their wedding plans. He took her along a path through a small copse at the back of the house.

"Where would you like to live when we're married?" he asked. "I do need to be near Egham."

"That's rather a long way from my daddy," she replied. "I think I would rather live in Richmond for the time being."

"I can catch a train from there," said Lionel. "I'm sure we could find a small flat somewhere near your home." He took hold of her hand. "When we get back, we'll go to Bond Street to get you a ring."

"I don't want to go there, if you don't mind, Lionel," she replied. "I would rather have an antique ring. I know of a shop in Richmond."

Lionel looked surprised, but he agreed.

Lionel asked Amanda if he could come round the following weekend to see her father. They hadn't seen each other since the unveiling of the memorial window at the regimental chapel. She smiled and nodded.

They continued strolling through the trees, enjoying the spring sunshine.

On her return, Amanda's father asked about her visit.

"Lionel's parents live in a very grand house," she told him. "They were both very welcoming. His mother is very beautiful. Lionel doesn't get on too well with his sister, but I liked her."

"They're very well off, then."

"Yes, very."

Lionel made his way to Amanda's home the following Saturday and was shown in by Amanda. He had a feeling of trepidation as he entered. She went to tell her father that he had arrived and then, giving him a quick kiss, said she was going to do some shopping but wouldn't be too long. Lionel stood waiting for about ten minutes.

Eventually, Mr. Craig emerged, pushing the draped curtain aside as he did so. "Hello again, young man," he said, extending his hand.

Lionel shook hands. "Mr. Craig, I think you know why I'm here. I would like to ask your daughter to be my wife."

Mr. Craig took his time in answering. "And do you think she will accept?"

"Yes, I do."

Mr. Craig looked at him intently. "So you've already asked her?"

"Yes."

"I see." There was a moment of silence. "Then what is the point of asking me?"

"We would both like your blessing."

Mr. Craig took off his spectacles and put them on the table. "My daughter is too young to marry. She still needs time to decide what she wants to do in life. I would rather see her do that than get married."

"Amanda has said she wants to get married, sir."

Mr. Craig looked at him sharply. "And I say she should not. She's too young to leave home. I have her best interests at heart."

"I'm afraid we shall have to disagree, Mr. Craig. I'm sorry for it."

"As you know, she's not yet twenty-one, so she must do as I say."

"Very well, but we will marry as soon as we can. Make no mistake about that."

Mr. Craig looked annoyed. "I don't like your tone, young man. I think you'd better leave."

Now angry, Lionel bid Mr. Craig good day and left.

He stood outside and waited until he saw Amanda coming back. She was carrying two bags of shopping. *He treats her like his housekeeper*, he thought.

Amanda set her bags down on the pavement and waited to hear what Lionel had to say.

"He's refused us permission, but we *shall* get married, come what may."

She put her arms round Lionel and kissed him. "I love you," she said.

CHAPTER TWENTY

MARRIED LIFE

ESPITE HER FATHER'S REFUSAL, AMANDA and Lionel decided to get married as soon as possible, and they set a date.

They were sitting in Richmond Park, watching the deer grazing in the distance. Lionel took Amanda's hand in his.

"It's going to be difficult if we do marry," said Lionel seriously. He had explained his parentage to Amanda, but now he needed to tell her the problems. "As you know, I have two families because I am illegitimate, although my stepfather has adopted me. We would need to ask both my fathers and families to the wedding. This is going to cause consternation about me amongst my wider family and be embarrassing to my mother and Ben and Sophie." He paused to hear Amanda's reaction.

"What do you think we should do, then?" she asked. "You do still want to get married, don't you?" She looked worried.

"Of course I do, darling! What I was going to suggest is that we get married quietly in a registry office."

Amanda's face fell. "No white dress, then?"

Lionel put his arms round her. "Do you mind very much?"

"I suppose not, if you think that's the best thing to do. It sounds as if it probably is."

"It will be worth it to be together. I'll get the licence as soon as I can."

Lionel began looking for somewhere for them to live. The places he found were mostly unsuitable, as they were either in the wrong location or dirty and run-down. He eventually found a basement flat near the park and took Amanda to view it one Saturday afternoon.

The small sitting room, bedroom, and an even smaller basic kitchen at the back were all basically furnished. In the garden was a privy and an outhouse where, suggested Lionel, she could keep her clay and perhaps set up her studio.

"It's a bit dingy and dark," Amanda said after taking a good look round.

"I was hoping you could use your artistic abilities to make it comfortable," replied Lionel hopefully.

Amanda frowned. "And it's very dirty. I don't think I could live here, Lionel."

"I'll hire some cleaners to give it a going over," he said. "And we can get it decorated. It will look much better when we get some more furniture in. The thing is, you wanted to be near your father, and this is literally round the corner."

Amanda reluctantly agreed.

Lionel felt uncomfortable, knowing the flat was unsuitable, but it was all he could afford. His salary at the law firm wasn't very substantial while he was being trained. He really didn't want to go to his stepfather to ask for money.

He arranged for the flat to be cleaned and spent his spare time doing a few maintenance jobs there. After discussing the decor with Amanda, he engaged a decorator, who painted the walls. When it was finished, Lionel had to admit the rooms were still dark.

He and Amanda went shopping for kitchen equipment and bed linen, which they took to the flat. Amanda made the bed, covering up a rather grubby-looking mattress. When she'd finished, she went to find Lionel.

He'd just finished cleaning out the fireplace in the sitting room, and he stood up and brushed the ash off his hands as she entered. "I know this isn't what you expected, darling, but it will only be until I finish my training."

Amanda nodded. "I do understand," she replied, managing a small smile.

On the day of the wedding, Amanda made her way to the registry office and met Lionel and Charles. They were both dressed smartly in suits and had even put flowers in their buttonholes. She was wearing a dress and coat she had bought for her interview at the art school a year ago, being the only nice clothes she had. Early that morning, she had filled two suitcases with her clothes and a few belongings, and Lionel had collected them from outside the front door.

Lionel embraced her when she arrived, asking her if everything was all right.

"Yes, I left a note for Daddy," she told him, then suddenly looked upset. "I wish Daddy was here," she said, her eyes welling up.

Lionel held her closer, and she clung tightly to him. "I love you," he whispered in her ear.

Taking her by the hand, he led her into the registry office.

The ceremony was brief and businesslike. Charles signed as one witness, and they asked the taxicab driver to be the other then they emerged from the building, with Amanda holding their marriage certificate. They went to a local hotel, where the wedding breakfast was to be.

When they had settled into their seats in the restaurant, Amanda said, "I can't believe I'm now married."

Charles raised his glass to them. "To your very good health and happiness," he said warmly. "Many congratulations to you both."

"Thank you, Charles. We are very grateful for your support," Lionel said.

"I suppose now you will have to tell your families?" Charles enquired.

"We'll settle into the flat first, then I'll do the rounds," Lionel replied. "I must say, I'm not looking forward to it." He turned his attention to his wife. "I think we'll see your father first."

After the meal, Charles left, and Lionel ordered a taxicab to take Amanda and him to the flat. As they entered their new home, Lionel's heart sank. He felt ashamed bringing his wife back to such a place.

He lit the fire he'd laid in earlier that morning, while Amanda unpacked her cases and then made some tea.

When she joined him, he put his arm round her and said, "I promise we shall have a wonderful honeymoon somewhere when my studies have finished."

Amanda had not told her father where they were living, but she knew she must see him soon. She and Lionel had decided that she should make the initial visit, as Lionel's last encounter with him had been difficult.

One morning a few days later, Amanda told her husband that she was going to see her father.

"He has every right to feel aggrieved, but I did try to tell him we were set on getting married," said Lionel. "I hope you can talk him round."

Amanda set off, and entering her home, she nervously went through to the dining room, where she found her father having a late breakfast. The letter she'd left for him lay opened on the table.

He looked at her coldly. "So you're now married."

Amanda braced herself. "Yes, I'm now married to Lionel, and we're very happy. You will have to accept that, Daddy. If you don't, I won't want to come here to see you. If you do, I'm happy to come round and look after you as best I can. Our flat is nearby. Lionel insisted that we live near to you."

"Well, it's all done now, and there's nothing I can do. I must say, Amanda, I'm very disappointed and hurt at the way you have treated me after all these years when I have loved and cared for you. I hope we can repair the damage that has been done and perhaps begin again."

His words cut into her, and she began to sob.

Her father put his arm round her to comfort her. "There, there, my dear. This will all blow over, I'm sure, and we shall be as we always were."

Amanda set about clearing her father's breakfast things while he went to his studio. Later that afternoon, when she walked back to the flat, she was in a much better frame of mind.

Lionel returned just after seven o'clock and asked about her visit to her father. Amanda told him they were reconciled. She didn't tell him she had been there for most of the day, getting her father's meals and doing his housework.

The following week, Amanda could not settle and got out of the flat as much as she could. Lionel had bought her a batch of clay, and she tried to make a start on a few ideas. It was chilly in the outhouse, so she tried to make do on the kitchen table. Then she lost interest and became increasingly lonely.

The days were long, and she would walk round to her old home every day to see her father. There she would prepare his meals and do the household chores as she had always done. Her old home made her feel secure and happy, and she dreaded going back to the flat each day.

Lionel expected a meal when he came back from his day's work, and it was sometimes gotten together in a hurry, as Amanda had been late getting home. He said nothing to begin with, feeling that Amanda needed time to get used to married life, with all its practical demands. *Surely she learnt how to cook decent meals for her father?* he thought.

He noticed other things, like the bedding needing changed and the ironing left untouched. He hesitated to say anything, thinking perhaps she had been working on her sculptures.

One Saturday he went to the outhouse and saw that the rag covering her work was dry, as if she had not done anything for a time. He decided to say nothing for the present, but one evening, he arrived home and Amanda wasn't there. She came rushing in eventually, apologising profusely, and explained that she had been helping her father with a particularly demanding piece of work that had taken longer than expected.

Lionel let it go, but he was not at all pleased.

When it happened a second time, he took his new wife to task. "Amanda, I have to ask you why you need to spend so much of your time at your father's?"

Amanda stood at the door, her eyes wide open.

Lionel went on, "You're my wife, Amanda. Your place and home are here."

"But Daddy can't manage on his own."

"He'll have to get a housekeeper, then, or better still, a wife."

Amanda looked shocked. "He needs me!"

"So do I. As I said, you're my wife, and this is your home now."

"I can't abandon him, Lionel."

"Well, I'm asking you to!" answered Lionel, getting angry.

Amanda's eyes began to well up, and she flinched at her husband's raised voice.

"You'll have to make a choice. Either you go back to live with your father or you live here with me. You can't do both."

"Please don't ask me to do that." Her lips trembled as he stood before her, making demands.

He raised his voice. "I'm serious, Amanda. I'm asking you now to make that choice. I'm not prepared to go on like this anymore!"

Amanda gasped, put her hand to her mouth, and walked quickly past him, going into their bedroom. He heard the door close and the key turn in the lock, and then he heard sobbing. He didn't go and comfort her, thinking she had locked him out anyway.

He found some bread and cheese and settled down to study, but he couldn't concentrate. Tomorrow, things would be better. He had made himself clear, or at least, he hoped he had. He slept in the chair that night and set off early next morning to catch his train.

When he returned that evening, he was sure Amanda would be there to welcome him and they would make up.

He reached the flat, finding only darkness. As he unlocked the door, fear spread throughout his body. It didn't take him long to see that Amanda had taken her two suitcases and left.

He sank into the chair, his head in his hands. How had he let this happen? If only he had comforted her last night and told her he loved her. He realised he had spoken too severely to her. He had got too used to dressing down his men when the occasion arose.

He was in despair as he looked round. What had he been thinking, expecting her to live in this place? He realised his other mistake had been to let her live round the corner from her old home. If he changed these things, he might win her back and make a success of his marriage.

He also blamed her father, who he was sure had manipulated this. He was a selfish, controlling man who thought only of himself. If only Lionel could persuade Amanda to realise this.

He decided that he would give up the flat and find somewhere for them to live in Egham. He would get home earlier, and Amanda would be away from her father. He hoped that would persuade her to return to him.

For the next two weeks, he busied himself with finding a suitable place for them to live, and eventually, he found one near the river in Egham. It was a small house with two rooms downstairs, a kitchen and a scullery at the back, and an indoor privy and two bedrooms upstairs. It was well furnished and more expensive than the flat, and he had to make a substantial down payment.

Having come to the end of his savings, he knew he would have to ask his stepfather for a loan, which he hated doing. But he was prepared to do anything to save his marriage. *Was it a good idea to rush the wedding?* he wondered.

He hired a removal company to move all their furnishings and belongings from the old flat. He put Amanda's clay materials in the scullery and made sure there was a wet cloth over the clay in the bin. Then he filled the kitchen cupboard with provisions and put flowers in the sitting room.

When everything was ready the next weekend, he set off to Richmond to ask his wife to come back. It had been nearly three weeks since she'd left.

He rattled the knocker confidently, and it was Mr. Craig who answered.

"Oh, it's you," he said briefly. "She doesn't want to see you."

Lionel pushed past him. "Well, we'll ask *her*, shall we?"

Amanda came out of the kitchen with a teacloth in her hand. She looked pale and shocked at seeing him.

"Hello, Amanda," he began. "I've come to ask you to come home."

"*This* is her home," growled her father. "Her place is *here*."

"Amanda?" pleaded Lionel, maintaining eye contact with her.

She stood still, bewildered.

"Amanda, I love you. You know I always have. I'm asking you to come home with me to live with me and be my wife. I believe we are meant to be together. Please pack your case and come back with me."

He was almost ready to break down at the end of his short speech, but he waited.

Amanda put the teacloth down carefully and walked past both men.

"She doesn't want to go back to you after you threw her out," snarled her father.

Lionel ignored him and went out to wait in the hallway.

Amanda soon reappeared at the top of the stairs, and he went up to take both her cases from her.

He bent over and kissed her cheek. "Thank you," was all he said.

They got into the waiting taxicab. When they drove past the road where they had lived, Amanda asked Lionel where they were going.

"Somewhere better," he replied.

At Egham, they drew up at the small white house Lionel had found.

"This is where we live now," he said. He got out her two cases and paid the driver.

Amanda looked up at the house and said it was lovely. It had a gate and a small front garden with a tree and some shrubs.

They went inside, and she said she loved everything and assured him she would be much happier living there.

"My office is just down the road," Lionel told her. "I could even come home for lunch!"

She hugged him. "Oh, Lionel, I thought you would never come. I'm so sorry! I haven't been a proper wife, have I? I'm so sorry!"

Lionel put his hand gently to her lips. "No need for that," he said. "I, too, got it wrong. We must begin again, and we will succeed."

He took her through to the little studio he had created for her.

She looked in the bin. "You kept my clay wet!" she exclaimed.

"I knew you would come back," he replied.

CHAPTER TWENTY-ONE

LIONEL VISITS HIS FAMILY

WHEN LIONEL WOKE UP THE next morning, Amanda was already up. He lay in bed, listening to the joyful sound of the Sunday morning church bells, and closed his eyes, content that he and Amanda were reunited.

He then got up and went downstairs to their small kitchen, finding Amanda had lit the fire and was buttering some toast.

When she saw him, she laughed. "Go back to bed! This is a surprise. I was getting you breakfast in bed."

Lionel returned to his warm bed, and she brought up a tray of tea and toast. "Here you are, my lovely husband," she said.

"This is a treat. I'm not sure I deserve it."

She kissed his head. "Yes, you do," she replied.

He poured out his tea. "Amanda, I've been thinking. Can I ask you to promise me two things? The first is that you wait awhile before contacting your father, and the second is that you call this your home from now on."

She answered straight away, "Yes, of course, I promise."

"And I promise to take care of you better than I have done. I was wrong to expect you to live in that awful place. I hope here you can begin work on your sculptures. I very much want you to succeed in your work. I know you have talent."

"Thank you," she said as she got back into bed beside him.

As days and then weeks passed, Lionel knew he had to inform his family of his marriage. He had put it off long enough.

He told Amanda what he planned to do, and he suggested that Sapphire come to stay with her for the weekend. He was going to have lunch with his stepfather at his club in London first and then go home to tell his mother. After that, he would visit his father and Sophie.

Lionel said goodbye to his wife and sister and set off for London. He was escorted into the smoking lounge at Samuel's club, where he found his father reading a newspaper.

Samuel got up and stubbed out his cigar when he saw Lionel approaching. "Lionel! Good to see you, my boy!"

Lionel shook his hand warmly. "Hello, Father. I hope you don't mind this intrusion?"

"No, no, of course not. I'm always pleased to see you."

He took Lionel through to the dining room and his usual table, and the waiter came and presented the wine list. Samuel chose a vintage wine, and they chatted until the waiter returned and filled their glasses.

Samuel eyed Lionel, smiling, then said, "I have a feeling you are going to tell me something important or ask me for money."

It occurred to Lionel that his father had all the astuteness of a lawyer. "You're quite right. How clever of you to guess!"

"Is it something to do with that lovely girl you brought to see us?"

Here goes, thought Lionel. "Yes, it is. We're now married."

Samuel took a sip of his wine and put his glass down. "Then congratulations are in order. I wish I'd known. I would have ordered some champagne."

"You're not angry?"

"No, no, my boy. I think I know why you've done it. I'm not a great one for big family gatherings, and you have your other family to think of. Do they know?"

"Not yet. I was going down this afternoon to tell mother and then Ben and Sophie."

"I warn you, your mother will be very upset."

"Yes, I realise that."

"All I can say is good luck. I wish you and Amanda many congratulations." He raised his glass. "I expect you are wanting a wedding gift from me. I'll arrange to send some money through to your bank account."

"Thank you, sir. Thank you very much."

"And now I just need to marry off that wayward daughter of mine."

"She and Amanda have been getting along well," replied Lionel.

Samuel became serious. "We didn't have a very good start, you and I, if I remember," he began. "I want you to know how proud I am of you, and I hope I proved to be a decent stepfather."

"Yes, you have, sir, very much so."

Having exchanged these sentiments in their brief masculine way, they moved on to have an enjoyable lunch together. *One down, two to go*, Lionel thought when it was time to leave.

As his train rattled down to Exeter that afternoon, Lionel looked out of the window and let his thoughts wander. He knew he was going to upset his mother, but how could it be made less painful?

When at last he arrived, he found his mother was out, but the maid said she wouldn't be long. Lionel paced up and down their expensive carpet in the sitting room until she returned.

When he heard a cab pull up, he looked through the window and could see his mother getting out. She came into the hall, and he heard the maid informing her of his arrival as she took off her fur coat.

Lucinda came straight in and embraced him warmly. "Lionel, this is an unexpected pleasure!" She often had to spend her weekends alone, with Samuel away for work, so she was very pleased to see her son.

"Sit down, please, Mother," he said. "I want to tell you some news."

She looked slightly alarmed. "Good news, I hope," she said.

He took a deep breath. "Amanda and I are married."

Lucinda gasped and put her hand to her mouth. "Oh, Lionel! How could you do this without telling your stepfather and me?"

He put his arm round her to try and comfort her, but she shook him off. She had now begun to cry.

"You must know I have always wanted to see you married and ask all our family and friends. What am I to tell them now?" She looked at him reproachfully, dabbing her eyes with her handkerchief.

"Mother, please don't! I'm sorry I've upset you so much, I really am."

"Does your stepfather know?"

"Yes, I saw him earlier today."

"What did he say?"

"He said he understood my reasons."

"And what are they?"

"I have two families to think about, and I wanted to prevent any embarrassment."

"I wish you had discussed it with me first."

"I don't think that would have changed my decision."

Lucinda sniffed, her expression shifting to one of anger. "I'm very upset and displeased about this, Lionel." She glared at him.

Lionel knew he had to console her somehow. "How about a small family dinner, after Christmas, to celebrate our marriage?" he suggested.

Lucinda sniffed again, now seeming to appear a little reconciled. "That will be better than nothing, I suppose," she said, fiddling with her handkerchief. "When are you going to tell Ben and Sophie?"

"I'm going over there now, and then I'll be back."

She nodded and dabbed her nose again. "I'll tell cook there'll be an extra place for dinner tonight, then," she said.

Lionel set off, and as he approached Clayden village, he decided to call at Ben's workshop on the main road first, since Ben and Danny opened the garage on Saturdays, when the roads were busy. He found Ben working on a motor and Danny tinkering with a motorbike.

Ben looked surprised. "Hello, Lionel, is everything all right?" he asked.

"I've come to tell you something, Pa. I think I ought to tell you and Sophie together."

"Fancy knocking off early, Danny?" Ben asked.

Danny needed no persuading. They cleared up quickly, locked up, and then followed Lionel to Forge Cottage.

Surprised to see them all arrive, Sophie met them at the door. "What's all this about?" she asked.

"Lionel has something to tell us," said Ben, winking at his wife.

Danny excused himself, heading off to his room to give them some privacy.

Sophie embraced Lionel, then they went into the parlour and sat down. Sophie and Ben looked at him expectantly.

Lionel began, "As you know, I've met a lovely young lady, and we are very much in love. There have been a few problems with her father, and we decided it would be best if we married quietly."

Sophie nodded and gave Ben a smile.

"I've come here today to tell you we got married a few weeks ago."

Sophie gasped and looked at Ben, but his face showed no emotion. "Have you told your mother?" she asked.

"Yes, she was very upset."

Ben then spoke. "As far as I'm concerned, you've probably done the right thing."

"I'm so sorry. We did it for the best of reasons and out of no disrespect to you," said Lionel.

Sophie looked across at Ben. "I think we are both glad you and Amanda are happy, and we wish you well, don't we, Ben?"

Ben shook his son's hand. "Of course we do!" he said. "Congratulations, son!"

"How about your stepfather, Lionel, does he know?" asked Sophie.

"Yes, I saw him earlier today. He thinks it's for the best as well. My mother wants to have a family dinner after Christmas to celebrate," he added. "I don't know how you feel about that."

"I think we would like to go," said Sophie quietly, again looking at her husband.

"Splendid!" exclaimed Lionel. "I know she will like that." He told them he had to go, apologising for not staying longer. He had the drive back still ahead, then a train home to his new wife the following day, so he had too little time for visiting on this trip.

When he eventually arrived home, Sapphire had left and Amanda was preparing their evening meal.

"Have you told her?" he asked.

"Yes," replied Amanda. "Sapphire said she was very happy for us and had always wanted a sister. She told me people should always do what they think best."

"For once my sister has said something sensible," replied Lionel.

"How did you get on?"

"My stepfather took it in good part when I told him, and he's even going to give us a gift of some money."

"How generous of him!"

"My mother was very upset, and it pained me to hurt her. She said she always wanted us to have a big celebratory wedding, so I suggested we have a family wedding banquet after Christmas. Just close family."

"That sounds a perfect idea! What did she say?"

"She seemed very enthusiastic about it."

"I'm sorry she was so upset."

"I think she will forgive me. We parted on good terms. Ben and Sophie were fine and thought we had probably done the right thing. I'll write to my stepsisters. It will be good to have a family gathering."

"Yes, I'll look forward to meeting them all."

The weeks passed, and Lionel and Amanda's married life settled into a comfortable routine.

As they ate their dinner one night, Lionel noticed Amanda seemed distracted, so he put down his knife and fork. "Amanda, what is it?"

She looked at him sadly. "I'm concerned about Daddy. I wrote and told him our address, but I haven't heard anything back. I don't like the thought of him being all alone."

Lionel felt a little guilty. He had encouraged Amanda to pursue her desire to make clay sculptures, and she had been working hard at it. He really wanted her to gain some independence from her father, so he had discouraged her from getting in touch.

"Hasn't he got any family he could stay with?" asked Lionel.

"He has a brother, but they're not very close."

"Let's go and see him next weekend. You could then invite him over."

Amanda brightened up. "Oh, Lionel, thank you!"

As he lay in his bed that night, he thought about her father's continuing hold on her emotions. He reached out and drew Amanda closer to him. He had certainly slain enough dragons to win her, but would it make their union the stronger for it?

The next Saturday, after an early lunch, they caught the train to Richmond. It was only a few stops and a short walk to her old home. When they entered the house, all seemed very quiet. Amanda went through to the studio, but her father was not there, and she came back, looking worried. The fire hadn't been lit, there was no sign of a meal having been prepared, and the house was in some disarray.

"Oh, Lionel, where could he be?" she asked.

"He's probably gone out shopping or visiting a client or friend," he suggested. "Let's sit down in the living room and wait for him."

They waited for nearly an hour before hearing him come in.

When he entered and saw them waiting, he looked startled. "Hello, Amanda," he said, ignoring Lionel, who had stood up, ready to shake his hand.

"Oh, Daddy, there you are! We've been so worried about you!"

They followed as Mr. Craig went through to the dining room and sat down at the table.

"If you must know, I've been to the café for my lunch," he said. "It's about a two-mile walk." He looked tired and downhearted. He put his elbow on the table and rested his head on his hand. "I don't know what I am to do," he said. "I do so miss you, my love."

Amanda sat beside him, and he reached out and held her hand.

"Let's see what we can do to sort this out," Lionel said firmly. "Can I make some suggestions? How about if Amanda comes over three mornings a week to help you in the house and prepare a couple of meals, and then on Sundays, you could catch the train and come have lunch with us?"

Amanda smiled thankfully at him.

Mr. Craig nodded. "Thank you, I would like that. Thank you," he said quietly.

Amanda got up to make some tea and tidy up the kitchen.

"It will be nice to see where you're living," Mr. Craig said to Lionel.

Lionel described the house and its situation. "Like you, we're not far from the station," he added.

Amanda came in and began to lay the table for tea as Lionel told her father how much the memorial window had been admired since the dedication ceremony.

"Do you miss the army?" asked Mr. Craig.

"Sometimes," replied Lionel. "On the whole, I prefer my independence."

Lionel realised he should explain the circumstances of his family background, and Mr. Craig listened intently.

After hearing about Lionel's two families, Mr. Craig smiled. "Chalk and cheese," was his comment.

When Lionel had finished, Mr. Craig regarded him seriously. "I think I have misjudged you, young man. You have not had an easy time of it, and you have apparently served your country well. I'm sorry for my behaviour."

"Think no more of it," replied Lionel, and Amanda gave him a grateful smile.

The arrangements worked out well, and Amanda made sure she kept to the schedule.

One weekend at the beginning of December, Lionel and Amanda called on Mr. Craig.

"We came over to ask you to spend Christmas with us," Amanda said cheerfully.

"My mother has issued us an invitation to go there," added Lionel. "She would be delighted if you could come too."

Mr. Craig looked pleased at the invitation. "That would be lovely," he said.

It was decided they would all travel down on Christmas Eve together. Lionel booked the train reservations, then they collected Mr. Craig and travelled to Paddington Station. He had suggested to Mr. Craig that he take one or two of his sketchbooks to show his mother, as she was interested in the arts.

When they arrived, Lucinda was as charming as ever. She immediately took to Mr. Craig, who insisted she call him David, and she later told Lionel that he looked like "a true artist" in his green velvet jacket and round, flat, embroidered hat. They sat together on the sofa for some time, looking through his sketchbooks.

Samuel and Sapphire arrived later, and the family gathering was complete.

Lucinda had arranged an impressive dinner for Christmas Day and spoke about the banquet to celebrate Lionel and Amanda's marriage, which she was planning for the end of January.

Lionel was relieved that his marriage was to be celebrated privately, although he wasn't sure how the two families would get on together. Only time would tell.

CHAPTER TWENTY-TWO

THE WEDDING BANQUET

LUCINDA SENT OUT INVITATIONS TO the family after Christmas. Millie and Harry declined because of the shop, and Danny said that he preferred not to go and would stay behind to help Millie and Harry.

On the day of the banquet, Sophie spent more time than usual to get ready, fussing over her appearance nervously. Ben said she looked very elegant and "showed him up." He had put on a little weight over the years, and Sophie had to get him some new clothes.

Ben and Sophie set out early with Florrie and they collected Stephen from the schoolhouse on the way. Charles was to come later with Billy and Dorothy, after he had finished morning surgery.

When they arrived, Sophie was overwhelmed by the grandeur of Lucinda's home. In front of the house was a sweeping drive, curving round a patch of grass where a stone sundial stood.

Ben's motor drew up alongside the house, and Lucinda came down the steps to greet them. She embraced Sophie briefly and awkwardly, and then Sophie stood back as Lucinda enthused over Ben.

"Oh, Ben! I'm so glad you've come. It's so lovely to see you all!"

Sophie felt somewhat intimidated by how elegantly dressed Lucinda was and that she was still very attractive. Taking a deep breath, she put her arm through Ben's, ready for him to escort her inside.

They were shown into the spacious sitting room and introduced to Samuel and Sapphire. Samuel seemed genuinely pleased to see them again, having last visited Forge Cottage many years before. They shook hands enthusiastically as they were all introduced. Sophie studied him. His brown eyes and his hair, just greying round the temples, made him a distinguished-looking man, and she could see that he and Lucinda made a handsome couple.

Ben introduced Florrie and her fiancé Stephen. Samuel busied himself pouring drinks and passing round glasses of champagne. He gave one to Sophie, smiling kindly as he handed it to her.

Rosa was talking to Sapphire and Amanda, their bursts of girlish laughter adding to the excitement of the occasion.

Lucinda's brother, William, and his wife, Phoebe, were also there, together with their son and daughter, Francis and Madelaine.

William came over to greet Ben. "Hello, Ben! It's been a few years since we met."

"It must be at least twenty-five years, as I last came when Lionel was very young."

"Look at him now," said Lionel's uncle, nodding towards the tall, confident figure chatting to his guests.

As Ben and William continued talking together, Sophie looked round the room. It was so strange for her to be in a such a beautifully furnished room with a glass of champagne in her hand. How different all this was from life at Forge Cottage.

As she stared up at the portrait of Lucinda above the fireplace, someone speaking to her drew her attention to a short man in a brightly coloured waistcoat and an embroidered fez-type hat.

"It's a fine likeness, isn't it?" he said, then he gave a small bow.

"How do you do? I'm Ben's wife, Sophie," she said, introducing herself.

"Ah! The chalk," he responded.

"I'm sorry?" Sophie replied, giving him a puzzled look.

"How do you do? I'm David Craig, Amanda's father." He apologised about his remark and explained why he had said it. "I hope you don't think it rude," he said.

"Not at all. It's quite a perceptive remark to make," Sophie replied, thinking he looked a bit eccentric.

Luncheon was announced, and everyone began moving into the dining room.

As Sophie looked round for Charles, Lionel came over, kissed her on the cheek, and said he was delighted she had come. Ben stepped in to escort her into the dining room, where they found that Lucinda had placed everyone's names round the table, and only Lionel and Amanda were sitting together. Sophie found herself sitting next to William, and Ben was sitting opposite Lucinda.

William was relating a humorous incident about one of his parishioners to Sophie, when she happened to look over at Lucinda and saw her give Ben a charming smile, which he acknowledged. They looked at each other for a few moments before Ben resumed his meal. Suppressing her feelings, Sophie turned her attention back to what William was telling her.

After the luncheon, the guests retired to the sitting room, and Sophie sat down by herself on the window seat. She looked round the room at all the guests. *These well-off people are my family*, she thought.

Her mind went back to the time when Ben had confessed that another woman was expecting his child. The hurt she'd felt then had reverberated over the years. *When will I be able to fully forgive Ben and free myself of this feeling of betrayal?*

"May I?" Samuel gestured to the seat next to her.

She moved to one side so there was room for him. "Of course. Please, sit down."

"I hope you don't mind my saying, but you look a little dejected," he said.

Sophie tried to smile.

"You and I have something in common," he added, leaning forwards and lowering his voice. "We are both celebrating the marriage of a son who isn't ours."

Sophie looked at him with serious eyes, her lashes wet as she fought to contain herself. She took a deep breath. "It hasn't been easy for me, Samuel."

"We need to accept things sometimes," he responded. "I have had to accept my wife's past because I love her."

Sophie nodded at his wise words. *Haven't I always loved Ben?* she thought. *Why, then, did he betray me?* She had never been able to understand it. She glanced over at Lucinda enjoying the company round her.

"Lionel's a fine young man," Samuel went on. "In a way, he's your son too. Try and share him with Ben."

Sophie felt comforted by Samuel's kind words and decided that, in the future, she would try to be less resentful. "Thank you, Samuel," she said. "You've been very understanding."

"Come along, we'd better be sociable."

He took her arm to raise her up, then led her towards the other guests. He stayed with her for some time, engaging her in a conversation with William and his wife.

Billy and Dorothy soon arrived, bringing Charles with them, and Lucinda arranged for some food to be served to them.

Ben came over and asked his wife if she was enjoying the occasion. She gave a noncommittal reply and said she had liked meeting other members of the family.

After a while, the gathering began to form groups, as is always the case at parties. The young people went into the drawing room, where there was a piano, and Sapphire persuaded Dorothy to play. Soon jazz tunes were heard along with lots of laughter as they sang and danced.

Charles had stayed behind and was sitting in an armchair, his long legs crossed and his hands folded in his lap. Sophie noticed he looked pensive. *Why isn't he happy?* she wondered.

"Why don't you join the others?" Sophie asked him. "It sounds as if they're having a good time."

Before he could reply, Lionel came over and said, "Come on, Charles! The girls are wanting dance partners."

Charles reluctantly got up and followed Lionel into the drawing room, where Florrie was leaning on the piano, beating time to the music with her hand while the others danced.

Madelaine needed a partner, so he put out his hand to take hers.

"Hello," he said. "I'm not really used to this sort of dancing."

Madelaine threw back her head and laughed. "I'll show you how!" she said.

Charles shrugged but took hold of both her hands and let her twirl him round a few times. She was an attractive girl, and he found he was enjoying himself.

Soon the dancing came to an end, and they all gathered round the piano to sing some well-known songs. When tea was brought in, the excitement died down.

Charles handed Madelaine a cup of tea and engaged her in conversation.

"Let me work this out," she said. "You are Lionel's half-brother, and I am his and Sapphire's cousin, so what does that make us?"

"Some sort of half cousin, maybe?"

"It's all a bit complicated!" She laughed again. "What do you do, Charles?" She sipped her tea as she looked at him, her eyes alert and showing interest.

"I'm an assistant to a doctor. His wife is a friend of my mother's. I hope to have my own practice one day."

"That sounds very rewarding."

"I'm particularly interested in childhood illnesses."

"Daddy sometimes conducts funerals of children. It always upsets him."

"What about you?"

"I help Daddy with parish work. I'm engaged, but goodness knows when I shall get married. It's been over two years now."

Charles raised his eyebrows in surprise. "That's a long time!"

"My fiancé is a curate waiting to be appointed to a church," she explained. "My father won't hear of us getting married until we have somewhere to live."

Charles kept company with his new friend for the rest of the afternoon, which didn't escape the attention of her father, William. A tall man, William could see them over the heads of the other guests, and Charles noticed this several times.

While Lucinda swept round the room in her expensive silk dress, talking to her guests, Samuel was outside on the terrace, having a quiet smoke. After a while, Lionel joined him, and they stood side by side, surveying the garden.

"I think your mother has done you proud, Lionel," observed Samuel.

"Yes, it's been a wonderful day. Very successful, I would say. Amanda and I would like to thank you both very much."

"All your mother's work, Lionel."

"Yes, but you will have paid for it."

They continued talking together for a while longer until Lucinda came to find them.

"People are beginning to leave, Samuel," she said.

They both went to see their guests out and thank them for coming, standing opposite the pile of wrapped gifts that had been deposited on the hall table.

At the door, Ben said to Lionel, "I have new bicycles for you and Amanda. I shall bring them over here in parts, and hopefully you can put them together and get them to your home at some point."

Lionel thanked him and told him that there were lots of paths along the Thames where they could go and they would look forward to their rides.

The door closed, and the guests were gone, leaving the house suddenly silent. The maids began clearing up the teacups and plates littering the elegant rooms.

Lucinda went over to the window to watch Ben help Sophie into their motor. He glanced over to the window, then got in the motor and drove away.

Charles went over the events of the afternoon as he sat in the back of Billy's motor on their return journey.

Considering Madelaine's long engagement, he thought, *I would never keep a girl waiting that long*. He had found her attractive and liked the confident way she'd held his hands and danced with him.

A few days later, he wrote to Lionel and asked for Madelaine's address. When he received it, he put it aside for a few days to think about it a bit longer. Finally, deciding he wanted to tell her he had enjoyed her company, he found a sheet of writing paper and took out his fountain pen. After several attempts, he wrote what he hoped was an acceptable letter and posted it the next day.

An answer came quickly. Madelaine thanked him for writing and said she was pleased to have met him and other members of her cousin's family.

Charles replied, expressing a wish to see her again.

Two weeks passed before he received her answer, a polite refusal because she was already engaged and felt it would not be appropriate.

Instead of feeling rejected, Charles rallied to his cause, determined to win her over. *After all*, he thought, *that other fellow has been keeping her waiting far too long, and all is fair in love and war.*

He wrote again, saying he regarded her as a good friend and would like to continue corresponding with her. This time, he was more successful, as she wrote back, agreeing and asking to see him in Exeter one Saturday. They arranged to meet outside the cathedral.

It was a chilly morning in March when Charles took the early train and arrived before Madelaine. It was a chilly morning, and he walked briskly down to the Cathedral Close and sat on one of the seats on the green, hoping she would not be too long.

Soon he saw her coming along the diagonal path towards the cathedral, wearing a fitted coat and a cloche hat, looking very smart. He stood up, uncertain how to greet her.

She smiled kindly and said, "Hello, Charles."

She allowed him to kiss her lightly on the cheek, and he asked her how she was. She assured him she was well, and they walked together to a nearby café. Charles got them two hot cups of coffee and sat down.

"I expect you're wondering why I asked to meet up like this," she said, taking off her gloves and smoothing them out on her lap.

"Yes, I am," he answered.

She sighed and stared into the distance. "I've been thinking of your comment about my engagement being rather a long time. In fact, it's getting on for nearly three years now. You were right, and it made me see it in a new light. Edward is a curate, and plenty of curates get married. He's ambitious and wants to live in a grand rectory, whereas I would be content with a smaller house. My father wants me to marry well, and Edward is the son of his best friend, another clergyman, which is how we met."

"Are you trying to tell me it was almost arranged?" asked Charles.

"Yes, I suppose it was taken for granted, and I complied."

"Do you love him?"

"I thought I did, but looking back, I think I was trying to please my parents."

They sat in silence for a while.

At last, Charles felt compelled to speak. "You have every right, Madelaine, to spend the rest of your life with whoever you want, whether it is with him or me, or anyone else."

She looked at him and said, "You are that serious, then?"

"Yes, I am serious."

She sighed again. "I think, Charles, you may have saved me from making the biggest mistake of my life. I know it will hurt and offend him, but I have decided to break off my engagement with Edward." She looked upset as she continued, "You need to be a woman, Charles, to realise how hard it is to be able to make your own decisions. My parents will be very upset and angry with me. They are supporting me, so they think they have the right to tell me how I should live my life."

"I'm sure they love you, Madelaine. I hope they'll understand your decision."

"Please write to me." She looked at him earnestly. "If I don't reply, it will be because my father has forbidden it, but I will try to get letters to you somehow."

They drank their coffee and got up to go.

"I would like to take you out to lunch," said Charles.

"That's kind, but I would like to go home now," she replied. "Just see me back to the station, please."

He took her arm, and they walked back to St. Davids station in silence. They sat in the gloomy waiting room until it was time for her to leave.

"Goodbye, Charles. Thank you for being such a splendid friend."

"Am I no more than that?"

"I need some time. I must deal with this situation first. I do value your friendship very much." She kissed him gently on the cheek and turned to board her train.

All Charles could do was hope for a letter.

CHAPTER TWENTY-THREE

A SAD DEATH

Sophie was preparing breakfast, humming softly to herself as she laid the table, when a frantic knocking at the door startled her. Ben opened it, finding Agnes standing there, holding a telegram. Sophie ripped the small yellow envelope open and read it out.

STEPFATHER DIED UNEXPECTEDLY STOP
LETTER TO FOLLOW STOP
LIONEL

They looked at each other, horrified.

Sophie spoke first. "Oh, the poor man, the poor man!" She sank into a chair and shook her head in disbelief.

Also in a state of shock, Ben sat down beside Sophie and put his arm round her. "Poor Lionel," he whispered. *And poor Lucinda,* he thought.

Agnes said she was sorry it was such bad news and left to open the post office, leaving them wondering what could have caused his sudden death.

Ben told Danny he wouldn't be going to work in the garage, but he would take him in. It was a strange day spent remembering Samuel and reminiscing on past events. Ben wanted to go and see Lionel straight away, but Sophie suggested he wait for his letter to arrive.

Agnes appeared with the letter first thing the next morning, before she began her rounds. Lionel wrote that his stepfather had died of a heart attack at his club. Lionel had immediately gone there, and the manager had assured him all was being taken care of; they had experience dealing with this sort of thing, as many of their members were elderly. Lionel said his stepfather was only fifty-seven. He was now back home, comforting his mother, and Sapphire was there too. He said he would inform them about the funeral arrangements.

Sophie put the letter down and looked at Ben. Taking in his earnest expression as he looked back at her, she knew he was desperate to go.

"You had better wait a day or two, Ben, then go to see her. I'll write a letter."

Ben put his arms round her and kissed her gently. "Thank you," was all he said.

Lionel replied that he thought his mother would welcome a visit from Ben. He was arranging for his stepfather to be brought home by train and buried at their local church, and he would let them know the date.

Ben left later that morning and drove to Exeter. When he arrived at Lucinda's house, he was met by the maid, who took his coat just as Lucinda came into the hallway.

She waited until the maid left and then came running towards him. "Oh, Ben, I'm so glad you've come!" She flung her arms round his neck and embraced him.

With some awkwardness, Ben untwined himself and then guided her into the sitting room, where they sat together on one of the sofas.

"Oh, Ben! What am I to do? I don't know what I'm going to do!" She sobbed, covering her face with her hands.

Ben tried to calm her, putting his arm round her.

"I would spend all week here on my own," she continued. "I would wait until he came home late on Fridays. I would hear his key in the lock—the maid had gone to bed by then—and he would come in and I would be so happy to see him. I would get him a drink, and we would talk, and I lived for him to come back to me every weekend, and…"

He let her ramble on until she dissolved into uncontrollable sobbing, then he comforted her like he would a child. "It's all right, Lucinda. I understand. I'm here now." He looked round towards the door. "Are Lionel and Sapphire out?" he asked.

"They're…with…the rector," she managed to say between sobs. She dabbed her eyes with her handkerchief. "Ben, you will…stay here with me…won't you? Don't go."

"Lucinda, you know I can't do that."

"I'm sorry, Ben. I don't know what I'm saying. Please forgive me."

He hugged her to show that he did. "Lucinda, we are all so very sorry for your loss. It was such a shock. Samuel was a kind and honourable man, and I'm glad it was he and no one else who brought up my—*our*—son."

Lucinda looked at him admiringly and drew closer to him.

Ben heard the maid open the front door, so he sat up and moved a little away from Lucinda.

Lionel and Sapphire entered the room and greeted him, both looking tired and drawn. Sapphire went to comfort her mother, and Lionel poured some drinks.

"Brandies all round, I think," said Lionel, handing them to everyone.

He had brought with him a copy of *The Times* newspaper, which he showed to Ben. It contained an obituary of his stepfather, and when Ben read the article, he realised what a prominent lawyer Samuel had been.

Ben expressed his condolences again.

Lionel thanked him for coming and told him the funeral was to be the following Friday. "My uncle will take the service," he said. "The rector was fine about it."

The maid came and announced lunch. After the meal, Ben stayed for a short while and then said he should go.

Lucinda looked at him anxiously. "You will come to the funeral, Ben?" she asked.

"Yes, I'll be there. I believe Sophie will want to come too." He bid them all goodbye and left.

He got back late, but Sophie had sat up waiting for him.

He put his arms round her. "I'm glad to be back home," he said.

"How was Lucinda?" she asked.

"Very emotional. She seems incapable of anything now."

On that Friday, they set off very early, collecting Charles on the way. They eventually found the little country church and made their way to a pew.

The organ began playing, and the coffin was brought in, followed by Lucinda leaning on Lionel's arm. She was wearing a black hat with a veil and a long black coat, and she appeared a sad figure as she walked slowly past Ben and Sophie.

Sapphire and Amanda came next, together with William's wife, Phoebe, and their children, Madelaine and Francis. Other members of Samuel's family followed behind. Several of his colleagues had also attended, looking smart in their expensive suits.

The service commenced, and Lionel delivered the eulogy. He described his stepfather as a fine man who had been successful in his profession and helped many receive justice. He said Samuel would be very much missed, as he was well respected and well loved. With tears in his eyes, he said Samuel was a kind and generous man who had been the best of stepfathers.

Sophie glanced at Ben, who was leaning over, clasping his hands together, and staring at the floor.

Sapphire then stood up to do the reading.

Ben looked up and over at Lucinda. She was sitting upright in her pew, and lifting her veil, she dabbed her eyes with her handkerchief.

When the service finished, they proceeded slowly to the graveside, where the ceremony concluded. It was early April, and a recent shower had wetted the grass. It glistened as they all filed along the narrow path that led to the graveside. The family stood watching the coffin being lowered carefully into the grave, and Lucinda and Sapphire each placed a flower into the grave after William had read a few more words committing Samuel to rest.

The mourners began slowly moving away, but Lucinda lingered. Suddenly, she turned, knelt by the grave, and began to sob.

Sophie stepped forwards and bent down to put her arm round her.

Lucinda stopped her sobbing and looked at Sophie in a strange way. Then she grasped her arm and whispered, "Have you forgiven me?"

Sophie smiled gently. "I forgave you many years ago," she said as she helped Lucinda up.

By then, Lionel had seen his mother in distress and came hurrying over. "We need to go now, Mother," he said, leading her away.

They made their way back to the house, where refreshments were being served.

Ben and Sophie had begun talking to William, but Charles hung back, staying by himself.

The room was crowded, and Ben and Sophie got separated as everyone circulated, sharing condolences. Ben looked round for his wife and saw that she was talking to Lucinda.

Charles didn't join his parents in conversing with William because he'd noticed the rector giving him a look when he first arrived for the service.

He was taking a glass of wine from a maid when Madelaine came up behind him.

"Hello, Charles," she said.

He bowed slightly and offered to get her a drink, but she declined. "Your father took a wonderful service, Madelaine," he said.

She said, "Thank you. I'm thinking of leaving home and living with Aunt Lucinda for a while. I hope it will help her and be company for her. I think she gets rather lonely."

"That sounds a wonderful idea."

"Would you be able to visit us?" she asked, looking at him hopefully.

"I would be delighted to visit you," he said with a smile. "As long as your aunt doesn't mind."

Madelaine glanced at her father, putting a finger to her lips.

Charles's gaze followed her as she walked away to talk to the other guests. She was a tall young woman with an air of confidence that he admired. He was pleased she had spoken to him.

He wanted to visit Madelaine very soon, but he only had one weekend off a month, so it would be a while before he could manage a visit.

Surprised to find Sapphire there, he asked her how she was.

She looked straight back at him and gave a slight smile. "Thank you for asking," she replied. "I'm not too bad. I'm glad you've come. We're here to cheer Mummy up."

After dinner, Madelaine played the piano, and they gathered round to sing songs.

When Charles heard Sapphire's voice, he told her she should have gone on the stage. She laughed at him, and he found he couldn't take his eyes off her. He was excited that he would be spending the whole weekend with her.

William had been named as one of the executors of Samuel's will, and a colleague of Samuel's was the other. Lucinda, Sapphire, and Lionel attended the reading, which had been arranged to be held at a solicitor's office in Exeter.

They entered the dark, formal room and sat on the brown leather chairs. The solicitor sat behind his large desk piled high with files and papers. He coughed, cleared his throat, and began reading the document he was holding.

When he finally came to an end, he took off his spectacles and said, "Basically, this means that you are all well provided for in your lifetimes."

He went on to explain that Lionel was to be Samuel's heir, but Lucinda was to live in their house in Exeter for her lifetime, and she had also received a very generous bequest, as had Sapphire. There were other smaller bequests to members of his family, together with several charities. Everyone seemed content, Sapphire especially so.

"That should see me married off," she said as they left. "Men want well-off wives these days!"

Lionel would be able to buy a reasonably smart house in Richmond for Amanda and him when he finished his training. Lucinda told her children that she had decided to stay in her home, for the time being, but she expressed her intention of travelling abroad and taking Madelaine with her.

When Lionel returned to his home in Egham, he told Amanda how much he was now worth.

Wide-eyed, she replied, "Lionel, I am so pleased for you, but I'm happy living here, and I don't want to move anywhere grand yet."

Lionel reassured her that he needed to obtain his qualifications first and they would stay where they were in the meantime.

Lucinda wanted to go to Paris for the first part of her planned tour. She and Madelaine set sail from Portsmouth in May and were seen off by Lionel, Amanda, and Sapphire. Charles had come too, wanting to wish Madelaine bon voyage.

Lionel expressed his approval of his mother's decision to take this trip. "I think it's the best thing she could do," he said.

"And Madelaine will make an ideal companion," added Sapphire.

Lionel and Amanda returned home to Egham, and Charles drove Sapphire back to Exeter in her father's motor. When they arrived, the house was empty and quiet.

Sapphire led Charles to the kitchen. "Have something to eat before you drive home," she suggested. "I can cook, you know," she added when he hesitated. She opened a few cupboards and found some eggs. "Scrambled eggs?"

"Sounds good."

After their meal, they sat in the sitting room and had coffee.

"I wonder when you'll see your Madelaine again?" said Sapphire.

"She's not *my* Madelaine," he replied shortly.

"Don't be grumpy, Charles. You've always got me."

Charles looked at her, then laughed. "Yes, I've always got you, missy!"

She came and sat beside him and attempted to tickle him, but he took hold of her arms, saying, "Stop it, Sapphire! I must go. I have a long drive." He thanked her for his meal and got up. At the door. he gave her a quick kiss. "Goodbye, old girl!"

"Goodbye, Charles. See you again soon."

CHAPTER TWENTY-FOUR

WEDDING PLANS

IT WAS A QUIET AFTERNOON as Sophie took the iron off the range and wetted a finger to see if it was hot enough. She looked over at Ben sitting at the table, refilling the oil lamps and trimming the wicks.

"I'm glad Lucinda has decided on her trip to Paris. Samuel's death was such a shock to us all," she remarked.

"Do you want me to take you to Paris as well?" he asked mischievously. "We could go and see the cancan dancers."

Sophie gave him a look, but before she could reply, a tap at the door interrupted them.

Millie's head appeared and then she popped into the kitchen, waving about an envelope. "I've had a letter from Tom!" she said. She took the letter out and read it out to them.

Dear Ma and Pa,

I hope you are both well. Life over here is going fine. In fact, I have got engaged to Louise, my boss's daughter, so I've done okay there. We are going to wed in September, when it gets a bit cooler over here.

We very much want you both to be here, and Agnes too. I will wire you the money for the tickets. Please, please come.

Has Agnes got engaged yet? Tell her that her little brother has beaten her to it!

All my love, Tom

PS I'm enclosing a photograph of me and Louise and an invitation to our wedding.

Millie showed Sophie the photograph.

She put on her reading glasses and peered at it. "What a lovely couple they make! Look, Ben."

"Getting married, well, well! I'm pleased he's doing well," he said.

"All thanks to you!" said his sister.

"I'm glad I was able to help him on his way," answered Ben modestly.

Sophie looked at her sister-in-law. "Well, are you going?" she asked.

"It would mean leaving the shop for rather a long time, and I don't know who would run it for us. I will have to talk it over with Agnes," said Millie wistfully.

"You must go, Millie! It would be the trip of a lifetime!" urged Sophie. "And you want to see Tom again."

"I feel nervous at going such a long way. I've never been farther than Plymouth!"

"Harry will take care of you. He likes travelling," added Ben.

Millie replied, "Yes, I know, and he very much wants to go. Who would have thought it, Sophie, the likes of us going to America!"

"We must find a way to enable you to leave the shop. You really must go."

"If Agnes comes, she'll have to train someone to take her place."

"I'm sure that can all be taken care of," said Ben reassuringly. "You deserve a break."

Millie said she would talk it over with Harry. "You're right, we must go somehow."

She rushed off back to the shop, and Sophie picked up her iron again, but it needed reheating.

While she was waiting, she said to Ben, "I wonder who they can find to run the shop?"

Ben put down the lamp oilcan. "They should go," he said.

Ben and Sophie welcomed Rosa home on her final leave. Danny followed her like a shadow, and they could often be seen, their heads together, talking. Sophie wondered if they were making plans.

While Danny and Rosa were walking down the lane together towards the village, she told him, "My course is ending in July. I want to apply to the hospital in Plymouth where you had your operation. At least that will be a bit nearer than Exeter. I have missed not seeing you."

He put his arm round her waist and drew her close. "Rosa, I know you're keen to continue nursing, but I want to ask you to marry me."

Rosa stopped walking and looked at Danny, hardly believing what he had just said. What could she say? Her nursing meant everything to her. *I don't want to lose Danny. We've been through so much together. What am I to do? Perhaps there's a way I can marry and carry on nursing. I've known colleagues who've done that.* Her thoughts were in turmoil.

"I want us to get married," she replied. "I really do, but I've just worked really hard for two years to get qualified."

"Is there no way you could marry me and continue working?" he asked.

"I could continue and not inform the hospital I'm married. I know of some nurses who have done that. If I'm found out, though, I shall be dismissed."

"Would you be prepared to do that, at least for the time being?"

"Yes, I think so. The ruling is so unfair. I don't see why married women can't continue working, at least until they start a family. Let me apply for this new job first and then we can decide what to do," she replied.

Danny kissed her. "Thank you. I'll try and get a job in Plymouth and then we can start looking for somewhere to live."

"You'll have to tell Pa. I wonder how he'll take it if you leave?"

"I hope he can find someone to replace me. We have a lot of work coming in."

"Danny, we ought to contact your mother."

"Yes, I know," he replied. "We'll visit her as soon as possible."

They wrapped their arms round each other and continued strolling down the lane.

In July, Rosa completed her final exams and packed her bags, ready to leave the nurses' home. She said a fond farewell to her roommate, Betty. She had proved to be a good friend, and they each promised to keep in touch.

Ben collected his daughter from the station, and Sophie hugged her as she came through the door.

"Home at last, Rosa! I can't believe that two years have gone by!" her mother exclaimed. "Will you be going back to the hospital in Kingsbridge?"

"No, I have other plans," replied Rosa. "Danny and I want to tell you them later."

Sophie gave her an intrigued expression. "All right, then. Why don't you go up and get settled into your room. Supper will be ready soon."

After their meal, Ben and Sophie were excited for Rosa and Danny to tell them their news.

"Well," said Ben, folding his arms and leaning back in his chair, "what have you got to tell us?"

Danny took a deep breath and reached out to hold Rosa's hand. "I've asked Rosa to marry me, and she has accepted."

Sophie clapped her hands together. "Another wedding!" she exclaimed.

"But surely that will mean you won't be able to continue nursing, Rosa, after all that work," said Ben, looking bewildered.

"I've applied for a job at Plymouth Hospital, and I've just been given an interview. If I'm successful, Danny and I will get married quietly and I won't tell the hospital."

"Are you sure that's the right thing to do?" asked her father.

"I know a few girls who have done that and seem to get away with it. It's not fair making us leave if we marry. I think the hospital authorities know what's going on but turn a blind eye."

"I'm good at doing that," remarked Danny with a twinkle in his eye.

"Oh, Danny!" exclaimed Rosa, laughing at him.

"When do you plan to get married?" asked Sophie.

"As soon as I get a job in Plymouth, probably in September." Danny then turned to Ben. "I'm afraid I'll be leaving you, Ben. I'm sorry if you feel I've let you down."

"I don't feel let down at all. It's your life, Danny, and you must decide what's best for you. I'm sure Sophie joins me in offering our congratulations and wishing you well on the future."

Rosa was successful in her application and was to begin work at the beginning of September.

Danny began looking for work in Plymouth and was eventually offered a job at a family-run garage. He was to lodge with the owner, Stan, until he found other accommodation. He wanted to begin as soon as possible, but Ben said he should give his customers a month's notice.

Florrie was very excited when Rosa told her she was engaged to Danny. "I always knew you two should be together," she said. "You have always been fond of him, haven't you? Ever since you nursed him at the hospital. What are you going to do now?"

"We're moving to Plymouth next month, after we've got married. I have a job at the hospital, and Danny has found work at a local garage."

"You're giving up nursing, then?"

Rosa grinned. "No, I shall carry on," she said, putting a finger to her lips.

"You have more determination than me," said her sister. "I shall be giving up teaching." She looked wistfully at Rosa. "I wish you both luck," she added.

When Florrie found out Rosa was moving to Plymouth, she had an idea and spoke to Stephen about it after school.

"Do you think your parents would like a lodger?" she asked.

"Anyone in mind?" he replied.

"Yes, my sister, Rosa. She wants to start a new job at Plymouth Hospital, and I think she's had enough of nurses' accommodation."

"I think that's an excellent idea. It would give my parents some much-needed extra income and provide some companionship and support for them. I think there's an omnibus nearby that could take her to the hospital. I'll contact them straight away."

Florrie smiled to herself at his reply. Stephen was always so practical.

While busy making plans for Florrie's wedding, to be held in the summer holidays, Sophie couldn't help but reminisce about her own wedding, at Clayden's church, and what had proceeded it.

She had told her children the story, how she and their father had met and how she had been warned not to marry him. She knew that Florrie's choice was a good one, so she had not faced the dilemmas Sophie had all those years ago. Here she still was with Ben, loving him and having three wonderful children.

No, she thought, reminding herself of Samuel's words. *Four.*

She felt very happy for her daughter and wanted to organise a good wedding for her. She returned to her list, adding a few more reminders.

Two weeks later, the day before the wedding, Ben and Sophie made their way to the village hall, where the reception was to be held. Ben was carefully carrying the wedding cake Sophie had made. They found Florrie there, decorating the walls with garlands she had made with strands of ivy and white crepe-paper bows.

Florrie climbed down carefully from the ladder she had been standing on and stood back to look at her work. "I think that brightens things up a bit," she observed.

"It all looks wonderful," commented her mother.

Florrie looked at the cake Ben had placed in the centre of the table in the middle of the room.

"You've made a really good job of that," she said admiringly. Florrie put her arms round her mother. "Thank you for all you are doing for me," she said.

"Thank you, darling. Now, what else is there to do?"

Florrie and Stephen were married next day at the village church, which was full of friends and family. Many villagers also came to wish the couple well. A photographer from Kingsbridge took some photos and told them one was to be in the local paper, as it concerned the local headmaster.

Florrie and Stephen left for the schoolhouse that afternoon to go straight on to Plymouth afterwards. Stephen's father had been too poorly to attend the wedding, though his mother had managed to come, having found someone to look after her husband for the day. They were going to return with her so they could see him before leaving on their honeymoon.

That evening, Ben and Sophie sat in the garden, under the apple trees, remembering what an exciting day it had been.

"It's going to be very quiet at home now," Sophie mused. "With all our children gone."

"None of them are far away," Ben reassured her. "We shall be kept busy visiting them." He turned to face her. "Sophie, I don't know if I can continue running the garage without Danny. There's so much work coming in."

"Couldn't you employ someone?" she asked.

"I suppose so, but I'm considering selling up."

Sophie looked shocked. "Oh, Ben! What shall we live on?"

"I'm thinking of setting up as a village handyman. I think I could make a modest living at it, and I wouldn't have the pressure I have now, trying to get these motors back on the road quickly."

Sophie sat down to think. "I suppose we could manage," she said. "As long as you're sure."

"I've no idea what the business is worth. I'll wait until Danny leaves, then I'll put an advertisement in the local paper."

Shortly after Florrie's wedding, Rosa and Danny stood by the kitchen door, surrounded by suitcases, ready to leave. Ben was to drive them to Plymouth—Danny to his lodgings at the garage and Rosa to Stephen's parents' house. Jenny had let her son know she would be delighted to have Rosa live with them until they got married.

"Goodbye, Ma," said Rosa, embracing her mother. "We'll let you know when we set the date for our wedding. I hope you don't mind, but we shall be getting married in a registry office in Plymouth."

"I quite understand," replied her mother. "I hope the new job goes well." She kissed her daughter and Danny goodbye as Ben picked up two of the cases, ready to leave.

"Goodbye, Mrs. Browne," said Danny as he took the other two. "Thank you and Ben for all you have done for me."

Ben had told Danny about his intention to sell up their repair business, and Danny had agreed. It wasn't long before Ben had an enquiry.

He had just finished a particularly difficult job on his own at the garage and was writing out the invoice when a well-dressed man walked in and looked round in an interested way.

"Can I help you, sir?" asked Ben.

"How do you do?" said the man. "My name's Harold Benson. I understand you are wanting to sell your business?"

Ben introduced himself, and they shook hands. "Would you like me to show you round?" he asked. As they walked, Ben explained there was plenty of work coming in, as motorcar ownership was increasing. "They are prone to breaking down," he added. "People drive them badly and forget to fill the radiator."

After the short tour, Harold suggested a sale price he'd be willing to pay for the business.

Ben raised his eyebrows at the price he was offered. "I'll need to think about it and ask my partner," he replied cautiously.

Harold nodded politely and said he would return the next day.

When Ben mentioned Harold's offer, Danny whistled through his teeth.

"It seems generous, but I suspect it's under the market price," said Ben. "I think I'll push him for a little more tomorrow."

Harold returned the next day and, after some discussion, agreed to pay more. The deal was made. Ben could now pay Danny back the money he had put into the business. It was a substantial sum but would leave Ben and Sophie enough to live on for the time being.

After the sale had gone through, Ben and Sophie discussed their future. Sophie rested her head contentedly on her husband's shoulder as they sat together in the parlour.

"I can't believe our birds have all flown the nest," she murmured. Suddenly she sat bolt upright. "Ben! Now you don't have the garage anymore, why don't we offer to run the shop for Millie and Harry so they can go to New York for Tom's wedding?"

Ben looked surprised. "It's a lot to take on. We would have to do it for a few weeks."

"Yes, I realise that. You could do the post round while I run the post office, and I'm sure we can both take care of the shop."

He thought for a moment. "Let's go and visit them tomorrow, see what they say."

The following afternoon, they walked the short distance to the shop and arrived as Harry was just sweeping up.

"Sorry, we're closed!" he said, laughing.

"We haven't come to buy anything," said Ben.

"Go round to the cottage, then. I'll be there in a moment."

When he had joined them, Millie asked what the occasion of their visit was, and Ben informed them of Sophie's proposition.

Millie jumped up excitedly and hugged her brother and sister-in-law. "Oh, now we can go!"

"That's so kind of you," Harry said. "It will mean the world to us."

"Thank you!" added Millie. "We've been racking our brains for who to ask."

Millie explained that she would have to appoint Sophie as a deputy post-office assistant, and she would have to be trained. Sophie promised to come round every day and work alongside Millie until it was time for them to leave.

"And I'll go with Agnes on her post rounds," added Ben. "I might be able to pick up a bit of work from the villagers at the same time."

Millie and Harry thanked them profusely, and Ben and Sophie strolled home.

"I hope we can manage," said Ben. "It's a great responsibility."

"I'm sure Millie will train us well," said Sophie confidently. "It will be something very different for us to do."

Millie and Harry booked their passage as soon as they could, surprised at how much it was going to cost.

"Tom must be doing very well if he can afford that," said Harry.

They booked three second-class tickets on the *Mauritania* to set sail from Southampton in September.

CHAPTER TWENTY–FIVE

DANNY VISITS HIS MOTHER

ANNY DECIDED TO USE HIS portion of the money from the sale of the business to put a deposit on a small house in Plymouth.

He and Rosa spent one weekend looking for a suitable property. They explored several streets, looking out for FOR SALE signs.

"Do you know where your mother is living?" asked Rosa, wondering where it might be.

"Yes, in my old family home, as far as I know," he replied. "It's not so very far from here."

"Shall we go and see her?" suggested Rosa. "She would want to be at our wedding, Danny. We should go visit her."

Danny looked away. "I know I should. I do feel guilty not having contacted her."

"When was the last time you saw her?"

"I had some leave during the war. I came to stay, but it was awful. Her new husband's a bit rough and ready, and his sons are no better. I had to sleep in a chair."

While Rosa took this in, Danny told her that they could catch an omnibus. They found a stop and waited. Soon an omnibus appeared, and Danny said it would take them to the top of his mother's road.

Having arrived, they made the short walk to Danny's childhood home. Rosa could see it was not a well-off district by the small houses built in terraces and packed tightly together. Each front door opened straight onto the pavement, and one or two figures were lounging about in doorways. A woman with her arms folded was chatting to a neighbour, and farther along, a man in braces, his collarless shirtsleeves rolled up, was having a smoke. Some grubby-looking children were playing in the street. Rosa and Danny attracted suspicious glances as they walked by.

Eventually, Danny stopped. "This is where I used to live," he said as he knocked on a door.

After a short wait, it opened, and a young man stood there.

"What ya want?" he said roughly.

"Could I speak to Mrs. Barford?" asked Danny.

"Who is it wants 'er?"

"It's Danny, her son."

The young man looked surprised but turned back into the house and yelled, "Mum! Yer son's 'ere!"

A smell of stale cabbage wafted out, and Rosa wrinkled her nose.

A woman came hurrying out, wearing a wraparound pinafore and her hair bundled into a net. "Oh, Danny, you're here! You're safe! Oh, thank the dear Lord!" She threw her arms round him and hugged him tightly. "I thought I was never going to see you again!" She stood back and looked at him. "Your face," she said, touching his cheek and stroking his face gently. "Oh, Danny! Whatever happened to you?"

"I'll tell you in a moment, Mum. First, let me introduce you to Rosa. We're going to be married."

Mrs. Barford turned towards Rosa and took hold of both her hands, her eyes full of joy. "It's lovely to meet you, my dear."

"Hello, Mrs. Barford. I'm so pleased to meet you too."

They followed her into a hallway painted half brown and half cream, with a shabby carpet on the floor. At the end, they entered a small room with a table covered with an oil cloth, and in the corner was an easy chair with a grubby-looking cushion. A small fire was alight in the grate, and the room was stuffy.

The young man who had opened the door followed them in.

"I expect you remember Clarence," said Mrs. Barford, turning towards the young man. "Ian, my other stepson, is at work."

Danny nodded a greeting. "Don't you have work?" he asked, giving Clarence a cold look.

"No, can't get a job," Clarence replied, shrugging.

"There's no jobs round here, especially for unskilled men," added his mother.

"Is your husband in work?" Danny asked his mother.

Clarence laughed, and Mrs. Barford looked abashed. "He left last year. I haven't seen him since, so I've no idea."

Danny glanced at Clarence. "Can I speak to you on your own, please, Mum?"

The young man put his hands in his pockets and slouched out.

Danny got up and closed the door. "Mum, what have you been living on?"

"Ian gives me money for food and helps to pay the rent, and I have a small pension from your father."

"So your husband went off and left you with his two boys?"

"Yes, they didn't get on with him. There were lots of rows." His mother looked dejected.

"He should be supporting you," Danny said angrily.

Rosa put a restraining hand on his arm. "We came to ask you to our wedding, Mrs. Barford," she said quietly.

"Just you, not those two boys," said Danny firmly.

"Thank you. I shall look forward to that," she replied. "I'll go make us some tea and be right back."

Rosa had noticed her shabby clothes and slippers. She was about her mother's size, perhaps a little shorter, so she wondered if Sophie could lend her a dress for the wedding. She whispered, "Don't have a go at your mum, Danny. She needs our help."

Mrs. Barford came back with a big brown teapot and some chipped cups and saucers on a tray. They drank their tea as Danny told her what had happened to him after the war and about his eye operation.

"Rosa's family has been so good to me," he said, reaching out and clasping her hand.

"I did try and contact you, Danny love," explained his mother. "I wrote to your regiment, but they couldn't tell me where you were."

"I'm sorry I walked out, Mum. They were difficult times."

She nodded and sighed. "I shouldn't have remarried," she said. "I thought it would give you a better home." She got up and went to the dresser drawer. "These kept coming for you," she said, handing him some buff-coloured envelopes. "They looked important, so I kept them all. I didn't know where to send them."

Danny examined them. "It's about my pension, Mum. We've managed to sort it out."

They finished their tea, and Danny and Rosa got up to go.

"I'll come and see you again, Mum, I promise," said Danny as he pressed some money into her hand. "For you," he said. "Not them."

As he and Rosa walked back to the bus stop, he said, "Now you know why I left and didn't want to go back. It wasn't always like that. My mum used to keep the house nice when my dad was alive."

"I liked your mother," said Rosa. "She's doing her best."

"I'd like to kick those two boys out," he said vehemently.

"Your poor mum looks worn out from looking after them, and I didn't like the look of that Clarence. We should do what we can to help her."

On a trip home, Rosa asked to borrow a dress from her mother for Mrs. Barford, and she described how she'd found Danny's mother when they'd visited.

"She sounds very run-down," observed Sophie. "I expect she was overjoyed to see her son again. I'll look out for some other things for her, if you like."

Rosa thanked her mother, and when she returned to Plymouth, she took the dress round to Mrs. Barford on her day off to see if it fitted.

When she knocked on the door, there was some delay, so she knocked again. The door opened slowly, and Mrs. Barford peered round.

"Oh, hello, Rosa," she said hesitantly. She opened the door a little more, revealing a nasty bruise on her face.

"Mrs. Barford, are you all right?" asked Rosa anxiously.

She shook her head. "You'd better come in, dear," she said. She led her through to the back room.

Rosa put her bag down and helped Mrs. Barford to a chair. "May I look?" She gently held her head and examined her face. "How did this happen?" she asked.

Mrs. Barford looked embarrassed. "Oh, I just knocked it," she said.

"Was it one of the boys?" asked Rosa.

After some hesitation, Mrs. Barford replied, "Yes, it was."

Rosa sat next to her and put her arm round her. "What happened?" she asked quietly.

"He, Clarence, is always asking me for money. I refused, and he hit me."

Rosa's anger welled up inside her. "Danny will be furious when he finds out," she muttered under her breath.

Just then, the front door banged, and Mrs. Barford looked startled. Clarence came in and stopped still when he saw Rosa.

She stood up to confront him. "How dare you hit your mother!" she said.

Clarence smirked. "What are you going to do about it?"

"You'll see," replied Rosa firmly, looking him in the eye.

He turned and went out again.

"Let me make you some tea," suggested Rosa. "And then we can talk about the wedding."

Mrs. Barford gave a weak smile. "Thank you, dear," she said.

Rosa went into the small kitchen and put the kettle on the stove, then looked round for a box of matches and lit one of the gas burners. The kitchen was clean, but everything looked old. She peeped into one of the cupboards and saw only a few jars and tins there. She got out the cups and saucers and put them on a tray. The milk was in a jug in the meat safe, a box-like structure made of wood and wire gauze. Inside were also the remains of a cold leg of lamb and a slab of cheese.

The tea made, she carried it into the small sitting room, reminding herself to bring a cake next time she came. Mrs. Barford was sitting at the table, her head bowed.

"Here we are!" announced Rosa, trying to sound cheerful. She showed Mrs. Barford the dress she had brought.

"It's lovely, my dear," she said, feeling the material. "Please thank your mother for me."

Rosa described what she herself would be wearing, and they talked about the wedding for a while. Mrs. Barford appeared to rally.

"We're hoping to buy a house not far away," Rosa told her. "We shall be able to come and visit you then."

"That would be lovely, dear," repeated Mrs. Barford gratefully.

Having finished her tea, Rosa got up to go. Before she left, she told Danny's mother how to treat the bruising.

"He's got no right to hit you, Mrs. Barford," she said adamantly. "My Danny will put a stop to it. You needn't be afraid of him anymore."

Mrs. Barford embraced her warmly. "Please, call me Hilda," she said. "And thank you for everything."

Rosa rode the omnibus back to her lodgings in a pensive mood. She realised Hilda needed help but was unsure what to do. When she returned, she spoke to Mrs. Faircross about the incident.

"It's really upset me," she said. "That poor woman is just a slave to that boy. She has no life and seems to live in fear. Her son frightened me."

"She can't stay there with that violent boy," said Jenny. "You'd best bring her here. You go and get Danny, and I'll get the spare room ready."

"Thank you, Mrs. Faircross. You're very kind."

Rosa set off for the garage where Danny worked, about a mile away. He was working under a car when she arrived.

"Hello, Rosa! What brings you here?" he said, standing up with a look of surprise on his face.

When she told him how she had found his mother, he looked alarmed and angry.

"I'll kill that Clarence!" he said. "Wait till I get hold of him!"

"Mrs. Faircross suggested we bring her to stay at her house, Danny. That will be the best thing. We don't want any more violence."

Danny nodded. "That sounds a good idea. We'll go and fetch her this afternoon. Wait here a minute. I'll just get cleaned up." He left, and when he returned, he had with him a well-built young man. "This is Archie," he said. "He's my mate." Then he explained that he'd asked his boss if he could have the rest of the day off. "Come on," he said resolutely. "Let's go and sort this out."

They walked back to Danny's old home, and he knocked deter-
minedly on the door.

Clarence answered and leered at Danny. "What yer want?" he
demanded.

"Any more trouble from you and you'll be sorry!" said Danny
angrily.

Archie was standing behind Danny, towering over him. Clarence
took one look at him, and his face changed. He took his jacket from a
peg in the hall, pushed past them both, and left.

Danny and Rosa entered, finding Mrs. Barford sitting in the back
room, looking frightened, so Rosa went forwards and put her arms round
her. Mrs. Barford looked forlornly at her son.

"It's all right, Mum. We're here now. Has he been threatening you?"

His mother looked near to tears, and Rosa sat down beside her.
"Hilda," she said gently. "We think it would be better if you left here
for your own safety. You can stay with me at my lodgings for a while.
Would you like to do that?"

Mrs. Barford nodded, getting out her handkerchief and dabbing her
eyes.

"I'll help you to pack your things."

They went up the dark, narrow staircase, and Rosa found a battered
suitcase on top of the wardrobe in the bedroom. She opened the wardrobe and found several drab-looking garments hanging there, which she
folded and put into the case. Mrs. Barford sat on the bed, still crying.
Rosa emptied the chest of drawers of her few undergarments and then
wrapped her battered shoes in a towel and put those in. She added her
hairbrush and a few other items and closed the case.

"Come along," she said, taking Hilda's hand. "It's time to go."

CHAPTER TWENTY-SIX

DANNY GOES MISSING

ROSA AND DANNY'S MODEST WEDDING at a registry office in Plymouth took place quietly one Saturday morning in early October.

Hilda looked transformed wearing Sophie's dress with matching hat, gloves, and shoes and a new pair of stockings that Rosa had bought for her. Ben and Sophie had managed to get someone to run the shop for the day, and they arrived with Florrie and Stephen.

Jenny Faircross had arranged for the wedding reception to take place in her local church hall. Sophie had been quite happy at this, saying one wedding had been quite enough for her to do. The cake Sophie had made stood in pride of place on the table, surrounded by plates of sandwiches and sausage rolls.

Although heavily outnumbered by members of Rosa's family, Hilda looked happy and cheerful, and she appeared to enjoy herself immensely.

The next day, Danny and Rosa took Hilda back to their new home to live with them.

As they carried out the last of Rosa's belongings to take to the new house, she bid farewell to Jenny. "Thank you *so* much for all you have done for us," she began when she and Hilda were leaving. "I'm so grateful."

Jenny waved them off and turned to go back indoors. "They've gone!" she called out to her husband. "It's just us again, for now."

Rosa and Danny's house, although small, had three bedrooms. At the back was a small walled garden looking out onto a row of terraced houses behind. It was a pleasant, friendly neighbourhood, mainly populated with families or elderly couples. At the end of the road was a Baptist church, and there was a school nearby.

Rosa settled into her new life with Danny. Hilda took a pride in their new home and kept their house clean and tidy, and there was always a hot meal when Rosa and Danny returned from their work each day.

Rosa felt glad they had given Danny's mother a better life, away from the two grown stepsons who had been living off her goodwill and, in the younger one's case, her money. She encouraged Hilda to have her hair permed, and they went shopping together, buying her new clothes and shoes. She was hardly recognisable from the woman who had opened the door for them when Rosa and Danny had first gone to see her.

Hilda was glad of Digger's company, and she took him for a walk every day, usually to the shops and back. Every evening, when Danny was due home, the dog would go to the door and wait for him.

A week later, Rosa was returning home from her shift at the hospital. She got off the bus and began the short walk to her home. It had been an extra busy time at work that day, and she felt especially tired.

She finally reached her house and greeted the two small children playing outside.

" 'Ello, Miss Collins!" they called out cheerfully.

"Hello! Isn't it time for your tea?" said Rosa, being that it was nearly seven o'clock.

They grinned. "Waiting for our dad!"

Rosa put her key in the lock and went inside, and as she was taking off her coat, Hilda came out of the kitchen at the back, looking worried.

"Is everything all right, Hilda?" asked Rosa, bending down to fondle Digger.

"Danny's not home yet," she answered, fiddling with her apron. "He's usually back by now."

"He's probably working late."

"He always tells me if he is," replied Hilda. "It's not like him to be this late."

"Perhaps he's working on an urgent job that needs finishing," suggested Rosa.

Hilda looked unconvinced, but she was an anxious woman and worried about things, so Rosa asked, "Shall I go and see if he's still at the garage?"

"Have a cup of tea before you go," said Hilda, turning back into the kitchen.

"No, I'll go straight away," replied Rosa, putting her coat back on.

She walked quickly back up the street, turned the corner at the end, and made her way to the garage, expecting to meet her husband on his way home. She wondered if he would come a different way, but it seemed odd that he would he do that when it would be longer.

When she reached the garage, it was closed, so she went round the back to the owner's house and knocked on the door. An older man opened it.

"Hello, Stan," said Rosa. "Has Danny left yet?"

"He left the usual time, miss," he replied. "Is there a problem?"

"He hasn't returned home. His mother's very concerned."

"Maybe he's gone to the pub," said Stan. "Wait there a minute."

He went back inside and then came out wearing his jacket and holding a bunch of keys. "I'll drive you round there, Rosa."

She followed him round to the forecourt and got into his motor. He drove the short distance to the tavern and parked, then hopped out, asking Rosa to wait, and went inside.

He emerged a little later, saying, "He's not there, and none of his mates have seen him."

While he was telling her this, two men came along. Rosa recognised one of them as Archie. They came over to the car.

"What's up, Mr. White?" Archie asked Stan.

Stan explained that Danny was missing, and they offered to help look for him.

Stan turned to Rosa. "I'll take you home first. If he doesn't turn up, we'll call the police."

Rosa nodded, now beginning to feel a little sick inside. The two men got into the motor, and Stan dropped her back home.

"Now don't you worry, miss," he said before he drove off. "We'll find him. I'm sure he'll be all right."

When Rosa went inside, she told Hilda what was happening and asked if this had ever happened before. As Rosa worked different shifts, she was not always there when Danny came home.

"No, never," replied Hilda. "He's always very punctual, and as I said, he always tells me if he'll be working late."

They both sat down, but neither had any appetite for their dinner. Digger flopped down on the floor beside them, seeming to sense something was wrong. Hilda made a pot of tea, which they drank slowly and without speaking much.

An hour later, there was a loud thumping at the door, and both Rosa and Hilda looked up startled. Rosa got up quickly to answer it and was shocked to see a policeman standing there.

"Mrs. Collins?" he asked.

"Yes," said Rosa, hardly audibly.

"I understand your husband is missing?"

She nodded.

"We've found him, but I'm sorry to say he's in a bit of a bad way. He's been taken to the hospital and we're making some enquiries."

Hilda had come into the hall, having heard what had been said, and exclaimed, "Oh, my Danny! Is he all right? What's happened?"

"He was found on the railway embankment by some friends of his, and they took him straight to the hospital. He was unconscious, and it looks as if someone, or some persons, have beaten him up," explained the policeman.

Hilda collapsed against Rosa, and Rosa and the officer held her between them and got her into the living room, where she fell into a chair. Rosa found some smelling salts and brought her round.

"Can we go to the hospital to see him?" asked Rosa.

"Yes, of course. I have a car outside," answered the policeman.

"Are you able to come?" Rosa asked Hilda, holding her hand.

Hilda nodded, and Rosa helped her to her feet. She put on her coat and grabbed her handbag, which she clutched tightly. Digger looked anxiously at them as they shut him in the kitchen before leaving.

They were both silent as they rode to the hospital. Rosa prayed that they had not damaged Danny's good eye. *What if he is blind again? He will have to stop work, and how will we pay for our house? We will have to rent some low-grade dwelling somewhere in a rough neighbourhood...* Her mind raced on, each fear feeding the next.

She looked at Hilda, who had gone very pale. Rosa knew she had to be strong, so she did not share her fears with her. She held Hilda's hand and squeezed it, saying, "The hospital will take care of him. I know the doctors, and they're the best."

They arrived, thanked the policeman, and got out of the car.

"We shall be back tomorrow to question him, if he's up to it," the officer told them. "If he tells you anything before then, let us know. Don't worry, Mrs. Collins. We'll find out who did this to him."

The two women went through the hospital entrance, and Rosa asked at the desk where to go to see Danny. They were directed to the ward, and when they got there, the sister recognised Rosa. "Hello, Nurse Browne. What are you doing here?"

Rosa suddenly went hot, her heart racing. "Don't tell them Danny's my husband," she whispered.

Hilda nodded.

"I'm here with Mrs. Barford," she replied confidently. "We believe her son has been brought in."

"Yes, he's over there," the sister replied, indicating which bed he was in.

"How is he?" asked Hilda.

"He's been sedated, so he's still sleeping, but he has a good pulse. The best thing is for him to rest. We can't ascertain his full injuries until he wakes."

They went over to see him. Rosa could see he had a cut over one eye but, thankfully, no other injury to his eyes. She looked him over, thankful the nurse had cleaned him up before his mother saw him. It was difficult to know the damage done to his body, and she just prayed he would survive this. She reached out and stroked his head, the tears welling up in her eyes. Hilda stood staring at him, holding her handkerchief over her mouth in disbelief.

The sister advised them to go home, get some rest, and come back in the morning. "He'll be asleep for some time," she said.

Reluctantly, Rosa and her mother-in-law left, knowing they would probably not get much sleep that night.

The next day, they caught the omnibus back to the hospital. When they arrived at the ward, a policeman was talking to Danny, who was sitting up in bed with a bandage round his head. They waited until the policeman got up to go. As he came out, he said he had a name and arrests would be made. Rosa and Hilda rushed to Danny's side.

He smiled at them. "I'm all right, Mum, Rosa."

They both kissed him gently, and Hilda began weeping.

"Shush, Mum, please don't," said Danny.

"Who did this to you?" asked Rosa.

"Clarence."

"What? On his own?"

"No, he's too much of a coward for that. He had two mates with him. They caught me unawares on the way home last night."

"Your mother raised the alarm," said Rosa. "She knew something was wrong."

"Thanks, Mum. I don't know how long I would have lain there otherwise."

"It was Stan and Archie and another of your mates who looked for you and found you," Rosa told him.

"Will you thank them, Rosa?"

"Yes, of course."

Danny wanted to know when he would be allowed home, so Rosa went to find the ward sister. When she returned, she told him they wanted to keep him in another day for observation. He began to look tired, so Rosa and Hilda said their goodbyes and left.

When they arrived back home, Rosa asked Hilda if she had seen Clarence since she'd left.

"No, not at all," she replied. "I thought it was strange he hadn't been round, bothering me, and I supposed Danny had seen him off for good."

"I just wonder why he left it so long to get his own back. Something must have prompted this attack. Danny must know a little more than he's telling us."

That afternoon, the policeman returned and informed them that Clarence had been charged with grievous bodily harm and would be appearing in court. He assured them that his two accomplices would be apprehended soon, and he said there would be a court order for him to stay away from them so there was no need to be afraid.

The next day, Rosa and Hilda collected Danny from the hospital and brought him home in a taxicab. He was very shaken up but put on a brave face.

Stan arrived later to see how he was, and Danny thanked him for all his help.

"I'm so glad we found you," said Stan. "I understand they've arrested somebody."

"Yes, my no-good stepbrother."

Stan raised his eyebrows. "Well, well, families, eh? Listen, Danny, I don't want to see you back at work until you're properly fit, okay?"

Danny nodded, and his mother looked relieved. Before Stan left, Danny asked him to thank his other two mates.

"What are mates for if not to help?" asked Stan.

Rosa returned to work, but she made sure her mother-in-law knew how to nurse Danny and change his dressings. Hilda listened carefully to her daughter-in-law's instructions and assured her that she could manage.

When Rosa returned that evening, she asked Danny if he had seen Clarence recently.

"Yes, last week he came to the garage and asked me to get him a job there. I told him he had no skills or training to do repair work and would be better off applying to a factory. He got very abusive and said he couldn't get work anywhere. I'm not surprised. He played truant from school and has been a layabout ever since. He asked me for some money, so I gave him five shillings. He said that his brother was getting married and he would have nowhere to live. I told him to contact his father and he wasn't to bother my mother anymore or there'd be trouble. He left, saying it was 'all right for some.'"

"That doesn't give him an excuse to beat you up. Why did he do it?" asked Rosa.

"Envy, I suppose. He could make a success of his life if he tried. He thinks the world owes him a living."

"I wish you'd told me," said Rosa. "I can understand you not telling your mother."

"I know, I should have done," said Danny. "I didn't want to worry you. Whatever I did for him, he would mess it up. I know he's been in some trouble with the police already, so he won't get much sympathy this time."

"He's his father's responsibility, not yours, Danny."

"I wish I hadn't given him any money. I think he just got drunk on it."

The policeman called round later that day to get a written statement from Danny. He informed him that they had apprehended the other two lads who had attacked him, and they had confessed, saying that they were paid to do it by Clarence. He said they would be fined, but Clarence was likely to have a custodial sentence, as he had a previous conviction. Danny told Rosa that at least it would keep him out of the way for a while.

Rosa wrote to her mother, giving her an account of events. She knew they would be appalled, but she assured them they were all safe, as Clarence was locked up. Rosa realised that the attack on Danny had been carried out by a gang and they could have killed him. She shuddered to think about it.

Danny improved slowly and soon went back to work, mornings only for the first week. Stan was concerned about him. He was one of his best mechanics, despite his disability.

Danny admitted to Rosa that he felt a little nervous walking home each day after work and sometimes varied his route. He told her that, although his attackers had been caught, he knew Clarence could be vindictive and might get back at him somehow.

Danny, Rosa, and his mother had to attend the court case, as Danny had to testify. On the appointed day, they were waiting in the entrance hall when the lawyer representing Danny asked to speak to him and led him to the side of the room to have their conversation.

A man tapped Hilda on the shoulder and said, "Hello there, Hilda. You're looking very glamorous."

She spun round and exclaimed in surprise, "Ken!"

"How are you doing?" he asked.

"A lot better since you left and lumbered her with your two sons," replied Danny, who had rushed over to his mother when his stepfather approached her.

Ken smirked. "I hear my youngest is in a bit of trouble."

"We have nothing to say to you," said Danny, ushering his wife and mother away, towards his lawyer.

Later, they saw Ken sitting not far from them in the visitor's gallery, but there was no sign of Clarence's brother, Ian. Rosa held Hilda's hand tightly as Danny had to wait outside until he was called.

The case progressed, and Danny entered the courtroom and gave his evidence. While he was describing the attack, Hilda began silently weeping. Then Danny's two friends and Stan gave their evidence. Clarence had given an alibi, but this was contested by the police and proved false.

At the end of the submissions, the judge deemed that Clarence was guilty and sent him down for six months. Rosa glanced at Ken, seeing he looked quite angry.

They met up with Danny outside afterwards, and thankfully there was no sign of Ken. They returned home in a subdued mood. Danny said he was concerned about Hilda being alone in the house when he and Rosa were at work, and he advised her to be careful who she opened the door to. He was glad they had Digger there.

Soon Danny was able to resume full-time work, and life settled down. Jenny invited Danny's mother to join her church, so Hilda caught the omnibus once a week to attend the Mothers' Union meetings. Rosa was glad that she was making friends. Hilda had been isolated while looking after her stepsons, leaving her no room to have a life of her own.

A letter arrived one morning, and after reading it, Hilda put it on the mantelpiece to show Danny and Rosa later.

Danny arrived home first, followed shortly by Rosa, who went straight upstairs to change out of her nurse's uniform. When she came back down, Hilda gave Danny the letter.

"This came this morning," she said.

Danny read it and passed it to Rosa. "Do you really want to go, Mum?" he asked.

The letter was an invitation to Ian's wedding.

"At least Clarence won't be there," observed Rosa, handing the invitation back.

"Yes, but Ken will be, I should think," replied Danny.

"Ian was never any trouble to me," said Hilda, "and he did pay his rent regular. I didn't know he was getting married."

"Well, you accept if you want to, Mum, but I won't be going."

"Oh, Danny! She can't go on her own!" exclaimed Rosa.

Danny eventually relented, and they all decided to attend the wedding.

Rosa encouraged Hilda to get a new outfit and hat, and they bought an embroidered tablecloth and set of napkins to give as a wedding present. Rosa said they would be just right for "special teas."

On the day of the wedding, Hilda looked nervous, as Ken would probably be there. They entered the church and spotted him sitting with a young woman by his side.

The organ began playing, and they tried to catch sight of the bride when she came in. It was difficult to discern her features through her veil, and when she lifted it, they could only see her back view throughout the ceremony. At the end, as she turned round, they could see she was an attractive girl with a lovely smile.

At the wedding reception, Ian came over with his bride to speak to his stepmother. "Hello, Mum. This is Pam," he said, introducing her.

"Hello, Mrs. Barford, lovely to meet you."

"Please, call me Hilda, Pam. It's lovely to meet you too. Congratulations to you both. This is Danny, my son, and his wife, Rosa."

"Thanks for coming," continued Ian. "I wasn't sure if you would after what happened to Danny."

"We were very shocked," said Pam. "Clarence deserved to go to prison."

"He's been bothering me for money for some time instead of looking for a job," said Ian. "I wouldn't give him any, so I suppose that's why he went to you, Danny. I hope we'll see more of you after this." He smiled and took his bride's hand. "We must go now and welcome our other guests."

As Ian led Pam away, Danny said, "That was a turn up, I must say. He seems quite a decent chap."

They sat down at their places, and the meal and speeches commenced.

Hilda said she was glad she had attended, even if she did have to see Ken. "I'm glad I met Pam," she added. "She seems very nice."

Two weeks later, Hilda answered the door to her new daughter-in-law coming to thank her for their wedding present and give her their new address. It turned out to be not so very far away, and they became firm friends.

CHAPTER TWENTY-SEVEN

CHARLES RECEIVES SOME NEWS

"I EXPECT THEY'RE GLAD IT'S OVER," Sophie said after reading that Clarence had been given a custodial sentence. She put Rosa's letter down on the table. "Not a good start to their married life."

Ben agreed. "I'd like to get my hands on that lout," he growled.

"I'd hoped your fighting days were over," said Sophie, giving him one of her looks.

Ben had just returned from doing a job in the village. He had put an advertisement in the shop and was beginning to get some work as a handyman.

Their conversation turned towards whether they should finish with the cycle club teas. It had been a busy summer that had tired Sophie out.

"We've been doing it for many years now," said Ben. "Now our girls are married, we will want to visit them, especially at the weekends."

"I wonder if anyone in the village could take them on?"

"I could ask round. It would be nice to have more free time."

Charles called in to see his mother and father. Sophie had written to tell him about what had happened to Danny, and he was concerned.

"Do you know the extent of his injuries?" he asked.

"I think they were mostly cuts and bruises and a mild concussion. No broken bones," replied Sophie. "He had a bad cut over one eye, but no black eyes, thank God."

"Thank God, indeed!" muttered Charles. He knew only too well the implications of a punch in Danny's good eye. "He didn't deserve that. He's been through enough."

"Some folk seem to have more than their fair share of misfortune," remarked Ben.

Sophie nodded in agreement.

"I have some news," Charles announced. "Dr. Bailey is retiring, and he and Caroline are moving to another property," he told them. "He said I could pay rent and stay on at Acacia House as long as I want. I certainly can't afford to buy him out!"

"Where are they going?" Ben asked.

"Another house in Modbury, not far. Donald's made me a partner, and we're going to appoint an assistant. Luckily, they're leaving some furniture, and I'll have to get some daily help."

"Will you be happy living in that house all alone?" asked Sophie.

"It will do for now. I need to be there for the surgeries."

"Have you heard from Lucinda and Madelaine?" asked his mother.

"Yes, they've left Paris and have been touring France. They're off to Italy soon."

Donald and Caroline Bailey moved to their new house, and Charles settled into Acacia House on his own and managed to find a housekeeper to come in each day.

What Charles had not told his parents was that he had been seeing Sapphire. After Lucinda and Madelaine had left, he'd received a letter from her inviting him to London to "have some fun." When he arrived at the flat, she announced that they were to attend a preview of an art exhibition that was to include some sculptures by Amanda.

"That sounds good," he told her. "I thought we might be trailing round cocktail bars all evening."

They arrived at the gallery and spotted Amanda among the well-dressed guests.

"Hello, darling," said Sapphire, kissing her on the cheek.

Amanda embraced Charles and then whispered excitedly to them both, "I've sold one already!"

"How exciting!" enthused Sapphire.

They followed Amanda as she squeezed through the crowded room. "This is it," she said, indicating a clay figurine.

"I'm very impressed," stated Charles when he saw it. "Your work has real merit."

"Is your father here?" asked Sapphire.

"Oh yes, he wouldn't miss this. He's invited all his friends and colleagues."

Amanda was looking radiant, and when they found Lionel, he looked very proud of his wife. "She's a clever, talented girl," he said, putting his arm round her.

Amanda told them she had been working hard to produce her sculptures and had also obtained a commission. Her father had helped her contact a potter friend of his who fired her work, and she was hoping to cast some in bronze in the future.

As the evening progressed, they drank cocktails and conversed with a variety of artists and their guests, some rather bizarrely dressed. The conversations were full of animated superlatives, and Charles smiled to himself as he listened. This was Sapphire's world, and he rather liked being part of it.

When they finally returned to the flat later that evening, Charles collapsed onto the sofa and spread out his legs. Sapphire sat beside him and snuggled up. She had drunk rather too many cocktails, as he had done.

"Charles, I'm sorry I treated you so badly. You will forgive me, won't you, as I do want to be your friend and you want to be my friend too, don't you?" She put her arms round his neck and looked up at him with sorrowful eyes.

Charles was completely smitten. He smiled and nodded, looking at her longingly, realising he wasn't over her at all. He felt helpless in her gaze.

"You'll stay, won't you?"

"Yes, I'll stay."

Charles continued going to London to see Sapphire whenever he had time off. He had attended a day conference in London on one occasion, and after it had finished, he went to see Sapphire. He had a key to the flat, so he let himself in and found her lying on the sofa.

"Hello, darling! Get yourself a drink. I've something to tell you," she said as he came in.

He poured a drink and bent down to kiss her.

She looked straight at him. "I'm expecting your baby, Charles."

Startled, Charles stood quite still for a moment, clutching his drink. He put it down and knelt beside her. "That's wonderful, darling. I'll have to make an honest woman of you, then."

She smiled and nodded. He laid his head on her stomach, and she stroked his hair. "Dear Charles," she said.

He looked up. "What are we to do? We'll have to tell our families. You do want this child, don't you?"

Sapphire looked shocked. "Yes, of course! We must get married quickly, though."

"But that would mean your mother will have to curtail her tour."

"I know, but we need to get married soon. I'll write to her. I'll use express."

"Yes, do that," replied Charles eagerly. "I'll have to tell my parents. God knows what they'll say."

CHAPTER TWENTY-EIGHT

LUCINDA'S TRIP ENDS

IT WAS LATE OCTOBER, AND Madelaine drew the curtains of their sleeping compartment aside as the train rattled onwards. "Oh, Aunt, look at this!" Her voice was full of wonder.

Lucinda slowly opened her eyes, sat up in bed, and turned her head to look. Out of the window, she could see a vast panorama of mountains tinged rose pink in the emerging dawn light. "How beautiful!" she gasped.

They continued to enjoy the view for some time as the sun gradually rose. The train they had boarded the day before was now passing through the Alps on their journey towards Italy.

"How I wish I was an artist and could capture this," said Lucinda softly.

"You should take up watercolour painting when we get back," suggested Madelaine.

The practicalities of the day began, and they took it in turns in the small vestibule washroom.

After dressing, they made their way to the dining car and sat at their usual table. Lucinda picked up the menu card to see what was on that morning as the waiter brought a pot of coffee and poured each of them a cup.

"Did you enjoy Paris?" asked Lucinda.

"Very much so, Aunt. It was wonderful. Thank you again for asking me to accompany you on this trip."

"I hoped it will help you get over your broken engagement, darling."

"And I hope it will help you too, Aunt."

Lucinda looked wistfully out of the window. Samuel had passed away only six months before.

She turned and smiled sweetly at Madelaine. "Yes, I think it will, and when we get to our hotel in Italy, I hope we have some letters telling us all the news."

Two gentlemen entered the dining car and acknowledged them with a "good morning" and a slight bow as they passed. They had become briefly acquainted at dinner the evening before. Lucinda and Madelaine certainly made an impression wherever they went, and they enjoyed the attention. They knew it was unusual to travel unescorted, but women were enjoying more freedom and independence after the war.

They arrived in Florence early that evening and booked into their hotel, both expressing their excitement at the prospect of exploring the city the following day.

Madelaine sat on her bed, studying the guidebook and reading out places of interest to her aunt. Lucinda was choosing her gown to wear for dinner.

In the smart dining room, the waiter was very attentive as he helped them choose a suitable wine. He knew a little English, which amused them when they heard his complimentary phrases and laughed at his attempts to charm the ladies.

The following day, after a morning's sightseeing, they found a small restaurant near the cathedral and ordered a light lunch, both glad to rest and watch the world go by for an hour.

Madelaine was still reading her guidebook when Lucinda said, "Have you decided what you are going to do about Charles?"

Madelaine picked up her glass and took a sip of wine. "No, I want to enjoy some freedom first. He is rather sweet, and I do like him, but as I said, I don't want to be tied down again just yet."

After buying some postcards, they walked back to their hotel for a siesta. The sun had been hot and tiring.

Lucinda ran a bath and relaxed for an hour, emerging refreshed. She dressed, then wrote some letters and postcards, sitting at the small desk by the open window. They were to stay in Florence for two weeks, so she hoped they might receive a reply before they moved on to Rome.

Madelaine took the post down to the reception desk and was handed a letter addressed to her aunt. She took it upstairs, and Lucinda recognised the writing.

"It's from Sapphire," she said, peering at the date on the envelope. Lucinda opened it and began reading. When she got halfway down the first page, she gasped and put her hand to her mouth. "Oh my goodness!" she exclaimed.

"What is it?" asked Madelaine. "What does she say?"

Lucinda looked up from the letter, shock etched in her face. "She tells me she's expecting Charles's child and they are to be married."

Madelaine opened her eyes wide. "Are you sure?"

Lucinda handed her the letter to see for herself.

Sapphire had written on behalf of herself and Charles to ask if they could shorten their holiday and return for the wedding. "You will understand the urgency if I am to get married in a church, as I think you will want us to do," she wrote. She told her mother she thought the baby was due in February or early March.

When she'd finished reading, Madelaine gave the letter back and looked steadily at her aunt. "You're to be a grandmother, then."

"I don't know what to think. It's all so unexpected." She put her hand gently on Madelaine's arm and said, "I'm sorry, darling. This is rather unfortunate for you."

"I had my chance, Aunt. How do *you* feel about it?"

"Life never ceases to surprise us, does it?" she replied, sounding surprisingly cheerful. "It's very strange that she is to marry Ben's son. I never would have thought this possible, but I suppose I must accept it. I'm feeling thrilled at having a grandchild, of course, and I'm pleased that Sapphire is settling down at last. She could have done worse. I'm sorry we must curtail our trip."

"Oh, Aunt! I've had a lovely time! I understand, we must get back."

Lucinda went to the desk to reply to her daughter's letter, and Madelaine went down to the reception desk to book tickets for the opera.

"To take our minds off things," she said when she returned.

"You'll have to leave your job," said Charles. Sapphire had just told him how unwell she was feeling.

"I get so tired!" she exclaimed.

"You need to rest, then."

"I hope Mummy's got my letter. Oh, Charles! What will she think of me? I wonder what Daddy would have said."

Charles was wondering what his father and mother would think when he told them. "I don't think my pa is going to be very pleased either. Ma will be upset too."

"They obviously don't think very highly of me."

"It's not that, Sapphire darling." He put his arm round her shoulders and bent down to kiss her head. "It's all the history between my pa and your mother."

When Charles went to see Ben and Sophie, he let his mother fuss round making tea as he listened to his father describing the jobs he'd been doing in the village.

How can I tell them? he kept thinking. *Will they be angry with me?*

Finally, when Ben had finished, Charles put his cup down on the table. "Pa, Ma, I have something to tell you."

They regarded him expectantly.

He gave a nervous cough. "For some time now, I have had a close friendship with a young lady."

Sophie and Ben exchanged smiles.

"Her name is Sapphire."

The smiles disappeared. A look of consternation spread across Ben's face, and Sophie sat impassively, her hands in her lap, not revealing her feelings.

Ben got up, strode across the floor, then turned and came back again. "You're telling us, out of all the young women, you have chosen her?"

"Yes."

Ben looked desperately at his wife.

Sophie reached out and put her hand on Ben's arm. "It's all right," she said, her calm grey eyes looking intently at him.

"That's not all," continued Charles, his hands tightly clenched as he spoke. "We are expecting a child."

Ben looked astounded. "What?" he shouted.

"Keep calm," said Sophie. She turned to her son. "This isn't what we would have liked to have happened, but, for my own part, I'm happy for you both. Does Lucinda know? She's abroad, isn't she?"

"Yes, she knows. Sapphire has written to her, asking her to return."

"I suppose you're going to marry her," Ben said bitterly. He continued to pace the room.

"As soon as we can. I believe her mother and Madelaine will be back by the end of this week."

Ben said nothing. He glared at Charles.

"I hope you'll give us your blessing, Pa. It would mean a lot to me. I'm so sorry I have disappointed you. I owe so much to you both, and I've not treated you well, behaving like this." He looked up at his father with pleading eyes. "I…I just fell in love."

"She must have led you on," said Ben, still with an angry look on his face.

Sophie's expression looked pained.

"I think I'd better go," said Charles, getting to his feet. "You will come to the wedding, won't you?"

His mother walked to door with him. "We shall *both* be there," she said, putting her arm round him and giving him a kiss on his cheek. "Tell Sapphire to take care of herself." She turned to Ben. "Can he bring her here?" she asked.

"I suppose so," said Ben truculently, glowering at Charles.

As soon as he'd gone, Ben thumped the table with his fist.

Sophie flinched. It had been a long time since she had seen her husband so angry. "Ben, what's done is done, we cannot change it."

"Why did he choose her, of all people?" he asked, flinging out his arms. "I made one big mistake, and it's come back to kick me in the face ever since."

"I'm sorry you see it that way. We must see this child as a blessing, not a curse."

"I'm going for a walk," he said, getting up and slamming the door behind him.

Two weeks later, Lucinda and Madelaine reached their hotel in Rome, where they found two letters waiting for them. One was from Lionel, hoping they were both well and enjoying their trip. Amanda sent her love and was looking forward to seeing them when they returned. The other letter was for Madelaine, from her father, William, and she read it silently, then handed it to her aunt. He had written to ask her to reconsider her engagement, saying that her fiancé and his parents were all very upset with her.

"You'd think my brother would allow you to enjoy yourself without referring to this," said Lucinda as she handed back the letter. "I hope it hasn't worried you, darling."

"On the contrary," replied Madelaine. "I'm now determined to enjoy myself all the more, as I now realise that coming on this trip is the best thing I can do."

"I'm sorry your holiday has been shortened, darling."

"I've had a wonderful time. I just hope we can do it again."

Madelaine had written to cancel their hotel reservations in Rome, and they were both intending to book train tickets home the following day. Lucinda carefully folded her gowns and placed them in her suitcase. Some she hadn't worn yet. Madelaine had her case ready and placed by the door for the hotel porter to take the next day. She had also ordered a taxi that would take them to the station. They were due to return in two days, having booked a sleeper.

Lucinda was very subdued as they travelled through France.

Catching the boat ferry, they at last arrived in Portsmouth and were relieved to see Lionel and Amanda, together with Sapphire, waiting to welcome them home. No one from Madelaine's family was there, as expected.

Sapphire was the first to hug her mother. "Thank you so much for coming home early, Mummy. I'm so grateful. Have you had a wonderful time?"

"Yes, darling, until I got your letter. What a surprise it was! Now I must set to and organise your wedding," she said, giving her a reassuring smile.

They piled the luggage into the car and set off home to Exeter.

When they arrived, Lionel lit the fires and Amanda helped Lucinda unpack. Sapphire announced she would cook the dinner.

Their meal was lively with conversation as both Lucinda and Madelaine recounted their adventures.

Eventually, they began to discuss the wedding and arrangements that needed to be made. Sapphire informed them that she and Charles had booked the church, so the date was set. Lucinda had never been so happy.

CHAPTER TWENTY-NINE
CHARLES AND SAPPHIRE WED

EN WAS SETTING ABOUT MENDING a gate that had suffered from the children swinging on it over the years. While he worked, he kept on turning over in his mind Charles's unwelcome announcement. He hammered the nails more ferociously than was necessary, feeling the fury building up inside him.

He had struggled to distance himself from Lucinda over the years, despite trying to maintain a relationship with Lionel. Now their two families were to be conjoined, and he would have to see Lucinda.

He was amazed how Sophie had taken it so calmly. Why hadn't she felt aggrieved too? Now they were to be family, how was he to manage his feelings towards the woman he had once made love to?

He heard a car approaching down the lane and thought it must be the visitors he had been expecting for some time. He sighed heavily, put down his hammer, and stood waiting.

Charles's motor appeared and drew up alongside. Sapphire was sitting beside him. Charles got out, greeted his father, and then went round to the other side of the car to open the door for his companion. She emerged smiling, but Charles looked nervous.

"Good to see you both. Sophie will be pleased you've come," said Ben, hoping his voice carried some sincerity. He stood to one side and allowed them to go by.

Sapphire avoided looking at him as she passed, holding Charles's hand tightly.

Sitting at the kitchen table, preparing lunch, Sophie looked up as they entered, her eyes growing wide in surprise. "Charles! Sapphire!" She stood up to embrace them. "I'm glad you've come."

Ben followed them in, hoping his set expression didn't fully betray his hostile feelings.

Sophie led them into the parlour, where they all sat down. "How are you feeling, Sapphire?" she asked.

Sapphire's pale face showed some strain. "Not too bad, thank you, Mrs. Browne. I do get very tired."

"That should get better after a while," replied Sophie. "When is the baby due?"

Charles relaxed a little and smiled at Sapphire. They were still holding hands. "Next March," he said. "We've set the date for the wedding. It's to be in two weeks' time, at the local church near Sapphire's home."

"We shall look forward to that, won't we, Ben?" answered Sophie, looking at him.

Ben nodded.

Sapphire smiled at him and said, "Which would you prefer, Mr. Browne, a grandson or a granddaughter?"

"I haven't really had any thoughts on the matter," he replied.

"Charles wants a son, don't you, darling?" said Sapphire, turning to him and patting his knee. "I would love a little girl."

Sophie got up to make coffee for everyone.

Charles turned to his father. "Has Ma been keeping well?" he asked.

"Yes, thank you."

After a short silence, Charles said, "I'm sorry, Pa, that we have sprung all of this on you and Ma. We are both very happy, and I hope you can be happy for us too."

"It was a surprise, Charles, but we're glad you're happy. That's all we want you to be. We're both looking forward to being grandparents." He spoke without smiling, and his words sounded flat.

Sophie came in with the refreshments, and Charles told her he missed her baking.

"I can make you cakes," said Sapphire. "If Mrs. Browne will show me how to make your favourites."

"Please call me Sophie, Sapphire, and yes, I can give you some recipes."

"How are the girls?" asked Sapphire.

"Florrie has left teaching now she's married," replied Sophie. "Rosa and Danny are living in Plymouth with his mother, and Rosa is still nursing."

"We have a lot of family to keep up with," said Sapphire, laughing nervously.

"It's been quite a year for weddings," declared Sophie. "Florrie, Rosa, and now yourselves." She turned to Ben. "Oh yes! And Ben's nephew, Tom. He got married in September, in New York, of all places."

"I'd love to go there!" exclaimed Sapphire, her eyes shining. "Not much chance now, though." She patted her stomach.

Ben noticed Charles looking proudly at her as she spoke. *The boy has completely fallen for her*, he thought. He remembered his own emotions when he first met Lucinda. He began to feel his anger subside.

"Aunty Millie and Uncle Harry are still over there," continued Sophie. "We're going to be looking after the shop for them until November. Your pa has enjoyed doing the post round."

"Pa, a postman!" Charles suddenly relaxed as he showed his amused surprise.

Ben looked at him and grinned. "None of your teasing, young man!" he said.

"I think postmen do a great job. We all love getting letters." Sapphire looked straight at Ben as she said this.

"Quite right!" he said, looking pleased she had spoken up for him.

"Where will you live?" asked Sophie, wondering what their plans were.

"In Acacia House, for now," replied Charles. "As long as Sapphire is happy there," he said, turning to her.

"I shall have to get used to being a doctor's wife as well as a mother," commented Sapphire, and Sophie gave her a reassuring smile.

At the end of the visit, Sapphire thanked them both and said she was looking forward to seeing them at the wedding.

Charles stood and reached out to shake his father's hand. "Thanks for having us, Pa. I'm very grateful."

Feeling overcome, Ben clasped his son round his neck and hugged him.

Thanks to a good dressmaker, when Sapphire walked down the aisle on her wedding day, no one could have realised she was expecting. Her dress was in ivory silk, and a swathe of material at the front had been gathered round to one side and left to hang down in folds, held by a floppy bow.

Lucinda wore pale blue with a matching hat. William was asked to give Sapphire away, and Madelaine was a bridesmaid and Lionel the best man.

It was late September, and the golden sun shone through the trees behind the church as Charles led his bride out.

Lucinda had arranged an impressive wedding breakfast for her guests. Madelaine managed to have a few words with Charles and congratulated him. She assured him she was happy for him and told him she was now determined to travel more, having enjoyed her trip with Lucinda so much.

"I'm sorry you had to come back early," he said.

"If it hadn't been for you, Charles, I probably wouldn't have gone."

Charles and Sapphire were to spend their short honeymoon in Torquay, as Sapphire had said she did not want a long journey in her condition. They set off the following day and arrived at their hotel at lunchtime.

Later that day, as they strolled along the promenade, he asked her if she would be happy living at Acacia House. She told him she would have to decide once she had seen it.

"The rooms are spacious, and there's a conservatory," he said. "I hope you like Modbury. It's a quiet little village, very different to what you have been used to," he added cautiously.

"I'll still have Mummy's flat in town," she answered. "I'm not going to go into tweeds and brown lace-ups just yet!"

He put his arm round her and kissed her. "I thought you looked beautiful yesterday," he said. "I'm a lucky man."

A week later, Charles put his key in the heavy wooden door of the surgery, opened it, and led Sapphire through into the hallway. The Baileys had taken some of their furniture, so the sitting room was looking somewhat empty.

Sapphire paused, taking it all in.

"It needs some refurbishment," said Charles, looking round.

"I shall have great fun doing that," replied Sapphire brightly.

Charles had a limited budget for this, but undeterred, he showed her the rest of the house, finishing with his surgery and the waiting room.

Sapphire appeared very interested in all she saw. "It's a large house to run," she observed. "What staff do we have?"

"Mrs. Harris comes every day and cooks my evening meal," he explained. "She does my shopping and laundry, and she keeps the house clean. There's also a gardener who comes once a week."

"You seem very well looked after."

"Mrs. Harris is here now. I haven't shown you the kitchen yet. Let me introduce you. I think she's longing to meet you."

Acacia House had been built on two levels, the back being lower than the front, which faced the road. They descended some stairs to the basement, where there was a large kitchen and storeroom. The kitchen had a large window that looked out into the garden. It was a homely looking room with an old black range as well as a gas stove, and a row of copper saucepans of diminishing sizes were hanging along the wall. There were two large sinks side by side, surrounded by blue and white tiles. A large wooden table in the centre of the room was covered in jars and bowls. Behind it stood Mrs. Harris with a rolling pin, working on a piece of pastry.

She looked thrilled to see them, brushed her hands together quickly, and came round the table to meet Sapphire, her eyes shining in admiration. "How do you do, Mrs. Browne? How lovely to meet you at last!"

"I'm so glad you're staying on," replied Sapphire.

Mrs. Harris reassured her that was the case. "We'll have to meet up in the morning, ma'am, to look at the menus."

"Yes, of course."

As Sapphire was leaving, she glanced up at a row of bells above the doorway, each with a number. Even at her mother's house, they didn't summon staff this way. As they went back upstairs, she asked Charles if he ever used the system.

"Goodness no!" he replied. "I've never dared to!"

At dinner, Sapphire thanked Mrs. Harris as she served up the chicken pie.

"She's a great cook," whispered Charles as she left.

Later, while the newlyweds sat together on the sofa, ready to enjoy a comfortable evening together, the front doorbell rang.

"Some emergency, I expect." Charles sighed, getting up quickly to answer the door.

It was an urgent callout, so he kissed Sapphire goodbye; picked up his hat, coat, and bag; and left.

Sapphire wanted to show her mother her new home and ask her advice about refurbishing. She said her mother had a good eye. Charles welcomed the idea, concerned that Sapphire would become bored while he was conducting surgery or out on calls.

Lucinda replied to Sapphire's invitation, accepting and asking if she could bring Madelaine, as she was still living with her.

Sapphire looked forward to receiving her first guests. They arrived the following week, and Sapphire enjoyed showing them round, discussing ideas as they went.

Lucinda thought the house needed traditional decor, but not too old-fashioned. "We should get samples of wallpaper and curtain material. I can give you some addresses of suppliers."

"I'll have to get some of this done quickly, before the baby comes," Sapphire said, showing some concern.

"We're here to help, darling," reassured her mother.

"I love your conservatory," enthused Madelaine when they were shown it. Caroline had left all her plants behind, together with the wicker furniture.

That evening, Lucinda retired early to bed after her journey, and Charles was out on a call. Sapphire and Madelaine sat together on the sofa in the sitting room, curled up before a crackling fire.

"How are things with your parents now?" asked Sapphire. "Are they still annoyed with you?"

"They're coming round," replied her cousin. "They insisted I wrote a letter to my fiancé's parents to apologise."

"He should apologise to you for keeping you waiting so long!" exclaimed Sapphire indignantly.

Sapphire told her cousin about Charles's father being unfriendly towards her.

"I'm sure he'll change in time, especially when you place baby Browne on his lap," said Madelaine. "It's not what you are, but *who* you are that maybe bothers him."

The following morning, Sapphire and her mother strolled into the village and explored several small shops along the High Street, making some purchases for the house in one of the antique shops.

At dinner, Sapphire suggested that she and her mother should take another shopping trip together to London sometime soon.

"I don't want you getting tired, Sapphire," said her husband.

"You can see I'm married to a doctor!" she replied, laughing.

"I have something to announce," said Lucinda when they were drinking their coffee after the meal. "I have decided to sell. The house is too big for me, and quite honestly, I can't really afford it. Now that you and Lionel are both married, I have no reason to stay there. Also, I have lost two of my good friends. One has moved away herself, and the other, sadly, has died. It's interesting that once you are widowed, people suddenly drop you from their social calendar. The wives think you are going to steal their husbands."

"Poor Mummy," said Sapphire. "It must be very lonely, then."

"I can't sit in that big house, waiting for you or Lionel to turn up. You have lives of your own. And Madelaine won't want to stay with me forever. I know she wants to travel." She looked over at her niece. "You've been a great comfort to me, dear, and I'm very grateful, but I can't expect you to spend the rest of your life with me."

Madelaine smiled gently at her aunt and held her hand.

Lucinda turned her attention back to Charles and Sapphire. "What I want to ask you both is…" She fiddled with her teaspoon, stirring her coffee and avoiding eye contact. "If I could possibly come and live here? I could help by buying this property and paying for an extension, or purchasing somewhere else in the village, if you would prefer."

Sapphire turned to Charles, her expression a mixture of surprise and hope.

Charles sat frowning slightly as he thought hard about what had been proposed. Finally, he said, "That's extremely generous of you, Lucinda. I personally have no objections to you living here, and I think your idea is a good one, as it will give Sapphire some company. I'm never happy when I'm called out at night, leaving her here on her own. But perhaps Sapphire should have the last word." He turned towards her.

"Oh, Mummy! I would love to have you come! I haven't told Charles, but I've been worrying about when I have the baby. I shall have no idea what to do, and it would be so wonderful to have you here."

"I would prefer to have my own rooms," continued Lucinda. "We shall need to respect each other's privacy."

They set about discussing how they would reconfigure the house, agreeing it would mean losing some of the garden if they built an extension.

Lucinda spoke to her daughter about the arrangements she had decided on regarding the sale of her home. "I'll write to Lionel to explain that I have decided to sell up and move here. The proceeds will be split between the three of us. It should be enough for Lionel to buy a decent house and for me to buy Acacia House."

"Oh, Mummy! Charles and I are so grateful. We would never be able to buy this house ourselves."

"I'm very happy to do so, but it's still your home. I shall be happy with my own apartment."

Sapphire embraced her. "Thank you, Mummy!"

Lucinda and Madelaine's visit came to an end, and Sapphire immersed herself in all the tasks needed in running a large house.

Charles was to conduct interviews for a new partner that week, and he had four applicants. Sapphire suggested he give each applicant a chance to meet them both for coffee in the conservatory, then conduct the formal interview in the surgery afterwards. In that way, she pointed out, she would be able to form an opinion of them as well.

After the interviews were all over, Sapphire thought about each candidate. One stood out for her, but she waited to hear what Charles had decided. He mentioned the same person, Brian Forster, who was married with two children and looking for a country practice, as he wanted to raise his children away from city life. He had a cheerful, round face and wore heavy-rimmed glasses. Sapphire said she thought he had a "dependable" look. They agreed that Charles needed to check Brian's references, and if they were satisfactory, he should offer him the partnership.

CHAPTER THIRTY
MILLIE AND HARRY RETURN

BY THE TIME MILLIE AND Harry had been away for nearly two months, Ben and Sophie had to admit that, while they enjoyed running the shop, it was hard work. Ben was often back late from his post round, having stopped to chat with villagers along the way. Sophie liked hearing all the news and gossip at the shop, but it did make her realise that her own family had probably been the topic of many a conversation in the past.

The first week in November was damp and chilly when Millie, Harry, and Agnes were due back from America. Ben, Sophie, and Billy travelled down to Southampton to welcome them home. They parked the two motors and made their way down to the dockside.

The huge ship had already berthed and was looming over the crowds of people waiting to meet the passengers once they were allowed to disembark. It was exceptionally busy and chaotic, with a thrill of expectation and excitement in the air.

Sophie turned to a stranger next to her. "What's happening?" she asked.

"I've been here over an hour," replied the woman good-naturedly. "There seems to be some delay."

Twenty minutes later, the gangplanks were let down and some passengers began to emerge. A huge cheer went up, and the shouting and waving was deafening as people yelled greetings. Sophie put her hands over her ears.

"This will be the first-class passengers," said Billy. "We won't see Ma and Harry yet."

After the first throng of passengers had left the ship and melted away into the crowd, the next contingent appeared.

Suddenly, Ben shouted, "There they are! There they are!" He pointed and waved excitedly, hardly able to contain himself.

Millie and Harry, followed by Agnes, made their way down the gangplank and stood looking round expectantly.

Ben pushed his way through the crowds, followed by Sophie and Billy, until they stood in front of them, their faces glowing with delight at seeing them.

"Oh, Ben!" exclaimed Millie, throwing her arms round his neck. "Sophie!" Millie hugged her tightly before turning to Billy and giving him the same.

Harry shook his brother-in-law's hand firmly, beaming as he did so, and then Agnes came forwards and embraced her aunt and uncle and, finally, her half-brother.

"Come on," said Ben. "This way." He led the way to the customs building, and soon after, the families were reunited.

Millie told them they'd had a good crossing and the whole trip had been wonderful. "We've *so* much to tell you," she exclaimed. "I'm so glad you talked us into going!"

As they walked along, Sophie reassured her sister-in-law that everything at the shop and post office was in order. Agnes said she was looking forward to resuming her post round and hoped Uncle Ben had managed to deliver all the letters to the correct addresses.

Ben grinned at her and said, "Just about!"

He and Harry pushed the trolley loaded with their luggage back to where their motors were parked, as all the porters had been taken. Millie and Agnes followed, carrying parcels and bags.

On the drive back to Clayden village, Sophie told Millie some of the news.

Millie's eyes opened wide when she heard about Sapphire and Charles. "I hope he knows what he's done," she said. "She'll give him the runaround. I hope he realises that."

"She'll have me to answer to if she does," Ben muttered, his eyes fixed intently on the road ahead.

When they arrived at the shop, Harry and Ben unloaded the suitcases. Agnes's fiancé, Ted, was there, waiting outside, and relieved to have his intended back. He put his arms round her and held her for some time, whispering something in her ear that made her laugh and blush. His parents came out of the shop, which they had been minding that day.

"Lock up early," Harry said to them. "And come into the cottage. We're all going to celebrate!"

They all piled into the small cottage, and Millie and Sophie began to serve the tea and sandwiches Sophie had prepared earlier. She had made a large iced cake with *Welcome Back!* written in icing on top.

Later, as they shared their evening meal together, Billy told everyone that Dorothy was expecting.

Overjoyed, Millie expressed her delight at coming home to such wonderful news. "We are both to become grandmamas," she said to Sophie, her eyes shining.

Sophie gave a gentle smile to her sister-in-law, showing she enjoyed sharing this news. "Sapphire and Charles are expecting their child in March. I'm so sorry you missed their wedding. It was a lovely occasion."

"I expect Sapphire looked a million dollars!" Millie suddenly put her hand to her mouth and laughed. "I've rather got used to these American expressions!"

"Oh, do tell us about your trip," said Sophie, leaning forward.

"It was all so different out there," said Millie. "There are so many motorcars. The roads in New York are very crowded and noisy—Tom was right about that. Everyone lives in apartment blocks, but Tom and Louisa are hoping to buy a little house in Brooklyn soon. There's such a lot of development going on, constant building, and they call it real estate. They have different words for everything, and different food, as there are so many foreign immigrants. Harry particularly liked some little sugar buns called *donuts*, didn't you?" She looked at her husband, who smiled and nodded enthusiastically.

"The buildings are so tall either side that they shut the sunlight out, and it's like walking along the bottom of a well. And the shops! I've never seen so many lovely things. They have department stores bigger than ours. Everything is bigger over there!"

Millie paused to draw breath. "The wedding was wonderful. Tom's wife, Louise, is lovely, and her family were so welcoming. I'm sorry you couldn't have been there too."

"I bought a camera, so I'll have some pictures to show you when they're developed," added Harry.

They continued talking together for some time, and finally, Sophie and Ben departed, thankful they would not have to get up quite so early the next day to see to the shop.

As they lay in bed that night, Ben held Sophie's hand and said, "I'm sorry I've not been able to take you to exciting places abroad, Sophie."

"Ben, I've had a good life here. I love this cottage, and I've enjoyed living here, bringing up our family, and helping with the business. I haven't wanted more."

The next day, Millie arrived loaded with parcels. "We bought you and Ben some gifts," she announced, piling them onto the kitchen table. "If you hadn't looked after the shop and post office, we would never have been able to go to see Tom. Harry and I are so grateful to you." She hugged Sophie and gave her a kiss.

Looking at all the presents, Sophie said, "You didn't have to do this, you know, Millie. We were very happy to help you out. Thank you for thinking of us, though. It feels like Christmas!" She called Ben, and together they opened their gifts.

Millie had chosen leather gloves and a silk scarf for Sophie and a gold watch for Ben, which he was thrilled with, having sold his father's Hunter years before. They were also given biscuits and chocolates.

"They call biscuits *cookies*, and chocolate is *candy*," Millie informed them. She left some other gifts for Charles, Florrie, and Rosa.

"How is Tom?" asked Sophie. "I expect his old partner Danny will be interested in what he's doing."

"He was hoping to start up his own repair business," said Millie. "But now he thinks Louise's father might make him a partner in his motor dealership. I'm so glad he's happily settled. That awful war nearly ruined his life."

"How are his injuries?"

"All fully healed, thank goodness," replied Millie.

Millie returned to the shop, leaving Sophie and Ben to admire their lovely gifts.

Sophie felt the luxurious silk scarf between her fingers. "It's beautiful!" she whispered to herself.

Ben was busy fastening his watch to his waistcoat pocket. They caught each other's eye and burst out laughing.

"What a posh pair we are!" said Ben.

The next day, Agnes brought a letter with their daily newspaper. It was from Sapphire, inviting them to tea the following Saturday afternoon. Sophie read it to Ben as they were finishing breakfast.

"If we go, you must be a bit more friendly," said Sophie.

"Yes, of course I will," replied Ben, not looking up from the newspaper he was reading.

They took Millie and Harry's present with them, and when Sapphire opened it, she found it to be a large box of chocolates.

"It's called *candy*," said Ben.

"I don't care what it's called," declared his son. "I shall enjoy those!"

After tea, Sapphire showed them round the house while describing what they were hoping to do to add extra rooms. When they went back to the conservatory, Charles informed them that Lucinda would be living with them.

"Lionel and I didn't want her living on her own anymore," he added.

Sapphire told them that she hoped her mother would be moving in after Christmas. That would give them time to get her settled in before the baby was born.

At tea, she reminded Sophie about the recipes. "I've time to do some baking now," she said.

When they were back home, Ben asked Sophie if she minded Lucinda living closer to them.

"No," she replied. "She is, after all, family now."

CHAPTER THIRTY-ONE

DANNY IS IN TROUBLE

ROSA WAS READING OUT TO Danny a letter she had received from Sophie, describing Millie, Harry, and their daughter's return from New York.

"They seem to have had an exciting time," she told him. "Does it make you feel like you should have stayed?"

"Not likely! It was the best thing coming home and getting back with you, Rosa. I was a right fool to have left you."

"And you were able to have your operation."

They smiled contentedly at each other, and Digger pushed his muzzle between them, demanding some attention.

Danny rubbed the dog's cheeks between his hands. "Come on, boy! Time for your walk!"

Pam called round to have a cup of tea with Hilda just as he was leaving. She often popped round, and the two women were now firm friends.

As they drank their tea, Pam said she had some news. "I think I ought to tell you that Ian's dad is seeing someone," she said, studying Hilda to see her reaction.

"I thought he was," replied Hilda, putting her cup down and sighing.

"I believe they're living together."

"If he wants a divorce, he knows where to find me." Hilda pursed her lips together.

Pam had some other news to tell her, and when Danny returned home that evening, he found his mother looking upset.

Before he had time to take off his coat, she blurted out, "They're letting Clarence out before Christmas!"

Danny stared in disbelief. "But he's only served about half his sentence!"

"Pam told me this afternoon," Hilda went on. "She said he was being released for good behaviour."

"Good behaviour!" said Danny. "He wouldn't know what that was if he fell over it in the street!"

"I believe the prisons are very full and he's being dealt with leniently because of his age."

"He'd better not show his face here," said Danny. "You'll have to check who's at the door before you open it, Mum."

"You're not to worry, Danny. I do that already," Hilda answered.

When Rosa got home and was told, she asked what he would do if Clarence bothered him again.

"I'll be on my guard from now on," he told her.

"Surely he wouldn't risk doing anything again," she said. "He would be given a much longer sentence."

"I hope he goes back to his father."

"I don't think his so-called wife would want him round. Aren't there hostels for young men like him?"

"I expect so, but he would probably get thrown out if he continued to get drunk."

"He needs a lot of help, Danny. Could the Salvation Army do something for him?"

Danny shrugged. "I've no idea why Clarence is like he is, or why." He squeezed Rosa's hand. "I'm so glad I have you," he added.

Hilda had been putting a little money aside each week to pay for Christmas. She went to the shops and bought some paper decorations and some presents, and Danny was to bring the tree home after work.

Two days before Christmas, Danny told Hilda and Rosa that he would be home late, as he was going for a drink with his friend Archie and his mates.

The following day, on Christmas Eve, Danny finished his work at the garage and called round to wish Stan and his family a Happy

Christmas. Stan asked him to step inside and presented him with a large food hamper. Danny was overwhelmed.

"You've been a good worker," Stan told him. "And the customers all like you. This is to thank you for helping my business along."

Danny expressed his appreciation but wondered how he could get it home.

Stan saw the problem and said, "Hang on, Danny. I'll give you a lift."

He dropped him off at the end of the road, and Danny proudly carried the hamper to his house.

When he opened the door, he called out, "Mum! Rosa! Come and see what I have!"

There was no response, so he went on through to the back room. He saw that his mother was sitting down, looking pale and worried, and Rosa looked frightened. In the opposite corner of the room sat a policeman.

"Mr. Danny Collins?" he asked as soon as Danny walked in.

Danny put down the hamper. "Yes, that's my name."

"I have a few questions to ask you," the constable went on. "Can you tell me your whereabouts last evening?"

"I was at the tavern, having drinks with some friends," replied Danny, looking mystified.

"What time did you leave?"

Danny had to think. "It might have been about ten thirty, I'm not sure."

"Did you leave with anyone?"

"No, I stayed behind to pay the barman. I was treating my friends. They did me a big favour once."

"When did you get home?"

"About eleven, I suppose. Can I ask what this is about?" He looked round, perplexed.

"All in good time," said the constable as he wrote something in his notebook. When he finished, he looked up. "I have to inform you that Clarence Barford was found dead in the river last night."

Stunned, Danny grabbed a chair and sat down, his eyes wide in disbelief.

Hilda began sobbing, and Rosa got up to put her arm round her.

"I understand that you and he appeared in court a few months ago and he was sent to prison for assaulting you."

"Yes, he and his friends beat me up on my way home from work."

"He was recently released. Did you know that?" The constable eyed him carefully.

"Yes, his sister-in-law told us."

"And were you lying in wait for him to get your own back?"

"No. No! I was at the pub."

"Did anyone see you when you arrived home?"

Danny looked at Hilda and Rosa. "I'm not sure. My wife and mother had gone to bed."

"We have strong evidence that Mr. Barford was murdered."

Danny looked round at everyone as if in a panic.

The constable got up. "We shall probably need to have you in for more questioning, Mr. Collins. Please don't attempt to leave Plymouth. All this will have to wait until after Christmas now. I wish you all good night." With that, he left.

"Oh, Danny, what are we going to do?" asked Rosa anxiously.

Danny frowned. "They can't pin this on me. They won't have any evidence," he said.

Hilda wiped her eyes. "Oh, Danny!" she kept saying.

"I think we should put all this behind us until after Christmas," said Rosa firmly. "As you say, they can't prove anything, so we shall probably hear nothing more."

Hilda got up and announced she wanted to go round and see Ian and Pam.

When she returned, she said that they were shocked and upset by the news but would still like to come round for Christmas. They said that blaming Danny was ridiculous, and they would stand by him. This put Hilda in a better frame of mind, and she and Rosa began their Christmas preparations.

On Christmas morning, Danny laid and lit the fire in the sitting room and then sat in the armchair to think. What if he was somehow found guilty of this? What would happen to Rosa and his mother? He put his hand to his mouth to stifle a sob.

Rosa called him into breakfast, and he got up, sighed heavily, and went through to the kitchen.

After Christmas, the constable returned and asked to see Danny's coat that he had been wearing on the night. He examined it carefully and said it would be kept as evidence.

The following day, two officers arrived at the house and told Danny he was under arrest.

Both distraught and clutching each other, Hilda and Rosa watched helplessly as Danny was marched out of the house, into the waiting police car.

Hilda collapsed into a chair, crying.

Rosa knelt beside her. "I'm sure they'll realise their mistake," she said. "They'll have to release him."

"If only I hadn't married that man and then left the boys, none of this would have happened," she sobbed. "It's all my fault."

"No, it isn't," replied Rosa emphatically. "The responsibility for all this is with their father. He was the one who abandoned you and his boys. You've just done your best."

Hilda nodded and wiped her eyes. "Thank you, dear," she said.

Later that afternoon, there was a knock on the door, which made both Rosa and Hilda jump. Rosa looked through the net curtain and saw Stan standing outside. She quickly opened the door.

"Oh, Stan! Have you heard?" she asked.

Stan told her he had just come from the police station. "I'm afraid they've charged Danny. I tried to stand bail for him, but they're not letting him have it, as it's a murder charge."

Rosa was speechless.

"The case won't be heard for some months," he added. "The press has been to the garage, wanting his address, so it will only be a matter of time before they find out where he lives and then they'll be round here, banging on the door."

"What can we do?" asked Rosa.

"Is there anywhere you can go?" asked Stan. "We could put you up, but they would soon find you."

"I think we could go to my old lodgings. Hilda knows them there, and it is a little way from here."

"Well, don't delay," said Stan. "Look, I'll call round this evening after work and take you there."

"Oh, Stan, thank you!"

Rosa and Hilda packed their bags, ready to leave. Hilda took Digger round to Pam, and she agreed to look after him. She warned Pam about the press.

"Ian will deal with them if they come round here," said Pam.

While Hilda was gone, Rosa wrote to Ben and Sophie, explaining what had happened. She told them they were going to Jenny Faircross's house. She hurried out and posted it in the pillar box at the end of the road, hoping to catch the last post.

Stan drove them to Jenny's house, a few miles away. He lifted out their cases and then drove away.

Rosa explained to Jenny what had happened, and she asked them both inside.

"What a dreadful thing!" she exclaimed. "You are both welcome to stay here for as long as needed."

They went inside, greeting Mr. Faircross, who looked alarmed by their surprise visit. Rosa explained to him what had happened to Danny.

He leant forward, looking concerned. "You mustn't worry. As you said, the police have no evidence and are just making assumptions. It would never stand up in court. I hope they're investigating it thoroughly."

His words calmed Hilda, and Rosa thanked him. All they could do was wait.

Ben arrived with Sophie the next day and said he couldn't stay at home and do nothing. They decided that Rosa would return home, but Hilda should stay on at Jenny's.

Ben was very indignant about the police. "They have very little evidence to arrest him with," he commented.

"Will he need a lawyer?" asked Rosa anxiously.

"I wish Samuel was still with us," said Sophie.

Rosa returned to her home with her parents, collecting Digger on the way. It was all very surreal, and she felt very anxious as she prepared the evening meal for them.

After they had eaten, Ben announced he was going to see Stan and would then begin making some enquiries. He walked to the garage and, after introducing himself, asked Stan what he knew about the incident.

"When Clarence was fished out of the river, they found an injury on his head, so they think he was knocked out first, then pushed in," replied Stan.

"And all this happened late at night?" asked Ben.

"Yes, about eleven o'clock, after the pubs closed."

While Ben was thinking, Stan had an idea. "How long will you be staying, Ben?"

"As long as it takes to get Danny freed," he replied.

"Would you consider working for me, as I've lost Danny? He tells me you and he were motor mechanics together. It would help me out."

"It would certainly help with expenses," Ben replied. "Yes, Stan, I could do that. I'll see you tomorrow morning, then."

Ben walked back along the dark streets. *What can I do to help the lad?* he wondered. Passing by a lively pub, he had a thought—the pub might be where he could get some information.

When he got home, Rosa told him a reporter had knocked on the door, but she and Sophie had ignored it.

Ben told them what he had found out and that he was going to work for Stan. He then said he would visit some pubs after work the following day to see what he could find out, saying, "I'll start with the ones Clarence frequented."

"I hope asking questions won't put you in any danger," Sophie said to him, looking troubled. "Please be careful."

"I'll speak to the publican first," he reassured her. "I promise not to get drunk," he added with a twinkle in his eye.

After his day's work at the garage the next day, Ben ate his evening meal hurriedly and then grabbed his coat and went out. Rosa had given him Danny's old address, and he set off to find the nearest pub. It was a dull-looking building, more like a house, and was situated on the tow path beside the river.

Ben stood outside and looked round, then pushed open the door, letting out a warm, unpleasant smell of stale beer and cigarette smoke. The bar room was full of working-class men in cloth caps and shabby jackets. Ben went up to the bar and bought himself an ale.

The barman regarded him with interest. "Haven't seen you in here before," he remarked, eyeing him.

"Er, no." Ben put down his glass. He looked round, then lowered his voice. "My name's Ben, and my son-in-law Danny has been arrested for the murder of Clarence Barford."

The barman looked surprised. "Oh yes. I read all about that. That Danny wouldn't hurt a fly," he said emphatically. "Clarence was a whole load of trouble. He left a tab here as long as your arm, and he was always getting into fights after he left here drunk. I banned him in the end, so he went to the Kings Arms, I understand. I haven't seen Danny for some time. Years, in fact."

"Did Clarence have any enemies you know of?" asked Ben.

"Maybe one or two that he picked on, but I don't think they would have done him in for it."

"And you could swear that Danny wasn't in here the evening before Christmas Eve?"

"Definitely. The police came round, asking me this. They think Danny lay in wait for him outside somewhere."

Ben thanked the barman and sat down with his drink, writing down what he had been told in his notebook.

He then made his way to the Kings Arms, which turned out to be a rougher pub. He got much the same story from the landlord there, that Clarence was known to be a violent young man who hardly ever paid for his drinks. Ben looked round, seeing several groups of rowdy young men who looked as if they wouldn't welcome being questioned.

The landlord must have spoken to someone, because soon a thin-faced young man sidled up to him and said quietly in his ear, "Round the back in five minutes."

Ben was taken by surprise but continued to drink his beer. Then he slowly got up and sauntered towards the back door. Outside, he scanned the darkness and saw a figure lurking behind some outbuildings.

"Over here!" a voice hissed.

Ben went over to him, glancing round nervously. "Yes? You wanted to tell me something?" he asked.

The young man held out his hand, palm up.

Ben felt in his pocket and got out some coins.

The young man looked at them and shook his head. "No, not enough!" he said.

Ben produced a ten-shilling note.

The young man snatched it and shoved it into his pocket. Then he began, "I knows what happened to old Clarence. We'd all been drinking 'ere, and 'e got very drunk. We left, and 'e started on one of the lads outside and got shoved over and hit 'is head on the ground like. Then 'e gets up and runs off up the path, towards the river, and that's the last I saw of 'im."

"And this was the evening before Christmas Eve?" asked Ben.

"It was."

"Look, I don't know your name, but I'm grateful to you for this. My son-in-law Danny has been arrested for the murder of Clarence, who was his stepbrother. Do you think Clarence might have fallen into the river accidentally?"

"Could 'ave, 'e was that drunk."

"Would you be prepared to be a witness?"

"Maybe, for the right price."

"What would that be?"

The young man shuffled his feet and looked down. "Ten pounds."

"Five."

"All right, yeah."

"If I come tomorrow and pay you, I shall want a signed statement from you and your name and address."

"Yeah, okay."

"I'll see you tomorrow, then, with the money."

When Ben arrived home, it was late, and Sophie and Rosa were asleep.

He undressed and got into bed, and Sophie woke and put her arm round him. "You're back safely," she said sleepily.

"Yes, I'm back safe, and I think I've some good news," he replied.

Next morning, Ben told Rosa and Sophie what he had found out.

"Oh, Pa! Where will we get five pounds from?" asked Rosa desperately.

"I'll ask Stan if he'll advance it from my wages."

When he got to work that morning, Ben explained the reason for wanting five pounds, and Stan gave him the money straight away.

"Are you sure you know what you're doing?" Stan asked. "Can you trust this fellow?"

"I hope so, Stan. What else can I do? I hope to God he turns up tonight."

Later that evening, Ben arrived at the Kings Arms again and found a quiet corner to drink his beer. He sat for an hour, and nobody came. He went round the back a few times, but no one was there.

He decided to wait a little longer, and eventually, the door opened and the thin-faced young man entered and looked nervously round. He spotted Ben and, without acknowledging him, went straight out of the back door.

After some minutes, Ben finished his drink and followed him out. The young man was waiting.

"Hello, fellow," said Ben. "Am I glad to see you."

The young man mumbled something, and Ben gave him his money. Having already written down all that the man told him, he handed the document to him. The young man read it through quickly and then signed it. Ben looked at the name and asked him for his address, which he wrote down.

"Well, Joe, I can't thank you enough for this. Can I ask you something? Are you looking for work, by any chance?"

Joe looked surprised. "Yeah."

"You've done me a favour, albeit for a price, so I'd like to do you one. Would you like me to help you find work? I could speak up for you, say what a decent fellow you are." Ben was wanting to help him, but he also wanted to keep in touch.

Joe looked dumbfounded.

"I work in a garage as a mechanic," Ben went on. "With the owner's permission, I could train you."

"I dunno," said Joe, putting his hands in his pockets and looking down at his feet. "I'm not sure."

"Just give it a go," Ben went on. "Nobody's going to make you stay if you don't like it."

Ben explained where he worked and told him to call in one day. *I hope I've done the right thing*, he thought as he left.

Rosa was very relieved when Ben returned with Joe's signed statement. "I'm going to see the police and show them this," he told her. "I wonder if they've managed to find any witnesses. It will be interesting to find out."

"Oh, Pa, I pray it will work and they let my Danny go," she said tearfully.

Ben put his arm round her. "I'll make sure it does," he replied resolutely. "Poor Danny has had enough in his short life. He doesn't need this."

The next day, Ben went to the police station and asked to see the sergeant. He was taken to a side room, and the sergeant appeared and sat down in front of him at a table.

"Mr. Browne," he began, "I understand you wanted to see me about the murder we are currently investigating. Do you have some information?"

"Yes, I think I've found a witness. He was with Clarence at the pub the night he died." Ben produced the statement and handed it to the sergeant.

After examining it carefully, the sergeant eyed Ben suspiciously and asked, "How do I know you didn't bribe this fellow to say this?"

"If you don't believe me, I suggest you send one of your men down to the Kings Arms and ask round. I'm sure someone saw the fight and Clarence injured."

The sergeant looked slightly embarrassed. "We have made some enquiries," he replied. "But I will send an officer down there again."

"One more thing," added Ben. "Danny Collins has an alibi, and the publican at the pub where he was drinking can tell you what time he left that night. His wife knows he returned at about eleven, so he wouldn't have had time to get over to the Kings Arms."

"Leave this with me," said the sergeant. "I will certainly look into it."

When Ben got home, he told Sophie and Rosa about his meeting and said he thought it likely they would have to release Danny soon.

"I do hope so!" Sophie looked earnestly at him. "You've done your best."

Ben continued working at the garage each day, but he saw no sign of Joe. *Well, if he wants to spend all the rest of his life in the pub, it's up to him*, he thought.

At the end of that week, while Ben was walking home from work, he passed by a newsagent. On an A-board outside, he saw a poster announcing, "Local Man Released."

He stopped in his tracks, staring at it in disbelief. *It could only mean Danny, surely?*

CHAPTER THIRTY-TWO

DANNY COMES HOME

BEN RUSHED HOME AS FAST as his legs could take him, through the front door and down the passage. Danny was there, hugging Rosa. Sophie stood beside them, beaming broadly, and Digger was looking up at him, his tail wagging furiously.

When he saw Ben, Danny exclaimed, "How can I thank you enough? Rosa tells me you were the one who got me freed!"

"I was just doing the police's job for them," said Ben. "They should never have arrested you. I'm so relieved to see you!" He gave his son-in-law a hug.

"I think Pa has missed his vocation in life," added Rosa. "He would have made a first-rate detective!"

Sophie was examining Danny. "You look pale, Danny, and you've lost some weight." She turned to her daughter. "You'll have to feed him up, Rosa. He needs some good hearty meals and plenty of rest."

"Yes, Ma, I'll be taking great care of him." She was holding on to him as if she were about to lose him again.

"How are you feeling, Danny?" asked Ben.

"Not too bad. After three weeks of prison food, I'm not surprised I'm thinner."

"We should let your mother know they've released you," suggested Sophie. "Ben and I can go over to Jenny's and collect her. You two stay here. You have a lot of catching up to do."

After they'd left, Danny sat down with Rosa and clasped her hand. "I've never been so glad to be home. It was all I could think of when I was in the cell—coming home to you, Rosa. I'm sorry you had to go through all this."

"It wasn't your fault, Danny. The police jumped to conclusions. I hope they apologised."

"Not really. I suppose they were having to save face. I was just glad to get out of there."

"I think you ought to have some time off work. I'm sure Pa will agree to continue working for Stan for another week."

Rosa began to prepare a meal for Danny, busying herself until her parents returned.

Hilda came hurrying through the door, overcome at seeing her son again, and flung her arms round him. "I thought I'd lost you again," she exclaimed through her tears. "I'm so glad you're safe back with us."

"It's all right, Mum. I'm okay. Don't cry, this is a happy time!"

Rosa came in with a steaming plate of hot food. "Here you are, Danny. Tuck into this!" She placed it in front of him and watched him devour it.

Stan called round later to welcome Danny back and readily agreed to let Ben carry on while Danny recovered from his ordeal.

After he'd left, Ben related to Danny how he had found out that Clarence wasn't murdered. He told him about Joe, who Danny knew was one of Clarence's drinking mates.

"I wonder why they didn't question Joe?" asked Rosa.

"He probably didn't want to talk to the police," said Ben. "When he found out I was making enquiries, he thought he would make some money."

"I expect they'll be releasing the body," said Sophie. "Do you want to go to the funeral?"

The general feeling was that they should all stay away. Clarence had disrupted Danny's life enough.

Ben continued working at the garage for another week, but there was no sign of Joe until, one day, he saw him lurking across the street. Ben called out to him, "Over here, Joe! I'm glad you decided to come."

Joe slouched across the road, with his hands in his pockets. " 'Ello, Mr. Browne," he mumbled.

"Hello, Joe. Have you spent all your money?"

"Gave it to me Mum," he replied.

"That was a decent thing to do, Joe. Let me take you to see the boss."

Joe followed Ben to Stan's office round the side of the garage. Ben introduced him, having had already asked Stan if he could take him on.

Stan eyed him carefully. "Well, young man, this is a great chance for you if you're serious about it. If you finish your training, I may be able to take you on."

Ben took Joe back to the workshop and began to show him some of the tools he would be using. Then he lifted the bonnet of the motor he had been working on and explained the parts of the engine to him.

When he'd finished, he turned to Joe and said, "Now, you tell me what the parts are and what they do."

Joe managed to remember most of what he had been shown, and Ben was surprised he had been listening so carefully. He continued to help Joe work on the engine, and Ben shared his lunch with the young man.

At the end of the day, Ben told him to come back at eight thirty the next morning and to bring a packet of sandwiches with him. "I'm not sharing my lunch with you every day," he said.

To Ben's surprise, Joe did turn up the next day and arrived every day at the correct time for the rest of the week.

"I'm pleased you haven't been late," Ben remarked.

"Me mum gets me up," Joe told him. "Then she kicks me out."

Ben hid a smile. He was getting to really like Joe.

Danny was pleased when Ben told him about Joe turning up. He persuaded Rosa he was ready to return to work, and the following Monday morning, she and Hilda fussed round him getting him ready. He walked confidently down the road, towards the garage, with Ben.

When Joe appeared, Ben introduced his son-in-law.

"Hello, Joe," said Danny. "Do you remember me?"

Joe looked at him. "Nope. What's wrong with yer eyes?" he asked.

Danny explained what had happened to him.

"Blimey," said Joe.

Danny explained that he was Clarence's stepbrother. "I'm afraid we didn't get on," he said.

"No one got on with Clarence," Joe replied. " 'E 'ad no friends, only me."

"I'm sorry about what happened to him," continued Danny.

Joe shrugged. "Me mum says she's glad 'e's not round to lead me into 'is bad ways anymore."

Danny and Ben looked at each other. Joe was certainly not one to grieve.

"He's a bit of a character," Ben told Sophie later. "I hope he'll make a success of the training I've given him. How do you feel about taking him on, Danny? I must say, it's rather useful having someone to pass you your tools, especially when you're underneath the motor."

Danny said he would continue training him and that something good should come out of what had happened.

That evening, Ben announced it was time for Sophie and him to go home, and they packed up and left the following day. Before they went, Danny thanked Ben again for all his help.

"Joe helped too," said Ben. "I'm afraid I still owe Stan five pounds." He had told Danny about the bribe.

"Don't worry, we'll pay that off," said Danny.

Ben and Sophie returned to Forge Cottage, admitting that had been a fraught and emotional time, something they never wanted to experience again.

Rosa wrote to say that their lives had quietened down. The local press had been a nuisance, so they had given one interview to the local paper, and she enclosed the article. There was grainy photograph of Danny, accompanied by an account of the inquest and his subsequent release. No mention was made of Ben or Joe. The police just stated that new evidence had come to light. Sophie folded it up and put it in the dresser drawer.

CHAPTER THIRTY-THREE

A BABY IS BORN

Lucinda moved into Acacia House after Christmas, and Charles employed an architect to design the extension they wanted. Donald and Caroline had agreed to sell the property to Lucinda, who hoped they could have everything completed before the baby was born in March.

Although Lucinda was looking forward to the birth of her first grandchild, Sapphire was not. She told Charles she would be glad when it was all over. As the months went by, she had become tired of carrying the child inside her and just wanted her slim figure back again.

Charles fussed over her, listening to her tummy with his stethoscope and telling her to put her feet up. When the time for the birth grew near, Charles arranged for the local midwife to visit Sapphire.

A few days before the due date, things began to happen. Sapphire went into labour, and Charles sent for the midwife, who bustled him out of the bedroom and took over very efficiently.

He and Lucinda waited for over an hour in the sitting room until, finally, the door opened, and the midwife asked him to come and see his new baby daughter. Charles insisted that Lucinda come with him, and together they went up to the bedroom to congratulate a tired but contented Sapphire. Charles hugged her, then looked at his little red-faced baby daughter and said he couldn't imagine being happier.

"How are you, darling?" asked Lucinda. "How was it?"

"Well, I don't want to do *that* again anytime soon!" replied Sapphire adamantly. She looked exhausted and said she had to feed the baby, so they left her with the midwife.

Lucinda asked Charles about a name.

"We decided on Charlotte if it was a girl," replied Charles. "Charlotte Elizabeth."

He set off to the post office to send telegrams as Lucinda poured herself a drink.

Sophie couldn't settle once she knew the baby was to be born soon. Every day she would look out of the window, hoping news would arrive.

At last, Agnes appeared, late one afternoon, with a telegram. She waited while Sophie read it out.

BABY CHARLOTTE ELIZABETH
ARRIVED THIS AFTERNOON STOP
MOTHER AND BABY DOING WELL STOP
CHARLES

"Oh, Ben!" was all Sophie could say.

"Do you want to send a reply?" asked Agnes.

"Yes, just a minute," replied Sophie, and then she went to find paper and a pencil. "What shall I say?" she asked, looking at Ben. She had never written a telegram before.

"You have to pay for every word," said Agnes. "You'd better make it short."

Sophie scribbled down her message and read it out. "Congratulations. God bless little Charlotte Elizabeth. Love Ben and Sophie."

Agnes took it from her, said they could pay later, and cycled back to the post office.

Ben looked stunned. The reality of the birth of his first grandchild dawned on him, followed quickly by the fact, hitting him as well, that it was related to both his wife and Lucinda.

He went into the parlour and took out the brandy bottle from the cupboard. "We need to drink to the baby's health," he said as he poured the drinks.

They raised their glasses.

"Good old Charles!" said Ben. "I never ever thought he would present us with a grandchild before the girls. May she be one of many!"

"I can't see Sapphire having a large family," observed Sophie. "I strongly suspect one will be enough!"

Sapphire was grateful her mother was with her. Everything to do with her baby seemed stressful, but Lucinda was there to help and support her. The feeding routines settled down, and Mrs. Harris asked her daughter to come and assist with the less attractive aspects of caring for a baby.

Charles's patients were delighted at the news and sent messages of congratulations and best wishes as well as little gifts.

Eventually, Sapphire felt fit enough to venture out, and one morning, she and Lucinda steered the large, bulky pram through the front door of the surgery and up the street to the shops.

They returned at the end of morning surgery, and Charles and Dr. Forster seemed to be having a serious discussion. The door of the surgery was open, and Sapphire could hear the words "just not safe" as she passed by.

She went upstairs to feed Charlotte, and when she came down later, Charles said he wanted to talk to her and Lucinda.

They sat down together, and Charles said Brian had told him there was an outbreak of diphtheria in the village, and a mother had brought a child suffering from it into the surgery that morning. He explained that it was highly contagious and life-threatening, especially to a young baby.

"Are there no vaccines for it?" asked Lucinda.

"I read that one had been developed and is used in America, but not here yet," replied Charles. "Doctor Forster and I are worried about the baby."

"What do you suggest we do?" asked Lucinda.

"It would probably be best if Sapphire and the baby stayed somewhere for the duration of the outbreak."

"How long would that take?"

"Possibly several weeks. It's always hard to tell."

Sapphire looked alarmed. "Where would we go?" she asked. "And what about Mummy?"

"You could stay with Sophie and Ben. That way I could get over to see you and Charlotte Elizabeth."

"But, Charles, I couldn't stay there!" said Lucinda, looking dismayed.

"Could you stay with Lionel?" suggested Charles. "I'm sorry, Lucinda. It would only be for a short while, I'm sure."

Sapphire looked at her mother and burst into tears.

Charles sat down beside her and comforted her. "We all have to play our part in keeping little Charlotte Elizabeth safe," he said. "We would never forgive ourselves if anything happened to her."

Sapphire nodded, then dried her eyes and said she would go and pack some things, and Lucinda went to help her.

Later that day, Charles drove Sapphire and the baby over to Forge Cottage. Sophie and Ben were delighted to see them and, when the situation was explained, readily agreed that it was the best thing to do. Charles kissed his wife and child goodbye and left.

Sophie took Sapphire upstairs to feed Charlotte. "Use our bedroom for now," she said. "I need to get the other bedroom ready and air the bed."

Sapphire sat quietly while her daughter guzzled contentedly. Was she going to like living here with Ben and Sophie, and how long would it be for? If things didn't work out, she would insist that Charles take her somewhere else.

When she had finished, Sophie came in and sat on the bed, and Sapphire gave her the baby to hold.

"She has a lovely bloom," Sophie said. "I think she's going to inherit your looks and your mother's."

"I hope she has your brains as well!" said Sapphire, laughing.

They went downstairs as Ben came in with wood for the fire. "We need to keep the place warm for you and the child," he said. He went out to the scullery and washed his hands carefully, then returned to sit in his old chair. "Now, let's have a look at her!" he said, holding out his hands.

Sapphire placed Charlotte Elizabeth into her grandfather's strong arms, and he gazed at her. "She's a beauty!" he said.

Charles came as often as he could to see his wife and child. His partner was very supportive and took on extra duties so he could visit regularly.

Charlotte Elizabeth was thriving, but Sapphire was finding it hard to settle and couldn't wait to get back home.

"Sophie and Ben have been very kind," she reassured Charles. "But I do want to go home soon."

Charles told her they had lost a child from the village to diphtheria.

"That's very sad," said Sapphire. "The poor mother. Why can't we have the vaccine if they have it in America?"

"I read in the newspaper that they have had a serious outbreak there in the past two years. I suppose that was why it was introduced. They need to test these vaccines very carefully. I expect it will come over here eventually." Charles held his precious daughter and smiled at her. "She's doing very well," he said.

Ben came in and looked at them. "That child's going to be a real daddy's girl," he said.

When Charles had gone, Sapphire and Sophie took Charlotte Elizabeth to the shop to show Millie and Harry. Sophie bought a few provisions and then they went to the cottage next door.

Harry was at the table in the parlour, looking at something, and he got up to admire the baby, then said, "The photographs are here, Sophie. We'll bring them over this evening and show them to you."

After dinner, Millie and Harry arrived, and they all looked at the photographs together.

Sapphire was very interested. "It looks a wonderful place," she said. "Those buildings are huge."

"They're called skyscrapers," explained Harry.

"The men are all wearing straw boaters," observed Sophie, peering at a street scene.

"They're the office workers. The manual workers wear flat caps," said Millie. "It gets very hot in the summer but much colder in the winter."

They enjoyed studying the photographs, especially those of Tom and Louisa's wedding. Sapphire repeated her desire to go to New York one day.

"You and your mother would love the shops," said Millie. She explained that she was going to put the photographs into an album and would write out all the descriptions. She had little idea that this would be passed down in Billy's family and be looked at for years to come, providing a historical record of life in New York in the 1920s.

As they lay in bed that night, Ben shared his concerns with Sophie. "I suppose Sapphire will be gadding off again," he whispered. "She seems very taken with New York."

"Young people want to see something of the world, these days," said Sophie. "I'm sure she won't abandon her child. We must allow her to live her life."

CHAPTER THIRTY–FOUR

GOING HOME

TWO WEEKS AFTER EASTER, CHARLES thought it was time for Sapphire and the baby to come home. He drove over to Forge Cottage to collect her, and he said there had been no new cases of diphtheria for over a week, so he and Dr. Forster thought it safe for her to return.

Sapphire thankfully packed her things and wrapped the baby in a blanket. She went downstairs and kissed Sophie goodbye. "Thank you for looking after me, Sophie. I hope it hasn't been too much for you." She turned to Ben. "Thank you too, Ben. I'm pleased you've been able to spend time with your granddaughter."

Ben said, "I shall miss her, but I expect you want to get back to your own home. I'm glad we could help."

After they left, the cottage was quiet again. The old clock ticked steadily in the parlour and then chimed the hour. Sophie continued with her day's chores and Ben set off to the village to do some repairs.

Two weeks after Sapphire and her baby had left, Sophie was beginning to prepare dinner when she suddenly felt faint and had to sit down. The following day, it happened again, this time when she was taking a bucket of ashes out to throw on the garden. She thought she was going to pass out.

The third time it happened was at breakfast a day later, while Ben was there. He saw her, unsteady on her feet, as she tried to grab a chair.

"Sophie! Are you all right?" Ben held her arm and helped her sit down.

She told him that she had felt faint, and he asked her if it had happened before. "Yes, twice. Yesterday and the day before."

"I don't like the sound of that. I'm taking you over to see Charles."

"We can't bother him," Sophie replied. "I'll be all right."

"I insist," he replied firmly, and taking her arm, he led her to the motor and drove her to Acacia House.

Charles was surprised to see them and looked concerned when Ben told him the reason for their visit. He said he would see Sophie straight away, before morning surgery.

He escorted her through to his room and gave her a thorough examination, asking several questions. When they came out, Charles asked Ben to come through, while Sophie remained in the waiting room.

"I have detected a slight weakness in her heart, so I'd like to send her to Plymouth Hospital for further tests. I'll write to the consultant, and you'll get a letter. You mustn't worry," he went on. "She'll be fine, but she must take it easy until then."

As they drove home, Ben told Sophie what Charles had told him.

Sophie sat in silence for the rest of the journey.

He took her hand again and squeezed it reassuringly. "I love you, and I'm here to take care of you."

The letter from the hospital arrived, and Ben drove Sophie to her appointment. After her examination, they drove to the clifftop to sit and enjoy the view, where they continued to discuss their future.

"Do you intend to carry on with the bicycle repairs?" Sophie asked.

"Yes, and I have my repair jobs in the village. That should keep us going." He squeezed her hand reassuringly.

A week later, Ben took Sophie back to see Charles. He had the results from the hospital, and he told Sophie she had a slight weakness of her heart, as he had suspected. There were pills he could prescribe, and they would take her symptoms away. He added that she would have to take things a little easier and do no heavy lifting.

"Ben has already promised to do the heavier chores," she replied.

"Let me know how you get on," Charles said as he showed them out. "Don't hesitate to contact me if you need me." He hugged his mother and told her not to worry.

Ben took Sophie home again. When they arrived, the sun was shining, and Sophie said she wanted to sit in the garden for a while. They strolled hand in hand down to the orchard and admired the apple blossoms on the trees.

"It looks as if we'll get a good crop of apples this year," said Ben.

They sat under the trees, on the bench Ben had made many years before. It was very peaceful, and Sophie leant back and closed her eyes.

"I love this place," she said.

TO BE CONTINUED...

DID YOU KNOW?

The decade following WWI was one of economic prosperity as well as social and cultural change. Nothing reflected the transformation of society more than the automation of road travel.

The role of the horse was rapidly replaced by horsepower, with motor car ownership more than doubling in the early 1920s. The Ford Model T, or Tin Lizzie, was the popular motor car of the decade.

The roads in big cities were becoming busy, noisy thoroughfares, with horse traffic being banned on some London streets. Open top omnibuses jostled for space with motor cars, lorries and the few horse-drawn cabs that remained.

Horse drawn wagons were in continual use until the beginning of WWII, delivering milk, ice, coal, and barrels of beer, especially in smaller towns and villages. Many folk living in the countryside kept their horses and traps for personal use up until WWII.

Before WWI, a programme of resurfacing roads had begun and was continued afterwards. In 1922, roads were numbered for the first time in the UK and A and B designated roads were introduced. Exploring the countryside by motor car became very popular as roads improved, giving the name Tourer to some makes of car.

Garages and motor car repair workshops sprung up rapidly, some replacing the old blacksmith forges. Car dealerships developed out of these as more motor cars were manufactured in the UK with the development of mass production techniques.

ABOUT THE AUTHOR

Penelope Abbott is a retired teacher who lives in the Chilterns with her husband, John. She has two grown up children, a son James, and daughter Ros. Her hobbies are writing, painting, gardening, and playing her violin.

To find out more about the background of *Sophie's Story* and this sequel, *Sophie's Children*, please contact pennyabbott.author@btinternet.com or visit the website penelopeabbott.com.

www.ingramcontent.com/pod-product-compliance
Lightning Source LLC
Chambersburg PA
CBHW020653120726
47906CB00001B/247